The Iliad & The Odyssey
for Boys and Girls

The Iliad & The Odyssey
for Boys and Girls
by Alfred J. Church

©2011 SMK Books

Wilder Publications, LLC.
PO Box 3005
Radford VA 24143-3005

ISBN 10: 1-61720-408-0
ISBN 13: 978-1-61720-408-1

Table of Contents:

The Iliad

The Odyssey

The Iliad for
Boys and Girls

Of How the War with Troy Began

Once upon a time there was a certain King of Sparta who had a most beautiful daughter, Helen by name. There was not a prince in Greece but wished to marry her. The King said to them: "Now you must all swear that you will be good friends with the man whom my daughter shall choose for her husband, and that if any one is wicked enough to steal her away from him, you will help him get her back." And this they did. Then the Fair Helen chose a prince whose name was Menelaüs, brother of Agamemnon, who reigned in Mycenæ, and was the chief of all the Kings of Greece. After a while Helen's father died, and her husband became King of Sparta. The two lived happily together till there came to Sparta a young prince, Paris by name, who was son of Priam, King of Troy. This Paris carried off the Fair Helen, and with her much gold and many precious stones.

Menelaüs and his brother Agamemnon sent to the princes of Greece and said, "Now you must keep your oath, and help us to get back the Fair Helen." So they all came to a place called Aulis, with many ships and men. Others also who had not taken the oath came with them. The greatest of these chiefs were these:—

Diomed, son of Tydeus; Ajax the Greater and Ajax the Less, and Teucer the Archer, who was brother of Ajax the Greater.

Nestor, who was the oldest man in the world.

The wise Ulysses.

Achilles, who was the bravest and strongest of all the Greeks, and with him his dear friend Patroclus.

For nine years the Greeks besieged the city of Troy, but they could not break through the walls; and as they had been away from their homes for all this time, they came to be in great want of food and clothes and other things. So they left part of the army to watch the city, and with part they went about and spoiled other cities. Thus came about the great quarrel of which I am now going to tell.

The Quarrel

The Greeks took the city of Chrysé and divided the spoils among the chiefs; to Agamemnon they gave a girl named Chryseïs, who was the daughter of the priest of Apollo, the god who was worshipped in the city. Then the priest came bringing much gold, with which he wished to buy back his daughter.

First of all he went to Agamemnon and his brother, then to the other chiefs, and begged them to take the gold and give him back the girl. "So," he said, "may the gods help you take the city of Troy, and bring you back safe to your homes."

All the other chiefs were willing, but Agamemnon cried, "Away with you, old man. Do not linger here now, and do not come again, or it will be the worse for you, though you are a priest. As for your daughter, I will carry her back with me when I have taken Troy."

So the old man went out in great fear and trouble, and he prayed to Apollo to help him. And Apollo heard him. Very angry was the god that his priest should suffer such things, and he came down from his palace on the top of the mountain Olympus. He came as night comes across the sky, and his arrows rattled terribly as he went. Then he began to shoot and his arrows carried death, first to the dogs and the mules, and then to the men. For nine days the people died, and on the tenth day Achilles called an assembly.

When the Greeks were gathered together he stood up in the middle and said: "Surely it would be better to go home than to stay here and die. Many are slain in battle, and still more are slain by the plague. Let us ask the prophets why it is that Apollo is angry with us."

Then Calchas the prophet stood up: "You wish to know why Apollo is angry. I will tell you, but first you must promise to stand by me, for King Agamemnon will be angry when he hears what I shall say."

"Say on," cried Achilles: "no man shall harm you while I live, no, not Agamemnon himself."

Then Calchas said: "Apollo is angry because when his priest came to buy back his daughter, Agamemnon would not listen to him. Now you must send back the girl, taking no money for her, and with her a hundred beasts as a sacrifice."

Then King Agamemnon stood up in a rage and cried:

"You always prophesy evil, ill prophet that you are. The girl I will send back, for I would not have the people die, but I will not go without my share of the spoil."

"You think too much of gain, King Agamemnon," said Achilles. "Surely you would not take from any man that which has been given him. Wait till Troy has been conquered, and then we will make up to you what has been lost three times over."

"Do not try to cheat me in this way," answered Agamemnon. "My share I will have at once. If the Greeks will give it to me, well and good; but if not, then I will take it from one of the chiefs, from you, Achilles, or from Ajax, or from Ulysses. But now let us see about the sending back of the girl."

Then Achilles was altogether carried away with rage and said: "Never was there a king so shameless and so greedy of gain. The Trojans never did harm to me or mine. I have been fighting against them for your sake and your brother's. And you sit in your tent at ease, but when the spoil is divided, then you have the lion's share. And now you will take the little that was given me. I will not stay here to be shamed and robbed. I will go home."

"Go," said Agamemnon, "and take your people with you. I have other chiefs as good as you, and ready to honour me, as you are not. But mark this: the girl Briseïs, who was given to you as your share of the spoil, I will take, if I have to come and fetch her myself. For you must learn that I am master here."

Achilles was mad with anger to hear this, and said to himself, "Now I will slay this villain where he sits," and he half drew his sword from its scabbard. But at that instant the goddess Athené stood behind him and seized him by his long yellow hair. And when he turned to see who had done this, he perceived the goddess—but no one else in the assembly could see her—and said: "Are you come to see this villain die?" "Nay," she answered, "I am come to stay your rage. Queen Hera and I love you both. Draw not your sword, but say what you will. Some day he will pay you back three times and four times for all the wrong he shall do."

Achilles answered: "I will do as you bid; for he who hears the gods is heard by them." So he thrust back his sword into the scabbard, and Athené went back to Olympus. Then he turned to Agamemnon and cried: "Drunkard with the eyes of a dog and the heart of a deer, hear what I tell you now. See this sceptre that I have in my hand. Once it was the branch of a tree; now a king carries it in his hand. As surely as it will never more shoot forth in leaves, so surely will the Greeks one day miss Achilles. And you, when you see your people falling by the swords of the Trojans, will be sorry that you have done this wrong to the bravest man in your army." And he dashed the sceptre on the ground and sat down.

Then the old man Nestor stood up and would have made peace between the two. "Listen to me," he said. "Great chiefs of old, with whom no one now alive would dare to fight, were used to listen to me. You, King Agamemnon, do not take away from the brave Achilles the gift that the Greeks gave him; and you Achilles, pay due respect to him who is the King of Kings in Greece."

So spoke Nestor, but he spoke in vain, for Agamemnon answered: "Peace is good; but this fellow would lord it over all. The gods have made him a great warrior, but they have not given him leave to set himself up above law and order. He must learn that there is one here better than he."

And Achilles cried: "You better than me! I were a slave and a coward if I owned it. What the Greeks gave me, let them take away if they will. But mark this: if you lay your hands on anything that is my own, that hour you will die."

Then the assembly was broken up. After a while Agamemnon said to the heralds: "Go now to the tent of Achilles, and fetch thence the girl Briseïs. And if he will not let her go, say that I will come with others to fetch her, and that it will be worse for him."

So the heralds went, but it was much against their will that they did this errand. And when they came to that part of the camp where Achilles and his people were, they found him sitting between his tent and his ship. And they stood in great fear and shame. But when he saw them he spoke kind words to them, for all that his heart was full of rage. "Draw near, heralds. 'Tis no fault of yours that you are come on such an errand."

Then he turned to Patroclus and said: "Fetch Briseïs from her tent and give her to the heralds. Let them be witnesses of this evil deed, that they may remember it in the day when he shall need my help and shall not have it."

So Patroclus brought out the girl and gave her to the heralds. And she went with them, much against her will, and often looking back. And when she was gone, Achilles left his companions and sat upon the sea-shore, weeping aloud and stretching out his hands to his mother Thetis, the daughter of the sea. She heard his voice where she sat in the depths by the side of her father, and rose from the sea, as a cloud rises, and came to him where he sat weeping, shaking him with her hand, and calling him by his name.

"Why do you weep, my son?" she said.

And he told her what had been done. And when he had finished the story, he said: "Now go to Olympus, to the palace of Zeus. You helped him once in the old time, when the other gods would have put him in chains, fetching the great giant with the hundred hands to sit by his side, so that no one dared to touch him. Remind him of these things, and ask him to help the Trojans, and to make the Greeks flee before them, so that Agamemnon may learn how foolish he has been."

His mother said: "Surely, my son, your lot is hard. Your life must be short, and it should be happy; but, as it seems to me, it is both short and sad. Truly I will go to Zeus, but not now; for he is gone with the other gods to a twelve days' feast. But when he comes back, then I will go to him and persuade him. Meanwhile do you sit still, and do not go forth to battle."

Meanwhile Ulysses was taking back the priest's daughter to her father. Very glad was he to see her again, and he prayed to his god that the plague among the Greeks might cease, and so it happened. But Achilles sat in his tent and fretted, for there was nothing that he liked so much as the cry of the battle.

What Thetis Did for Her Son

When the twelve days of feasting were over, Thetis rose out of the sea and went her way to Olympus. There she found Zeus sitting alone on the highest peak of the mountain. She knelt down before him, and her left hand she laid upon his knees, and with her right hand she caught hold of his beard. Then she made this prayer to him:—

"O father Zeus, if I have ever helped thee at all, now give me what I ask, namely, that my son Achilles may have honour done to him. Agamemnon has shamed him, taking away the gift that the Greeks gave him. Do thou, therefore, make the Trojans prevail for a while in battle, so that the Greeks may find that they cannot do without him. So shall my son have honour."

For a long time Zeus sat saying nothing, for he knew that great trouble would come out of this thing. But Thetis still held him fast by the knees and by the beard; and she spoke again, saying: "Promise me this thing, and make your promise sure by nodding your head; or, else, say outright that you will not do it. Then I shall know that you despise me."

Zeus answered: "This is a hard thing that you ask. You will make a dreadful quarrel between me and the Lady Hera, my wife, and she will say many bitter words to me. Even now she tells me I favour the Trojans too much. Go, then, as quickly as you can, that she may not know that you have been here, and I will think how I may best do what you ask. And see, I will make my promise sure with a nod, for when I nod my head, then the thing may not be repented of or undone."

So he nodded his head, and all Olympus was shaken.

Then Thetis went away, and dived down into the sea. And Zeus went to his palace, and when he came in at the door, all the gods rose up in their places, and stood till he sat down on his throne. But Hera knew that Thetis had been with him, and she was very angry, and spoke bitter words: "Who has been with you, O lover of plots? When I am not here, then you take pleasure in hiding what you do, and in keeping things from me."

Zeus answered: "O Hera, do not think to know all of my thoughts; that is too hard for you, even though you are my wife. That which it is right for you to know, I will tell you before I tell it to any other god; but there are matters which I keep to myself. Do not seek to know these."

But Hera was even more angry than before. "What say you?" she cried. "I do not pry into your affairs. Settle them as you will. But this I know, that

Thetis with the silver feet has been with you, and I greatly fear that she has had her way. At dawn of day I saw her kneeling before you; yes, and you nodded your head. I am sure that you have promised her that Achilles should have honour. Ah me! Many of the Greeks will die for this."

Then Zeus answered: "Truly there is nothing that you do not find out, witch that you are. But, if it be as you say, then know that such is my will. Do you sit still and obey. All the gods in Olympus cannot save you, if once I lay my hands upon you."

Hera sat still and said nothing, for she was very much afraid. Then her son, the god who made arms and armour and cups and other things out of silver and gold and copper, said to her: "It would be a great pity if you and the Father of the gods should quarrel on account of a man. Make peace with him, and do not make him angry again. It would be a great grief to me if I were to see you beaten before my eyes; for, indeed, I could not help you. Once before when I tried to come between him and you, he took me by the foot and threw me out the door of heaven. All day I fell and at evening I lighted in the island of Lemnos."

Then he thought how he might turn the thoughts of the company to something else. There was a very beautiful boy who used to carry the wine round. The god, who was a cripple, took his place, and mixed the cup, and hobbled round with it, puffing for breath as he went, and all the gods fell into great fits of laughter when they saw him. So the feast went on, and Apollo and the Muses sang, and no one thought any more about the quarrel.

But while all the other gods were sleeping, Zeus remained awake, thinking how he might do what Thetis had asked of him for her son. The best thing seemed to be to deceive Agamemnon, and make him think that he could take the city of Troy without the help of Achilles. So he called a Dream, and said to it: "Go, Dream, to the tent of Agamemnon, and tell him that if he will lead his army to battle, he will take the city of Troy."

So the Dream went, and it took the shape of Nestor, whom the King thought to be the wisest of the Greeks, and stood by his bedside and said: "Why do you waste your time in sleep? Arm the Greeks, and lead them out to battle, for you will take the city of Troy."

And the King believed that this false dream was true.

The Duel of Paris and Menelaus

On the day after the False Dream had come to him Agamemnon called all his army to go out to battle. All the chiefs were glad to fight, for they thought that at last the long war was coming to an end. Only Achilles and his people stopped behind. And the Trojans, on the other hand, set their army in order.

Before they began to fight, Paris, who had been the cause of all the trouble, came out in front of the line. He had a panther's skin over his shoulders, and a bow and a quiver slung upon his back, for he was a great archer; by his side there hung a sword, and in each hand he carried a spear. He cried aloud to the Greeks: "Send out the strongest and the bravest man you have to fight with me." When King Menelaüs heard this, he said to himself: "Now this is my enemy; I will fight with him, and no one else." So he jumped down from his chariot, and ran out in front of the line of Greeks. But when Paris saw him he was very much afraid, and turned his back and ran behind the line of the Trojans.

Now the best and bravest of the Trojans was a certain Hector. He was one of the sons of King Priam; if it had not been for him the city would have been taken long before. When he saw Paris run away he was very angry, and said: "O Paris, you are good to look at, but you are worth nothing. And the Greeks think that you are the bravest man we have! You were brave enough to go across the sea and steal the Fair Helen from her husband, and now when he comes to fight with you, you run away. The Trojans ought to have stoned you to death long ago."

Paris answered: "You speak the truth great Hector; I am, indeed, greatly to be blamed. As for you, you care for nothing but battles, and your heart is made of iron. But now listen to me: set Menelaüs and me to fight, man to man, and let him that conquers have the Fair Helen and all her possessions. If he kills me, let him take her and depart; but if I kill him, then she shall stay here. So, whatever may happen, you will dwell in peace."

Hector was very glad to hear his brother Paris speak in this way. And he went along the line of the Trojans, holding his spear in the middle. This he did to show that he was not meaning to fight, and to keep his men in their places that they should not begin the battle. At first the Greeks made ready spears and stones to throw at him, but Agamemnon cried out: "Hold your hands; great Hector has something to say."

Then every one stood still and listened. And Hector said: "Hear, Trojans and Greeks, what Paris says, Paris, who is the cause of this quarrel between us. 'Let Menelaüs and me fight together. Every one else, whether he is Greek or Trojan, shall lay his arms upon the ground, and look on while we two fight together. For the Fair Helen and her riches we will fight, and the rest will cease from war and be good friends for ever.' "

When Hector had spoken, King Menelaüs stood up and said: "Listen to me, for this is my affair. It is well that the Greeks and Trojans should be at peace, for there is no quarrel between them. Let me and Paris fight together, and let him of us two be slain whose fate it is to die. And now let us make a sacrifice to the gods, and swear a great oath over it that we will keep our agreement. Only let King Priam himself come and offer the sacrifice and take the oath, for he is more to be trusted than the young men his sons."

So spoke Menelaüs; and both the armies were glad, for they were tired of the war.

Then Hector sent a messenger to Troy to fetch King Priam, and to bring sheep for the sacrifice. And when the herald was on his way, one of the gods put it into the heart of the Fair Helen as she sat in her hall to go out to the wall and see the army of the Greeks. So she went, leaving the needlework with which she was busy, a great piece of embroidery, on which the battles between the Greeks and the Trojans were worked.

Now King Priam sat on the wall, and with him were the other princes of the city, old men who could no longer fight, but could take counsel and make beautiful speeches. They saw the Fair Helen as she came, and one of them said to another: "See how beautiful she is! And yet it would be better that she should go back to her own country, than that she should stop here and bring a curse upon us and our children."

But Priam called to her and said: "Come hither, my daughter, and see your friends and kinsmen in yonder army, and tell us about them. Who is that warrior there, so fair and strong? There are others who are even a head taller than he is, but there is no one who is so like a king."

"That," said Helen, "is Agamemnon, a brave soldier and a wise king, and my brother-in-law in the old days."

And King Priam cried: "Happy Agamemnon, to rule over so many brave men as I see in yonder army! But tell me who is that warrior there, who is walking through the ranks of his men, and making them stand in good order? He is not so tall as Agamemnon, but he is broader in the shoulders."

"That," said Helen, "is Ulysses of Ithaca, who is wiser than all other men, and gives better advice."

"You speak truly, fair lady," said one of the old men, Antenor by name. "Well do I remember Ulysses when he came with Menelaüs on an embassy. They were guests in my house, and I knew them well. And when there was an assembly of the Trojans to hear them speak on the business for which they came, I remember how they looked. When they were standing, Menelaüs was the taller; but when they sat down, then Ulysses was the nobler of the two to look at. And when they spoke, Menelaüs said but a few words, and said them wisely and well; and Ulysses—at first you might have taken him to be a fool, so stiffly did he hold his staff, and so awkward did he seem, with his eyes cast down upon the ground; but when he began to speak, how grand was his voice and how his words poured out, thick as the falling snow! There never was a speaker such as he, and we thought no more about his looks."

Then King Priam asked again: "Who is that mighty hero, so big and strong, taller than all the rest by his head and shoulders?"

"That," said Helen, "is Ajax, a tower of strength to the Greeks. And other chiefs I see whom I know and could name. But my own dear brothers, Castor, tamer of horses, and Pollux, the mighty boxer, I see not. Is it that they are ashamed to come on account of me?"

So she spoke, not knowing that they were dead.

And now came the messenger to tell King Priam that the armies wanted him. So he went and Antenor with him, and they took the sheep for sacrifice. Then King Priam, on behalf of the Trojans, and King Agamemnon, on behalf of the Greeks, offered sacrifice, and made an agreement, confirming it with an oath, that Menelaüs and Paris should fight together, and that Fair Helen with her treasure should belong to him who should prevail.

When this was done, King Priam said: "I will go back to Troy, for I could not bear to see my dear son fighting with Menelaüs." So he climbed into the chariot, and Antenor took the reins and they went back to Troy.

Then Hector for the Trojans, and Ulysses for the Greeks, marked out a space for the fight, and Hector put two pebbles into a helmet, one for Paris and one for Menelaüs. These he shook, looking away as he did so, for it was agreed that the man whose pebble should first fly out of the helmet, should be the first to cast his spear at the other. And this might be much to his gain, for the spear, being well thrown, might kill his adversary or wound him to death, and he himself would not come into danger. And it so happened that the pebble of Paris first flew out. Then the two warriors armed themselves, and came into the space that had been marked out, and stood facing each other. Very fierce were their eyes, so that it could be seen how they hated each other. First Paris threw his spear. It hit the shield of Menelaüs, but did not pierce it, for the point was bent back. Then Menelaüs threw his spear; but first he prayed: "Grant, Father Zeus, that I may have vengeance on Paris, who has done me this great wrong!" And the spear went right through the shield, and through the armour that Paris wore upon his body, and through the tunic that was under the armour. But Paris shrank away, so that the spear did not wound him. Then Menelaüs drew his sword, and struck the helmet of Paris on the top with a great blow, but the sword was broken into four pieces. Then he rushed upon Paris and caught him by the helmet, and dragged him towards the army of the Greeks; neither could Paris help himself, for the strap of the helmet choked him. Then, indeed, would Paris have been taken prisoner and killed, but that the goddess Aphrodité helped him, for he was her favourite. She loosed the strap under his chin, and the helmet came off in the hand of Menelaüs. The King threw it among the Greeks, and, taking another spear in his hand, ran furiously at Paris. But the goddess covered him with a mist, and so snatched him away, and set him down in his own house at Troy. Everywhere did Menelaüs look for him, but he could not find him. It was no one of the Trojans that hid him, for they all hated him as death.

Then said King Agamemnon in a loud voice: "Now must you Trojans keep the covenant that you have made with an oath. You must give back the Fair Helen and her treasures, and we will take her and leave you in peace."

How the Oath Was Broken

Now, if the Trojans had kept the promise which they made, confirming it with an oath, it would have been well with them. But it was not to be. And this is how it came to pass that the oath was broken and the promise not kept.

Among the chiefs who came from the countries round about to help King Priam and the Trojans there was a certain Panda˘rus, son of the King of Lycia. He was a great archer, and could shoot an arrow as far and with as good an aim as any man in the army. To this Panda˘rus, as he stood waiting for what should next happen, there came a youth, a son of King Priam. Such indeed, he seemed to be, but in truth the goddess Athené had taken his shape, for she and, as has been before said, the goddess Hera hated the city of Troy, and desired to bring it to ruin.

The false Trojan came up to Panda˘rus, as he stood among his men, and said to him: "Prince of Lycia, dare you to shoot an arrow at Menelaüs? Truly the Trojans would love you well, and Paris best of all, if they could see Menelaüs killed with an arrow from your bow. Shoot at him as he stands, not thinking of any danger, but first vow to sacrifice a hundred beasts to Zeus, so soon as you shall get back to your own country."

Panda˘rus had a bow made out of the horns of a wild goat which he had killed. It was four feet long from end to end, and on each end there was a tip of gold on which the bow-string was fixed. While he was stringing his bow, his men stood round and hid him; and when he had strung it, he took an arrow from his quiver, and laid it on the string, and drew back the string till it touched his breast, and then let the arrow fly.

But though none of the Greeks saw what Panda˘rus was doing, Athené saw it, and she flew to where Menelaüs stood, and kept the arrow from doing him deadly hurt. She would not ward it off altogether, for she knew that the Greeks would be angry to see the King whom they loved so treacherously wounded, and would have no peace with the Trojans. So she guided it to where there was a space between the belt and the breastplate. There it struck the King, passing through the edge of the belt and through the garment that was under the belt and piercing the skin; and the red blood gushed out, and dyed the thighs and the legs and the ankles of the King, as a woman dyes a piece of white ivory to make an ornament for a king's war-horse.

Now Agamemnon was standing near, and when he saw the blood gush out he cried: "Oh, my brother, it was a foolish thing that I did, when I made a covenant with the Trojans, for they are wicked men and break their oaths. I know that they who do such things will suffer for them. Sooner or later the man who breaks his oath will perish miserably. Nevertheless, it will be a great shame and sorrow if you, my brother, should be killed in this way. For the Greeks will go to their homes saying: 'Why should we fight any more for Menelaüs, seeing that he is dead?' And the Fair Helen for whom we have been fighting these many years will be left behind; and one of these false Trojans will say when he sees the tomb of Menelaüs: 'Surely the great Agamemnon has not got that for which he came. For he brought a great army to destroy the city of Troy, but Troy still stands, and he and his army have gone back: only he has left his brother behind him.' "

But Menelaüs said: "Do not trouble yourself, my brother, for the wound is not deep. See here is the barb of the arrow."

Then King Agamemnon commanded that they should fetch Macha‾on, the great physician. So Macha‾on came, and drew the arrow out of the wound, and wiped away the blood, and put healing drugs upon the place, which took away all the pain.

After this King Agamemnon went through the army to see that it was ready for battle. When he found any one bestirring himself, putting his men in order, and doing such things as it was his duty to do, him he praised; and if he saw any one idle and slow to move, him he rebuked. When all was ready, then the host went forward. In silence it went; but the Trojans, on the other hand, were as noisy as a flock of sheep, which bleats when they hear the voice of the lambs.

The Great Deeds of Diomed

Many great deeds were done that day, and many chiefs showed themselves to be valiant men, but the greatest deeds were done by Diomed, and of all the chiefs there was not one who could be matched with him. No one could tell, so fierce was he, and so swiftly did he charge, in which host he was fighting, whether with the Greeks or with the sons of Troy. After a while the great archer Panda˘rus aimed an arrow at him, and hit him on the right shoulder. And when Panda˘rus saw that he had hit him, for the blood started out from the wound, he cried out in great joy: "On, men of Troy; I have wounded the bravest of the Greeks. He will soon either fall dead in his chariot, or grow so weak that he can fight no longer."

But Diomed was not to be conquered in this fashion. He leapt down from his chariot, and said to the man who drove the horses: "Come and draw this arrow out of the wound." And this the driver did, and when Diomed saw the blood spirt out from the wound he prayed to the goddess Athené: "O goddess, stand by me, as you did always stand by my father. And as for the man who has wounded me, let him come within a spear's cast of me, and he will never boast again." And Athené heard his prayer, and came and stood beside him, and took away the pain from his wound, and put new strength into his hands and feet. "Be bold, O Diomed, and fight against the men of Troy. As I stood by your father, so will I stand by you."

Then Diomed fought even more fiercely than before, just as a lion which a shepherd has wounded a little when he leaps into the fold, grows yet more savage, so it was with Diomed. And as he went to and fro through the battle, slaying all whom he met, Æne¯as, who was the bravest of the Trojans after Hector, thought how he might best be stopped. So he passed through the army till he came to where Panda˘rus the archer stood. To him he said: "Where are your bow and arrows? Do you see this man how he is dealing death wherever he goes? Shoot an arrow at him; but first make your prayers to Zeus that you may not shoot in vain."

Panda˘rus answered: "This man is Diomed. I know his shield and his helmet; the horses too are his. Some god I am sure, stands by him and defends him. Only just now I sent an arrow at him, yes, and hit him in the shoulder. I thought that I had wounded him to the death, for I saw the blood spirt out; but I have not hurt him at all. And now I do not know what I can do, for I have no chariot here. Eleven chariots I have at home, and my father would have had me bring one of them with me. But I would not, for I was afraid that the horses would not have provender enough, being shut up in the city of Troy. So I came without a chariot, trusting to my bow, and lo! it has failed me these two times. Two of the chiefs I have hit, first Menelaüs and then this Diomed. Yes, I hit them, and I saw the red blood flow, but I have not harmed them. Surely if ever I get back to my home, I will break this useless bow."

Then Æneᷱas said to him: "Nay, my friend, do not talk this way. If you have no chariot, then come in mine, and see what horses we have in Troy. If Diomed should be too strong for us, still they will carry us safely back to Troy. Take the reins and the whip, and I will fight; or, if you would rather, do you fight and I will drive."

Pandaᷱrus said: "It is best that the horses should have the driver whom they know. If we should have to flee, they might stand still or turn aside, missing their master's voice."

Now Diomed was on foot, for he had not gone back to his chariot, and his charioteer was by his side. And the man said to him: "Look there; two mighty warriors, Pandaᷱrus and Æneᷱas, are coming against us. It would be well for us to go back to the chariot, that we may fight them on equal terms." But Diomed answered: "Do not talk of going back. I am not one of those who go back. As for my chariot, I do not want it. As I am, I will go against these men. Both of them, surely, shall not go back, even if one should escape. And if I slay them, then do you climb into the chariot and drive it away. There are no horses in the world as good as these, for they are the breed which Zeus himself gave to King Tros."

While he was speaking the two Trojan chiefs came near, and Pandaᷱrus cast his spear at Diomed. It pierced the shield and also the belt, so strongly was it thrown, but it went no further. But Pandaᷱrus cried: "Aha! you are hit in the loin. This wound will stay you from fighting." "Not so," said Diomed, "you have not wounded me at all. But now see what I will send." And he threw his spear, nor did he throw in vain, for it passed through the warrior's nose and teeth and tongue, and stood out under his chin. And the man fell from his chariot, and the armour clashed loudly upon him. But Æneᷱas would not leave his comrade. He leapt from the chariot and stood with shield and spear over the body, as a lion stands over the carcase of some beast which it has killed. Now Diomed had no spear in hand, neither could he draw out from the dead body that which he had thrown. Therefore he stooped and took up from the ground a big stone—so big was it that two men such as men are now could scarcely lift it up—and threw it at Æneᷱas. On the hip it struck him and crushed the bone, and the hero fell upon his knees, and clutched at the ground with his hands, and everything grew dark before his eyes. Thus had he died, but for his mother, the goddess Aphrodité. She caught him up in her arms, and threw her veil over him to hide him. But Diomed did not like that he should escape, and he rushed with his spear at the goddess and wounded her in the arm, and the blood gushed out—such blood as flows in the veins of gods, who eat not the food nor drink the drink of men. She dropped her son with a loud shriek and fled up into the sky. And bold Diomed called after her: "You should not join in the battle, daughter of Zeus. You have to do not with men but with women." But Apollo caught up Æne⁻as when his mother dropped him. Even then Diomed was loath to let him escape, for he was bent on killing him and stripping him of his arms. Three times did he spring forward, and three times did Apollo put back his shining shield. And when he came to the fourth time, Apollo called out to him in an awful voice: "Beware, Diomed; do not think to fight with gods." Then Diomed fell back, for he was afraid. But Apollo carried Æne⁻as to the citadel of Troy, and there his mother Lato⁻na and his sister Arte˘mis healed the hero of his wounds. But he left an image of the hero in the midst of the battle, and over him the Greeks and the Trojans fought, as if it had been the real Æne⁻as.

Concerning Other Valiant Deeds

Now among the chiefs who came to help King Priam and the Trojans there was a certain Sarpe‾don, who was Prince of Lycia, and with him there was one Glaucus who was his cousin. When Sarpe‾don saw how Diomed was laying waste the army of the Trojans, and that no man was willing to stand up against him, he said to Hector: "Where are your boasts, O Hector? You used to say that you could keep the city of Troy safe, without your people, and without us, who have come to help you. Yes, you and your brothers and your brothers-in-law would be enough, you said; but now I look about me, and I cannot see one of them. They all go and hide themselves, as dogs before a lion. It is we who keep up the battle. Look at me; I have come far to help you, even from the land of Lycia, where I have left wife and child and wealth. Nor do I shrink back from the fight, but you also should do your part."

These words stung Hector to the heart. He jumped down from his chariot, and went through the army, telling the men to be brave. And Ares brought back Æne‾as with his wound healed, and he himself went back with Hector, in the shape of a man. And even the brave Diomed, when he saw him and knew that he was a god, held back a little, saying to his companions: "See, Hector is coming, and Ares is with him, in the shape of a man. Let us give way a little, for we must not fight with gods; but we will still keep our faces to the enemy."

Just then a great Greek warrior, who was one of the sons of Hercules, the strongest of men, was killed by Sarpe‾don the Lycian. This man cried out to Sarpe‾don: "What are you doing here? You are foolish to fight with men who are better than you are. Men say that you are a son of Zeus, but the sons of Zeus are braver and stronger than you. Are you as good as my father Hercules? Have you not heard how he came to this city of Troy, and broke down the walls and spoiled the houses, because the King of Troy cheated him of his pay? For my father saved the King's daughter from a great monster of the sea, and the King promised him a team of horses, but did not keep his promise. And you have come to help the Trojans, so they say; small help will you be to them, when I have killed you."

Sarpe‾don answered: " 'Tis true that your father broke down the walls of Troy, and spoiled the houses; the King of the city had cheated him and he was rightly punished for it. But you shall not do what he did; no, for I shall kill you first."

Then the two warriors drew their spears. At the same moment they threw them, and both of them hit the mark. The spear of Sarpe‾don went right through the neck of the Greek, so that he fell down dead; and the spear of the Greek hit Sarpe‾don on the thigh of the left leg and went through it close to the bone. It went very near to killing him; but it was not his fate to die that day. So his men carried him out of the battle with the spear sticking in the wound, for no one thought of drawing it out, so great was their hurry. As they were carrying him along, Hector passed by, and he cried out: "O Hector, do not let the Greeks take me! Let me, at least, die in your city which I came to help; for to Lycia I shall not go back, nor shall I see again my wife and my child." But Hector did not heed him, so eager was he to fight. So the men carried him to the great oak tree, and laid him down in the shade of it, and one of them drew the spear out of the wound. When it was drawn out he fainted, but the cool north wind blew on him and refreshed him, and he breathed again.

At this time the Greeks were being driven back; many were killed and many were wounded. For Hector, with Ares by his side, was so fierce and strong that no one dared to stand up against him. When the two goddesses, Hera and Athené, who loved the Greeks, saw this, they said to Zeus: "Father, do you see how furiously Ares is raging in the battle, driving the Greeks before him? May we stop him before he destroys them altogether?" Zeus said: "You may do what you please." Then they yoked the horses to Hera's chariot and went as fast as they could to the earth. Very fast they went, for every stride of the horses was over as much space as a man can see when he sits upon a cliff and looks over the sea to where the sky seems to come down upon it. When they came to the plain of Troy, they unharnessed the horses at a place where the two rivers met. They covered them and the chariot with a mist that no one might be able to see them, and they themselves flew as doves fly to where the Greeks and Trojans were fighting. There Hera took the shape of Stentor, who could shout as loud as fifty men shouting at once, and cried: "Shame, men of Greece! when Achilles came to battle the Trojans scarcely dared to go beyond the gates of their city, but now they are driving you to your ships." Athené went to Diomed, where he was standing and wiping away the blood from the wound which the arrow had made. "You are not like your father; he was a little man, but he was a great fighter. I do not know whether you are holding back because you are tired or because you are afraid; but certainly you are not like him."

Diomed knew who it was that was speaking to him, and answered: "Great goddess, I am not holding back because I am tired or because I am afraid. You yourself said to me: 'Do not fight against any god; only if Aphrodité comes into the battle, you may fight against her.' And this I have done. Her I wounded on the wrist and drove away; but when Apollo carried away Æne⁻as from me, then I held back. And now I see Ares rushing to and fro through the battle, and I do not dare to go against him."

Then said Athené: "Do not be afraid of Ares. I will come with you, and you shall wound him with your spear, and drive him away from the battle."

Then she pushed Diomed's charioteer with her hand, but the man did not see who it was that pushed him. And when he jumped down from the chariot she took his place, and caught the reins in her hand, and lashed the horses. Straight at Ares she drove, where he was standing by a Greek whom he had killed. Now Athené had put on her head the helmet of Hades, that is to say, of the god who rules the dead; Ares did not see her, for no one who wears the helmet can be seen. And he rushed at Diomed, thinking to kill him, and threw his spear with all his might. But Athené put out her hand and turned the spear aside, so that it flew through the air and hurt no one. Then Diomed thrust his spear at Ares, and Athené leant all her weight upon it, so that it pierced the god just below the girdle. And when Ares felt the spear, he shouted with the pain as loud as an army of ten thousand men shouts when it goes forth to battle. And Diomed saw him rise up to the sky as a thunder-cloud arises.

And this was the greatest of the deeds of Diomed, that he wounded Ares, the god of war, and drove him out of the battle.

Of Glaucus and Diomed

And now the Trojans, in their turn, were driven back, for they could make no stand against the Greeks. Now there was one of the sons of King Priam who was a very wise prophet, and knew all that men should do to win the favour and help of the gods, and his name was Hele˘nus. This man went up to Hector, and said to him and to Æne¯as, who was standing near him: "Make the army fall back and get as close to the walls as may be, for it will be safer there than in the open plain. And go through the ranks, and speak to the men, and put as much courage into them as you can. And when you have done this, do you, Hector, go into the city, and tell your mother to gather together the daughters of Troy, and go with them to the temple of Athené, taking with her the most precious robe that she has, and lay the robe on the knees of the goddess, and promise to sacrifice twelve heifers, and beseech her to have pity on us and to keep Diomed from the walls. Never did I see so fierce a man; even Achilles himself was not so terrible as he is, so dreadful is he and so fierce. Go, and come back as soon as you can, and we will do what we can to bear up against the Greeks while you are away."

So Hector went through the ranks, bidding the men be of good courage; and when he had done this he went into the city.

And now the Trojans had a little rest. The way in which this happened shall now be told.

Sarpe¯don and Lycian had a cousin, Glaucus by name: the two were sons of brothers. This Glaucus, being one of the bravest of men, went in front of the Trojan line to meet Diomed. When Diomed saw him, he said: "Tell me, mighty man of valour, who you are, for I have never seen you before; for this is a bold thing that you have done to come out in front of your comrades and to stand against me. Truly those men whose children come in my way in battle are unlucky. Tell me then who you are, for if you are a god from heaven, then I will not fight with you. Already to-day have I done enough fighting with them, for it is an unlucky thing to do. King Lycurgus, in the land of Thrace, fought with a god, and it was a bad thing for him that he did so, for he did not live long. He drove Bacchus, the god of wine, into the sea. But the other gods were angry with him for this cause, and Zeus made him blind, and he perished miserably. But if you are no god, but a mortal man, then draw near that I may kill you with my spear."

Glaucus said: "Brave Diomed, why do you ask who I am, and who was my father, and my father's father? The generations of men are like the leaves on the trees. In the spring they shoot forth, and in autumn they fall, and the wind blows them to and fro. And then when the spring comes others shoot forth, and these also fall in their time. So are the generations of men; one goes and another comes. Still, if you would hear of what race I come, listen. In a certain city of Greece which is called Corinth there dwelt a great warrior, Belleroˇphon by name. Some one spoke evil of this man falsely to the King of the city, and the King believed this false thing, and plotted his death. He was ashamed to kill him, but he sent him with a message to the King of Lycia. This message was written on a tablet and the tablet was folded up in a cover, and the cover was sealed. But on the tablet was written: 'This is a wicked man; cause him to die.' So Belleroˇphon travelled to Lycia. And when he was come to the King's palace, the King made a great feast for him. For nine days did the feast last, and every day an ox was killed and eaten. On the morning of the tenth day the King said: 'Let me see the message which you have brought.' And when he had read it he thought how he might cause the man to die. First he sent him to conquer a great monster that there was in that country, called the Chimæra. Many men tried to conquer it, but it had killed them all. It had the head of a lion, and its middle parts were those of a goat, and it had the tail of a serpent; and it breathed out flames of fire. This monster he killed, the gods helping him. Then the King sent him against a very fierce tribe of men, who were called the Solymi. These he conquered after much fighting, for, as he said himself, there never were warriors stronger than they. After this he fought the Amazons, who were women fighting with the arms of men, and these also he conquered. And when he was coming back from fighting the Amazons, the King set an ambush against him, choosing for it the bravest men in the whole land of Lycia. But Belleroˇphon killed them all, and came back safe to the King's palace. When the King saw this, he said to himself: 'The gods love this man; he cannot be wicked.' So he asked him about himself, and Belleroˇphon told him the whole truth. Then the King divided his kingdom with him, and gave him his daughter to wife. Three sons he had, of whom one was the father of Sarpe¯don and one was my father. And when my father sent me hither he said: 'Always seek to be the first, and to be worthy of those who have gone before.' This, then, brave Diomed, is the race to which I belong."

When Diomed heard this he was very glad, and said: "It is well that we did not fight, for we ought to be friends, as our fathers were before us. Long ago Œneus entertained Belleroˇphon in his house. For twenty days he kept him.

And when they parted they gave great gifts to each other, the one a belt embroidered with purple, and the other a cup of gold with a mouth on either side of it. Now Œneus was my grandfather, as Belleroˇphon was yours. If then you should come to Corinth you will be my guest, and I will be yours if I go to the land of Lycia. But now we will not fight together. There are many Trojans and allies of the Trojans whom I may kill if I can overcome them, and there are many Greeks for you to fight with and conquer, if you can. But we two will not fight together. And now let us exchange our armour, that all men may know that we are friends."

So the two chiefs jumped down from their chariots and exchanged their armour. And men said afterwards that Glaucus had lost his wits, for he gave armour of gold in exchange for armour of brass, armour that was worth a hundred oxen for armour that was worth nine only.

Hector and Andromache

When Hector passed through the gates into the city, hundreds of Trojan women crowded round him, asking what had happened to their sons or husbands. But he said nothing to them, except to bid them to pray that the gods would protect those whom they loved. When he came to the palace there met him his mother, Queen Hecuba. She caught him by the hand, and said: "O Hector, why have you come from battle? Have the Greeks been pressing you hard? or have you come, maybe, to pray for help from Father Zeus? Let me bring a cup of wine, that you may pour out an offering to the god, aye, and that you may drink yourself and cheer your heart."

But Hector said: "Mother, give me no wine, lest it should make my knees weak, and take the courage out of my heart. Nor must I make an offering to the gods with my hands unwashed. What I would have you do is this—gather the mothers of Troy together, and take the most beautiful and precious robe that you have, and go with them and lay it upon the knees of Athené, and pray to her to keep this terrible Diomed from the walls of Troy. And do not forget to promise a sacrifice of twelve heifers. And I will go and call Paris, and bid him come with me to the battle. Of a truth I could wish that the earth would open her mouth and swallow him up, for he is a curse to his father and to you his mother, and to the whole city of Troy."

Then Queen Hecuba went into her palace, and opened the store where she kept her treasures, and took out of it the finest robe that she had. And she and the noblest ladies that were in Troy carried it to the temple of Athené. Then the priestess, who was the wife of Antenor, received it from her hands, and laid it upon the knees of the goddess, making this prayer: "O Lady Athené, keeper of this city, break, we beseech thee, the spear of Diomed, and make him fall dead before the gates of Troy. If thou wilt have pity on the wives and children of the men of Troy, then we will offer to thee twelve heifers that have never been made to draw the plough."

So the priestess prayed; but Athené would not hear. And indeed, it was she who stirred up Diomed to fight so fiercely against Troy and had given him fresh strength and courage.

Meanwhile Hector went to the house of Paris. It stood on the citadel, close to his own house and to the palace of King Priam. He found him cleaning his arms and armour, and the fair Helen sat near him, with her maids, busy with needlework.

Then Hector thought to himself, "If I tell him that he went away from the battle because he was afraid, then I shall offend him and do no good: I will try another way." So he said: "O Paris, is it right that you should stand aside and not fight in the battle because you are angry with your countrymen? The people perish, and the fight grows hotter and hotter every minute about the city. Rouse yourself and come forth before Troy is burnt up. For, remember, it is you that are the cause of all these troubles."

Then Paris answered: "O my brother, you have spoken well. But it was not because I was angry that I came away from the battle; it was because I was so much ashamed of being beaten. But now I will come back, for this is what my wife would have me to do; maybe I shall do better another time, for the gods give victory now to one man and now to another."

Then the Fair Helen said to Hector: "Sit down now and rest a little, for you must be very tired with all that you have done."

But Hector answered: "You must not ask me to rest; I must make haste to help my countrymen, for indeed they are in sore need of help. But do you see that your husband overtakes me before I go out of the city gate. Now I am going to my house to see my wife and my little boy, for I do not know whether I shall ever see them again."

When he said this, Hector went to his house to see his wife Andromaché, for that was her name. But he did not find her at home, for she had gone to the wall, being very much afraid for her husband.

Hector asked the maids: "Where is the Lady Andromaché? Has she gone to see one of her sisters-in-law, or, maybe, with the other mothers of Troy, to the temple of Athené?"

Then an old woman who was the housekeeper said: "Nay; she went to one of the towers of the wall that she might see the battle, for she had heard that the Greeks were pressing our people very much. She seemed like a mad-woman, so much haste she did make, and the nurse went with her carrying the child."

Then Hector ran towards the gate, and Andromaché saw him from where she stood on the wall, and made haste to meet him. And the nurse came with her, carrying the child, Hector's only son, a beautiful boy, with a head like a star, so bright was his golden hair. His father called him Scamandrius, after the river which runs across the plains of Troy; but the people called him Astya˘nax, which means the "City King," because it was his father who saved the city. And Hector smiled when he saw the child. But Andromaché did not smile, for she caught her husband by the hand, and wept, saying, "O Hector, your courage will be your death. You have no pity on your wife and child, and you do not spare yourself. Some day all the Greeks will join together and rush on you and kill you"—for she did not believe that any one of them could conquer him. "But if I lose you, then it would be better for me to die than to live. I have no comfort but you. My father is dead; for the great Achilles killed him when he took our city. He killed him, but he did him great honour, for he would not take his arms for a spoil, but burnt them with him; yes, and the nymphs of the mountains planted poplars by his grave. I had seven brothers, and they also are dead, for the great Achilles killed them in one day. And my mother also is dead, for when my father had redeemed her with a great sum of money, Arte˘mis slew her with one of her deadly arrows. But you are father to me and mother, and brother, and husband also. Have pity on me, and stay here upon the wall, lest you leave me a widow and your child an orphan. And set your people in order of battle by this fig-tree, for here the wall is easier to attack. Here too, I see the bravest chiefs of the Greeks."

Hector answered her: "Dear wife, leave these things to me; I will look after them. One thing I cannot bear, that any son or daughter of Troy should see me skulking from battle. I hate the very thought of it; I must always be in front. Alas! I know that Priam and the people of Priam and this holy city of Troy will perish. But it is not for Troy, or for the people of Troy, nor even for my father and my mother, that I care so much; it is for you, when I think how some Greek will carry you away captive, and you be set to spin or to carry water from the spring in a distant land. And some one will say: 'See that slave woman there! She was the wife of Hector, who was the bravest of the Trojans.' "

Then Hector stretched out his arms to take the child. But the child drew back into the bosom of his nurse, making a great cry, for he was frightened by the helmet which shone so brightly, and by the horsehair plume which nodded so awfully. And both his father and mother laughed to hear him. Then Hector took the helmet from his head and laid it on the ground, and caught the boy in his hands, and kissed him and dandled him. And he prayed aloud to Father Zeus and to the other gods, saying:

"Grant, Father Zeus, and other gods who are in heaven, that this child may be as I am, a great man in Troy. And may the people say some day when they see him carrying home the bloody spoils of some enemy whom he has killed in battle: 'A better man than his father, this!' And his mother will be glad to hear it."

Then he gave the boy to his mother, and she clasped him to her breast and smiled, but there were tears in her eyes when she smiled. And Hector's heart was moved when he saw the tears; and he stroked her with his hand and said:

"Do not let these things trouble you. No man will be able to kill me, unless it be my fate to die. But fate no one may escape, whether he be a brave man or a coward. But go, dear wife, to your spinning again, and give your maids their tasks, and let the men see to the battle."

Then he took up the helmet from the ground, and put it on his head, and Andromaché went to her home, but often, as she went, she turned her eyes to look at her husband. And when she came to her home she called all the maids together, and they wept and wailed for Hector as though he were already dead. And, indeed, she thought in her heart that she should never again see him coming home safe from the battle.

Hector went on his way to the gate, and as he went Paris came running after him. His arms shone brightly in the sun, and he himself went proudly along like a horse that is fresh from his stable, and prances over the grass and tosses his mane. And he said to Hector: "I am afraid that I have kept you when you were in a hurry to get back to your comrades."

Hector answered: "No man doubts that you are brave. But you are wilful, and hold back from the battle when you should be foremost. So it is that the people say shameful things about you. But now let us make haste to the battle."

So they went out by the gate, and fell upon the Greeks and killed many of them, and Glaucus the Lycian went with them.

How Hector and Ajax Fought

Athene was very sorry to see how her dear Greeks were being killed by Hector and his companions. So she flew down from the heights of Olympus to see whether she could help them. When she had come to the plains of Troy she met Apollo. Now Apollo loved the Trojans, and said to her: "Are you come, Athené, to help the Greeks whom you love? Now I, as you know, love the Trojans. Let us therefore join together and stop them from fighting for to-day. Hereafter they shall fight till that which the Fates have settled for Troy shall come to pass."

Athené answered: "How shall we stop them from fighting?" Apollo said: "We will set on Hector to challenge the bravest of the Greeks to fight with him, man to man."

So these two put the thought into the mind of the prophet Hele˘nus. So Hele˘nus went up to Hector and said: "Hector, listen to me; I am your brother, and also the gods have made me a prophet, so that you should take heed to the things which I say. Now my advice is this: cause the men of Troy and the Greeks to sit down in peace, and do you challenge the bravest of the enemy to fight with you, man to man. And be sure that in this fight you will not be killed, for so much the gods have told me; but whether you will kill the other, that I do not know, for the gods have not told me."

This pleased Hector greatly, and he went to the front of the army, holding his spear by the middle, and keeping the Trojans back. And King Agamemnon did the same with his own people. Then Hector said:

"Hear me, sons of Troy, and ye men of Greece. The covenant which we made together was broken. Truly this was not my doing; the gods would have it so, for it is their will that we should fight together, till either you take our city or we drive you back to your ships, and compel you to go back to your own land. And yet listen to what I shall now say, for it may be that the gods will repent and suffer peace to be made between us. Do you Greeks choose out from those who are strongest and bravest among you some one to fight with me, man to man. And let this be agreed between us: if this man shall conquer me, then he shall take my arms for himself, but he shall give back my body to my people that they may burn it with fire. And in like manner, if I shall conquer him, then I will take his arms for myself, but I will give his body to his people that they may bury it and raise a great mound over it. And so in days to come men who shall see it, as they sail by, will say: 'This is the tomb of the bravest of the Greeks, whom Hector of Troy killed in battle, fighting him man to man.' So my name will be remembered for ever."

When the Greeks heard these words, they all stood still, saying nothing. They feared to meet the great Hector in battle, for he seemed to be stronger than he had ever been before, but they were ashamed to hold back. Then Menelaüs jumped up in his place and cried: "Surely now ye are women and not men. What a shame it is to Greece that no one can be found to fight with this Hector! I will fight with him my own self, for the gods give the victory to one man or to another as they will."

So spoke Menelaüs, for he was very angry, and did not care whether he lived or died. And, indeed, it would have been his death to fight with Hector, who was by much the stronger of the two. But King Agamemnon would not suffer him to be so rash. "Nay, my brother," he said, "this is but folly. Seek not to fight with one who is much stronger than you. Even Achilles was not willing to meet him. Sit still, therefore, for the Greeks will find some champion to meet him."

And Menelaüs hearkened to his brother's words and sat down. But when no one stood up to offer himself to fight with Hector, old Nestor rose in his place and said: "Now this is a sad day for Greece! How sorry old Peleus would be to hear of this thing. I remember how glad he was when I told him about the chiefs who were going to fight against Troy, who they were and whence they came. And now he would hear that they are all afraid when Hector challenges them to fight with him man to man. He would pray that he might die. Oh, that I were such as I was in the old days, when the men of Pylos fought with the men of Arcadia. The men of Arcadia had a great champion, who was the strongest and biggest of all the men of that day, and carried the most famous arms in Greece, and a club of iron such as no one else could wield. And when this man challenged the men of Pylos to fight with him, the others, indeed, were afraid, for the man was like a giant; but I stood up, though I was the youngest of them all, and Athené stood by me and gave me great glory, for I slew him, and took from him his arms and his great iron club. Oh! that I were now such as I was that day! Hector would soon find some one to fight with him."

When old Nestor sat down, nine chiefs stood up. First among them was King Agamemnon, and after him Diomed and Ajax the Greater and Ajax the Less and Ulysses, and four others. Then said Nestor: "Let us cast lots to see who of these nine shall fight with Hector."

So the nine chiefs threw their lots, each man a lot, into the helmet of King Agamemnon. And the people standing round prayed silently to the gods:

"Grant that the lot of Ajax the Greater may leap first out of the helmet, or the lot of Diomed, or the lot of King Agamemnon." Then Nestor shook the helmet, and it came to pass that the lot which first leapt forth was that very one which they most desired. For when the herald carried it round to the chiefs no one took it for his own, till the man came to Ajax the Greater. But Ajax had marked it with his own mark; he put out his hand, therefore and claimed it. He was very glad in his heart, and he threw down the lot at his feet and cried: "The lot is mine, my friends, and I am glad above measure, for I think that I shall conquer this mighty Hector. And now I will put on my arms. And do you pray Father Zeus, silently, if you will, that the Trojans may not hear; or if you had rather pray aloud, then do so, for I fear no man. None shall conquer me either by force or by craft, for the men of Salamis"—it was from the island of Salamis he came—"are not to be conquered."

So Ajax put on his armour. And when he finished, he went forward, as dreadful to look at as the god of war himself, and there was a smile on his face, but it was not the smile that other men like to see. Taking great strides he went, and he shook his great spear. And when the Trojans saw him their knees trembled beneath them, and even the great Hector felt his heart beat more quickly than before. But he showed no fear, and stood firmly in his place, for he himself challenged his adversary.

So Ajax came near, holding his great shield before him, as it might be a wall. There was no such shield in all the army of the Greeks. It had seven folds of bull's-hide, and one fold, the eighth, of bronze. Then Ajax spoke in a loud voice: "Come near, Hector, that you may see what men we have among us, we Greeks, though the great Achilles is not here, but sits idle in his tent."

Hector answered: "Do not speak to me, Ajax, as though I were a woman or a child, and knew nothing of war. I know all the arts of battle, to turn my shield this way and that to meet the spear of the enemy, and to drive my chariot through the crowds of men and horses, and to fight hand to hand. But come, let us fight openly, face to face, as honest men should do."

And as he spoke he threw his great spear at Ajax. Through six folds of bull's-hide it passed, but the seventh stopped it, for all that it was so strongly thrown. It was no easy thing to pierce the great shield with its seven folds. But when Ajax, in his turn, threw his spear at Hector, it passed through his shield, and through the armour that covered his body, and through the garment that was under the armour. It went near to killing him, but Hector bent his body away, and so saved himself. Then each took a fresh spear, and ran together as fiercely as lions or wild boars. Again did Hector drive his spear against the great shield, and again did he drive it in vain, for the spear point was bent back. But Ajax, making a great leap from the ground, pierced Hector's shield with his spear, and pushed him back from the place where he stood, and the spear point grazed his neck, so that the blood spirted out. Then Hector caught up a great stone that lay upon the ground and threw it. And yet once more the great shield stayed him, nor could he break it through, and the stone which Ajax threw was heavier by far, and it broke Hector's shield and bore him to the ground, so that he lay on his back upon the ground, with the broken shield over him. Truly it had fared ill with him but that Apollo raised him up and set him on his feet. Then the two warriors drew their swords, but before they could get close together, the two heralds came up and thrust their staves between them. And the Trojan herald said: "It is enough, my sons; fight no more; you are great warriors both of you, and Zeus loves you both. But now the night is at hand, and bids you cease, and you will do well to obey."

Then said Ajax: "Yes, herald; but it is for Hector to speak, for he began this matter, challenging the bravest of the Greeks to fight with him. And what he wills, that I will also."

Hector said: "The herald speaks well. Verily the gods have given you, O Ajax, stature and strength and skill. There is no better warrior among the Greeks. Let us cease then from fighting; haply we may meet again another day, and the gods may give victory to you or to me. But now let us give gifts to each other, so that the Trojans and Greeks may say, 'Hector and Ajax met in battle, but parted in friendship.' "

So Hector gave to Ajax a silver-studded sword, with a scabbard and a belt, and Ajax gave to Hector a buckler splendid with purple. So they parted. And the Trojans were right glad to see Hector coming back safe from the battle; on the other hand, the Greeks rejoiced yet more, for indeed their champion had prevailed. And King Agamemnon called all the chiefs to a feast, and to Ajax he gave the chine. The Trojans also feasted in their city. But Zeus sent thunder all that night to be a sign of trouble to come.

The Battle on the Plain

When it was morning Zeus called all the gods and goddesses to an assembly on the top of Mount Olympus, and said to them: "Now listen to me, and obey. No one of you shall help either the Greeks or the Trojans; and mark this: if any god or goddess dares to do so I will throw him down from here into the outer darkness, and there he shall learn that I am lord in heaven. Does any one of you think that I am not stronger than you, yes than all of you put together? Well, let it be put to the trial. Let down a golden chain from heaven to earth, and take hold of it all of you, and see whether you can drag me from the throne. You cannot do it, not though you pull with all your might. But if I should choose to put out all my strength, I could lift you up, and the earth and the sea with you, and fasten the chain round one of the peaks of this mountain Olympus here, and leave you hanging in the air."

So did Zeus speak, and all the gods sat saying nothing, for they were terribly afraid. But at last Athené said: "Father, we know right well that none of us can stand up against you. And yet we cannot help pitying the Greeks, for we fear that they will be altogether destroyed. We will not help them, for this you forbid. But, if you will permit, we will give them advice."

And Zeus smiled, for Athené was his daughter, and he loved her better than any other among the gods and goddesses, and he gave his consent. Then he had his horses yoked to his chariot and touched them with his whip, and they flew midway between heaven and earth till they came to a certain mountain which was called Ida, and was near to Troy. There he sat down and watched the battle, for the time was come when he would keep the promise which he had made to Thetis.

The Greeks ate their food in haste and freshened themselves for battle; and the Trojans also armed themselves inside the city, and when they were ready the gates were opened and they went out. So the two armies came together, and shield was dashed against shield, and spear against spear, and there was a great clash of arms and shouting of men. So long as the sun was rising higher in the sky, neither of the two prevailed over the other; but at noon Zeus held out in the sky his golden scales, and in one scale he laid a weight for the Trojans and in the other a weight for the Greeks. Now the weights were weights of death, and the army whose weight was the heavier would suffer most. And lo! the scale of the Greeks sank lower. Then Zeus sent a thunderbolt from the top of Mount Ida into the army of the Greeks, and there was great fear among both men and horses.

After this no man could hold his ground. Only old Nestor remained where he was, and he remained against his will, for Paris had killed one of his horses with an arrow, and the chariot could not be moved. So the old man began to cut the traces, that he might free the horse that was yet alive from the horse that was dead. While he was doing this Hector came through the crowd of fighting men. Then had the old man perished, but Diomed saw it and went to help him. But first he called to Ulysses, whom he saw close by, running towards the ships. "Ulysses," he cried, as loudly as he could, "where are you going? Are you not ashamed to turn your back in this way like a coward? Take care that no man thrust you in the back with a spear and disgrace you for ever. Stop now, and help me to save old Nestor from this fierce Hector."

So he spoke, but Ulysses gave no heed to his words, but still fled to the ships, for he was really afraid. When Diomed saw this he made haste, though he was alone, to go to the help of Nestor. When he got to the place where the old man was, he stopped his chariot and said: "Old friend, the young warriors are too much for you. Leave your own chariot for others to look after and climb into mine, and see what these horses of King Tros can do, for these are they which I took away from Æne⁻as. There are none faster, or better, or easier to turn this way or that. Take these reins in your hand, and I will go against this Hector, and see whether the spear of Diomed is as strong as it was of old."

So old Nestor climbed up into his chariot, and took the reins in his hand and touched the horses with the whip, driving straight at Hector. And when they were near him, Diomed threw his spear at him. Him he missed, but he struck down his charioteer, and the man fell dead to the ground. Hector was greatly grieved, but he let him lie where he fell, for he must needs find another man to drive the horses. And when he went back from the front to look for the man, then the Trojans went back also, for it was Hector to whom they looked and whom they followed. But when Diomed would have pursued them, Zeus threw another thunderbolt from Ida. It fell right in front of the chariot, and the horses crouched on the ground for fear, and Nestor let the reins drop from his hand, for he was greatly afraid, and cried: "O Diomed, let us fly; see you not that Zeus is against us? He gives glory to Hector to-day; to-morrow, maybe, he will give it to you. But what he wills that will he do, and no man may hinder him."

Diomed answered: "Old sir, you speak wisely. Yet it goes to my heart to turn back. For Hector will say, 'Diomed fled before me, seeking to hide himself in the ships.' I had sooner that the earth should open her mouth and swallow me up, than that I should hear such things."

But Nestor answered: "O Diomed, be content: though Hector may call you coward, the sons of Troy will not believe him, no, nor the daughters of Troy, whose brothers and husbands you have tumbled in the dust."

So then he turned the horses to fly. And Hector cried when he saw the great Diomed fly before him: "Are you the man to whom the Greeks give the chief place in their feasts and great cups of wine? They will not so honour you after to-day. Run, girl! run, coward! Are you the man that was to climb our walls and carry away our people captive?"

Diomed was very angry to hear these words, and doubted whether he should flee or turn again to the battle. But as he doubted, Zeus made a great thundering in the sky, and he was afraid. Then Hector called to his horses; by their names he called them, saying, "Come, Whitefoot and Bayard and Brilliant and Flame of Fire; remember how the fair Andromaché has cared for you, putting you even before me, who am her husband. Carry me now as fast as you can, that I may take from old Nestor his shield, which men say is made all of gold, and from Diomed his breastplate, which was wrought for him in the forge of heaven."

So the Greeks fled as fast as they could within the wall which they had built for a defence for their ships, for Hector drove them before him, nor was there one who dared to stand up against him. And the space between the wall and the ships was crowded with chariots, and no spirit was left in any man. Then Hera put into the heart of King Agamemnon that he should encourage his people to turn again to battle. So the King stood by the ship of Ulysses, which was in the middle of the ships, for they were drawn up in a long line upon the shore, and cried aloud: "Shame on you, Greeks! Where are your boats which you boasted before you came to this land, how that one of you would be more than a match for a hundred, yea, for two hundred Trojans? It was easy to say such words when you ate the flesh of bullocks and drank full cups of wine. But now, when you are put to the trial, a single Trojan is worth more than you all. Was there ever a king who had such cowards for his people?"

Then the Greeks took courage and turned again, and set upon the Trojans. And the first of all to turn and slay a Trojan was Diomed. He drove his spear through the man's back, for now the Trojans were flying in their turn, and tumbled him from his chariot. And after Diomed came King Agamemnon, and Ajax and other chiefs. Among them was Teucer, the brother of Ajax, a skilful archer. He stood under the shield of his brother, and Ajax would lift the shield a little, and then Teucer would peer out and take aim and send an arrow at some Trojan, and kill him or wound him. Then he would go back, as a child runs to his mother, and Ajax covered him with his shield. Eight warriors did he hit in this way. And when King Agamemnon saw him, he said: "Shoot on, Teucer, and be a joy to your people and to your father. Surely when we have taken the city of Troy, and shall divide the spoil you shall have the best gift of all after mine."

And Teucer said: "I need no gifts, O King, to make me eager. I have not ceased to shoot my arrows at these Trojans; eight arrows have I shot, and every one has found its way through some warrior's armour into his flesh. But this Hector I cannot hit."

And as he spoke he let fly another arrow at Hector from the sling. Him he did not touch, but slew a son of Priam. And then he shot yet a tenth, and this time he laid low the charioteer who stood by Hector's side. Then Hector's heart was filled with rage and grief. He leant down from his chariot, and caught up a great stone in his hand, and ran at Teucer, that he might crush him to the earth. And Teucer, when he saw him coming, made haste, and took an arrow from his quiver and fitted it to the sling. But even as he drew back the string to his shoulder, the great stone struck him where the collar-bone stands out against the neck and the arm. It broke the bow-string, and made his arm and wrist all weak and numb, so that he could not hold the bow. And he fell upon his knees, dropping the bow upon the ground. But Ajax stood over him, and covered him with his shield, and two of his comrades took him up in their arms and carried him, groaning deeply, to the ships.

When the Trojans saw the great archer carried away from the battle, they took fresh courage, and drove back the Greeks to the ditch, for there was a ditch in front of the wall. And Hector was always in the very front. As a dog follows a wild beast and catches him by the hip or the thigh as he flies, so did Hector follow the Greeks and slay the hindmost of them.

Then Hera, as she sat on the top of Olympus, said to Athené: "Shall we not have pity on the Greeks and help them? Let us do it this once if we never do it again. I fear much that they will perish altogether by the hand of Hector. See what harm he has done to them already."

Athené answered: "This is also my Father's doing. He listened to Thetis when she asked him to do honour to her son Achilles. But, perhaps, he may now listen to me, and will let me help the Greeks. Make your chariot ready, therefore, and I will put on my armour. So we will go together to the battle; maybe that Hector will not be glad when he sees us coming against him."

So Hera made her chariot ready, and Athené put on her armour, and took her great spear, and prepared as for battle. Then the two mounted the chariot, and the Hours opened the gates of heaven for them, and they went towards Troy.

But Zeus saw them from where he sat on the top of Mount Ida. And he called to Iris, who is the messenger of the gods, and said to her: "Go now, Iris, and tell these two that they had better not set themselves against me. If they do, then I will lame their horses, and throw them down from their chariot, and break the chariot in pieces. If I do but strike them with my thunderbolt, they will not recover from their hurts for ten years and more."

So Iris made all the haste she could, and met the two goddesses on their way, and gave them the message of Zeus. When Hera heard it, she said to Athené: "It is not wise for us two to fight with Zeus for the sake of men. Let them live or die, as he may think best, but we will not set ourselves against him."

So Hera turned the chariot, and they went back to Olympus, and sat down in their chairs of gold among the other gods. Very sad and angry were they.

When Zeus saw that they had gone back, he left Mount Ida and went to Olympus, and came into the hall where the gods were assembled. When he saw Hera and Athené sitting by themselves with gloomy faces, he mocked them, saying: "Why do you look so sad? Surely it cannot be that you have tired yourselves by joining in the battle, and slaying these Trojans whom you hate so much? But if it is because the thing that I will does not please you, then know that what I choose to happen, that shall happen. Yes; if all the other gods should join together against me, still I shall prevail over them."

And when Zeus had so spoken, then Athené, for all that her heart was bursting with anger, said nothing: but Hera would not keep silence. "Well do we know, O Zeus, that you are stronger than all the gods. Nevertheless we cannot but pity the Greeks when we see them perishing in this way."

Zeus spake again: "Is it so? Do you pity the Greeks for what they have suffered to-day? To-morrow you shall see worse things than these, O Queen. For Hector will not cease driving the Greeks before him and slaying them till the great Achilles himself shall be moved, and shall rise from his place where he sits by his ships."

And now the sun sank into the sea, and the night fell. The Trojans were angry that the darkness had come and that they could not see any longer; but the Greeks were glad of the night, for it was as a shelter to them, and gave them time to breathe.

Then Hector called the Trojans to an assembly at a place that was near the river, where the ground was clear of dead bodies. He stood in the middle of the people, holding in his hand a spear, sixteen feet or more in length, with a shining head of bronze, and a band of gold by which the head was fastened to the shaft. What he said to the people was this: "Hearken, men of Troy, and ye, our allies who have come to help us. I thought that to-day we should destroy the army of the Greeks and burn their ships, and so go back to Troy and live in peace. But night has come, and hindered us from finishing our work. Let us sit down, therefore, and rest, and take a meal. Loose your horses from your chariots and give them their food. Go, some of you, to the city, and fetch thence cattle, and sheep, and wine, and bread that we may have plenty to eat and drink: also fetch fuel, that we may burn fires all the night, that we may sit by them, and also that we see whether the Greeks will try to escape in the night. Truly they shall not go in peace. Many will we kill, and the rest shall, at the least, carry away with him a wound for him to heal at home, that so no man may come again and trouble this city of Troy. The heralds also shall go to the city and make a proclamation that the old men and boys shall guard the wall, and that every woman shall light a hearth fire, and that all shall keep watch, lest the enemy should enter the city, while the people are fighting at the ships. And now I will say no more; but to-morrow I shall have other words to speak to you. But know this, that to-morrow we will arm ourselves, and drive these Greeks to their ships; and, if it may be, burn these ships with fire. Then shall we know whether the bold Diomed shall drive me back from the wall or whether he shall be himself slain with the spear. To-morrow shall surely bring ruin on the Greeks. I would that I were as sure of living for ever and ever, and of being honoured as the gods are honoured."

So Hector spoke, and all the Trojans shouted with joy to hear such words. Then they unharnessed the horses, and fetched provender for them from the city, and also gathered a great store of fuel. They sat all night in hope of what the next day would bring. As on a calm night the stars shine bright, so shone the watch-fires of the Trojans. A thousand fires were burning, and by each fire sat fifty men. And the horses stood by the chariots champing oats and barley. So they all waited for the morning.

The Repentance of Agamemnon

While the Trojans made merry, being full of hope that they would soon be rid of their enemies, the Greeks, on the other hand, were full of trouble and fear. And not one of them was more sad at heart than King Agamemnon. After a while he called the heralds and told them to go round to the chiefs and bid them come to a council. "Bid them one by one," he said, "and do not proclaim the thing publicly, for I would not have the people know of it." So the chiefs came, and sat down each man in his seat. Not a word did they say, but looked sadly on the ground. At last King Agamemnon stood up and spoke: "O my friends, lords and rulers of the Greeks, truly Zeus seems to hate me. Once he promised me that I should take this city of Troy and return home in safety, but this promise he has not kept. I must go back to the place from which I came without honour, having lost many of those who came with me. But now, before we all perish, let us flee in our ships to our own land, for Troy we may not take."

And when the King had finished his speech the chiefs still sat saying not a word, for they were out of heart. But after a while, seeing that no one else would speak, brave Diomed stood up in his place and said: "O King, do not be angry, if I say that this talk of yours about fleeing in our ships to our own land is nothing but madness. It was but two days since that you called me a coward; whether this be true the Greeks, both young and old, know well. I will not say 'yes' or 'no.' But this I tell you. Zeus has given you to be first among the Greeks, and to be a king among kings. But courage he has not given you, and courage is the best gift of all, and without it all others are of no account. Now, if you are bent on going back, go; your ships are ready to be launched, and the way is short; but all the other Greeks will stay till they have taken the city of Troy. Aye, and if they also choose to go with you, still I will stay, I and Stheneʾlus here, my friend: yes; we two will stay, and we will fight till we make an end of the city, for the gods sent us hither, and we will not go back till we have done the thing for which we came."

Then old Nestor stood up in his place and said: "You are a brave man Diomed, and you speak words of wisdom. There is not a man here but knows that you have spoken the truth. And now, O King Agamemnon, do you seek counsel from the chiefs, and when they have spoken, follow that counsel which shall seem to you wisest and best. But first let them sit down to eat and to drink. Also set sentinels to keep watch along the trench lest our enemies should fall upon us unawares, for they have many watch-fires and a mighty host. Verily this night will either save us or make an end of us altogether."

So the King bade his men prepare a feast, and the chiefs sat down to eat and drink; and when they had had enough, Nestor rose up in his place and spoke: "O King, Zeus has made you lord over many nations, and put many things into your hand. Therefore you have the greater need of good counsel, and are the more bound to listen to wise words, even though they may not please you. It was an evil day, O King, when you sent the heralds to take away the damsel Briseïs from Achilles. The other chiefs did not consent to your deed. Yes, and I myself advised you not to do this thing; but you would not hear. Rather you followed your own pride and pleasure, and shamed the bravest of your followers, taking away from him the prize which he had won with his own hands. Do you, therefore, undo this evil deed, and make peace with this man whom you have wronged, speaking to him pleasant words and giving him noble gifts."

King Agamemnon stood up and said: "You have spoken true words, old sir. Truly I acted as a fool that day; I do not deny it. For not only is this Achilles a great warrior but he is dear to Zeus, and he that is dear to Zeus is worth more than whole armies of other men. See now how we are put to flight when he stands aside from the battle! This surely is the doing of Zeus. And now, as I did him wrong, so I will make him amends, giving him many times more than that which I took from him. Hear now the gifts which I will give him: seven kettles, standing on three feet, new, which the fire has never touched, ten talents of gold, and twenty bright caldrons, and twelve strong horses which have won many prizes for me by their swiftness. The man who had as much gold of his own as these twelve horses have won for me would not be a beggar. Also I will give him some women-slaves, skilled with their needle and in other work of the hands, who were my portion of the spoil, when we took the island of Lesbos. Yes, and I will send back to him the maiden Briseïs, whom I took from him. And when, by favour of the gods, we shall have taken the city of Troy, and shall divide the spoil, then let him come and choose for himself twenty women the most beautiful that there are in the city, after the Fair Helen, for none can be so beautiful as she. And I will give him yet more than this. When we get back to the land of Greece, then he shall be as a son to me, and I will honour him even as I honour my own son Orestes. Three daughters have I in my palace at home. Of these he shall have the one whom he shall choose for his wife, and shall take her to the house of his father Peleus. Nor shall he give any gifts, as a man is used to give when he seeks a maiden for his wife. He shall have my daughter without a price. And more than this, I will give her a great dowry, such as a king has never given before to his daughter. Seven fair cities will I give him, and with each city fields in which many herds of oxen and flocks of sheep are grazing, and vineyards out of which much wine is made. And the people of these cities shall honour him as their lord and master. All these things will I give him, only he will cease from his anger. Let him listen to our prayers, for of all things that are in the world there is but one that does not listen to prayers, and this one thing is Death. And this, verily is the cause why Death is hated of all men. Let him not therefore be as Death."

When Agamemnon had made an end of speaking, Nestor said to him: "The gifts which you are ready to give to the great Achilles are such as no man can find fault with. Let us, therefore, without delay, choose men who may go to his tent and offer them to him. Let Phœnix go first, for he is dear to the gods, and Achilles also honours him, for, indeed, Phœnix had the care of him when he was a child. And with him Ajax the Greater should go, and Ulysses also, and let two heralds go with them. And now let the heralds bring water and pour upon our hands, and let each keep silence, while we pray to Zeus that he may have mercy on us, and incline the heart of this man to listen to our entreaties."

Then the heralds brought water, and poured it upon the hands of the chiefs, and they filled the bowls with wine. And each man took his bowl and poured out a little on the ground, praying meanwhile to the gods. And when they had done this, they drank, and came out from the King's tent. And, before they went to their errand, old Nestor charged them what they should say. All of them he charged, but Ulysses most of all, because he was the best speaker of them all.

The Embassy to Achilles

So they went along the shore of the sea, and as they went they prayed to the god who shakes the earth, that is to say, the god of the sea, that he would shake the heart of Achilles. And when they came to the camp of the Myrmidons, for these were the people of Achilles, they saw the King with a harp in his hand, the harp he had taken from the city of Thebé (which was also the city of Andromaché). He was playing on the harp, and as he played he sang a song about the valiant deeds which the heroes of old time had wrought. And Patroclus sat over against him in silence, waiting till he should have ended his singing. So the three chiefs came forward, Ulysses leading the way, and stood before Achilles. And he, when he saw them, jumped up from his seat, not a little astonished, holding his harp in his hand. And Patroclus also rose up from his seat, to do them honour. And Achilles said: "You are welcome, my friends: though I am angry with the King, you are not the less my friends."

And when he had said this he bade them sit down upon chairs that were there, covered with coverlets of purple. And to Patroclus he said: "Bring out the biggest bowl, and mix the wine and make it as strong and sweet as you can; and give each of these my friends a cup that they may drink, for there are none whom I love more in the whole army of the Greeks."

And this Patroclus did. And when he had mixed the wine, strong and sweet, and had given each man his cup, then he made ready a feast. Nor were they unwilling, though they had but just feasted in the tent of King Agamemnon, for the men of those days were as mighty in eating and drinking as in fighting. And the way that he made ready the feast was this. First he put a great block of wood as close as might be to the fire. And on this he put the back, that is to say the saddle of a sheep, and the same portion of a fatted goat, and also the same of a well-fed pig. The charioteer of Achilles held the flesh in its place with a spit, and Achilles carved it. And when he had carved the portions, he put each on a skewer. Then Patroclus made the fire burn high, and when the flames had died down, then he smoothed the red-hot embers, and put racks upon the top of them, again, the spits with the flesh. But first he sprinkled them with salt. And when the flesh was cooked, he took it from the skewers, and put portions of it on the platters. Also he took bread and put it in baskets, to each man a basket. Then they all took their places for the meal, and Achilles gave the place of honour to Ulysses. But before they began, he signed to Patroclus that he should sacrifice to the gods, and this he did by casting into the fire something of the flesh and of the bread. After this they put forth their hands, and took the food that was ready for them. When they had had enough, Ajax nodded to Phœnix, meaning that he should speak and tell Achilles why they had come. But Ulysses perceived it, and began to speak, before ever Phœnix was ready to begin. First he filled a cup and drank to the health of Achilles, and then he said: "Hail, Achilles! Truly we have had no lack of feasting, first in the tent of King Agamemnon, and now in yours. But this is not a day to think of feasting, for destruction is close at hand, and we are greatly afraid. This very day the Trojans and their allies came very near to burning our ships; and we are greatly in doubt whether we shall save them, for it is plainly to be seen that Zeus is on their side. What, therefore, we are come to ask of you is that you will not stand aside any longer from the battle, but will come and help us as of old. And truly our need is great. For this Hector rages furiously, saying that Zeus is with him, and not caring for god or man. And even now he is praying that morning may appear, for he vows that he will burn the ships with fire and destroy us all while we are choked with the smoke of the burning. And I am greatly afraid that the gods will give him strength to make good his threats and to kill us all here, far from the land in which we were born. Now, therefore, stir yourself if now, before it is too late, you have a mind to save the Greeks. Make no delay, lest it be too late, and you repent only when that which is done shall be past all recalling. Did not the old man Peleus, your father, on the day when he sent you from Phthia, your country, to follow King Agamemnon, lay this charge upon you, saying: 'My son, the gods will give you strength and will make you mighty in battle, if it be their will; but there is something which you must do yourself: keep down the pride of your heart, for gentleness is better than pride; also keep from strife, so shall the Greeks, both young and old, love you and honour you'? This charge your father laid upon you, but you have not kept it. Nevertheless there is yet a place of repentance for you. For the King has sent us to offer you gifts great and many to make up for the wrong he did to you. So great and so many are they that no one can say that these are not worthy." And then Ulysses set forth in order all the things which Agamemnon had promised to give, kettles and caldrons and gold, and women slaves, and his daughter in marriage, and seven cities to be her dowry. And when he had finished the list of these things he said: "Be content: take these gifts, which, indeed, no man can say are not sufficient. And if you have no thought for Agamemnon, yet you should have thought for the people who perish because you stand aside from the battle. Take the gifts, therefore, for by so doing you will have wealth and love and honour from the Greeks, and great glory also, for you will slay Hector, who is now ready to meet you in battle, so proud is he, thinking that there is not a man of all the Greeks who can stand against him."

Achilles answered: "I will speak plainly, O Ulysses, and will set out clearly what I think is in my heart, and what I intend to do. It does not please me that you should sit there and coax me, one man saying one thing and another man saying another. Yes, I will speak both plainly and truly, for, as for the man who thinks one thing in his heart and says another with his tongue, he is hateful to me as death itself. Tell me now, what does it profit a man to be always fighting day after day? It is but thankless work, for the man that stays home has an equal share with the man who never leaves the battle, and men honour the coward even as they honour the brave, and death comes alike to the man that works and to the man who sits idle at home. Look now at me! What profit have I had of all that I have endured, putting my life in peril day after day? Even as a bird carries food to its nestlings till they are fledged, and never ceases to work for them, and herself is but ill fed, so it has been with me. Many nights have I been without sleep, and I have laboured many days. I took twelve cities to which I travelled in ships, and eleven to which I went by land, and from all I carried away much spoil. All this spoil I brought to King Agamemnon, and he, who all the time stayed safe in his tent, gave a few things to me and to others, but kept the greater part for himself. And then what did he do? He left to the other chiefs that which he had given to them, but what he had given to me that he took from me. Yes; he took Briseïs. Let him keep her, if he will. But let him not ask me any more to fight against the Trojans. There are other chiefs whom he has not wronged and shamed in this way; let him go to them and take counsel with them, how he may keep away the devouring fire from the ships. Many things he has done already; he has built a wall, and dug a ditch about it; can he not keep Hector from the ships with them? And yet in time past when I used to fight, this Hector dared not set his army in array far from the walls of Troy; nay, he scarce ventured to come outside the gates. Once indeed did he gather his courage together and stand up against me, to fight man with man, and then he barely escaped from my spear. But neither with him nor with any other of the sons of Troy will I fight again. To-morrow I will do sacrifice to Zeus and to the other gods, and I will store my ships with food and water, and launch them on the sea. Yes, early in the morning to-morrow, if you care to look, you will see my ships upon the sea, and my men rowing with all their might. And, if the god of the sea gives me good passage, on the third day I shall come to my own dear country, even to Phthia. There are the riches which I left behind me when I came to this land of Troy, and thither shall I carry such things, gold and silver and slaves, as King Agamemnon has not taken from me. But with him I will never take counsel again, nor will I stand by his side in battle. As for his gifts, I scorn them; aye, and were they twenty times as great, I would scorn them still. Not with all the wealth of Thebes which is in the land of Egypt would he persuade me, and than Thebes there is no wealthier city in all the world. A hundred gates it has, and through each gate two hundred warriors ride forth to battle with chariots and horses. And as for his daughter whom he would give me to be my wife, I would not marry her, no, not though she were as beautiful as Aphrodité herself, and as skilled in all the works of the needle as Athené. Let him choose for his son-in-law some chief of the Greeks who is better than I am. As for me, if the gods suffer me to reach my home, my father Peleus shall choose me a wife. Many maidens, daughters of kings, are there in Phthia and in Hellas, and not one among them who would scorn me if I came a-wooing. Often in time past I have thought to do this thing, to marry a wife, and to settle down in peace, and to enjoy the riches of the old man my father, and such things as I have gathered for myself. For long since my mother, Thetis of the sea, said to me, 'My son, there are two lots of life before you, and you may choose which you will. If you stay in this land and fight against Troy, then you must never go back to your own land, but will die in your youth. Only your name will live for ever; but if you will leave this land and go back to your home, then shall you live long, even to old age, but your name will be forgotten.' Once I thought fame was a better thing than life; but now my mind is changed, for indeed my fame is taken from me, seeing that King Agamemnon puts me to shame before all the people. And now I go away to my own land, and I counsel you to go also, for Troy you will never take. The city is dear to Zeus, and he puts courage into the hearts of the people. And take this answer back to the man who sent you: 'Find some other way of keeping Hector and the Trojans from the ships, for my help he shall not have.' But let Phœnix stay with me this night that he may go with me in my ship when I depart to-morrow. Nevertheless if he choose rather to stay, let him stay, for I would not take him by force."

And when Achilles had ended his speech all the chiefs sat silent, so vehement was he.

The Story of Old Phœnix

After a while old Phœnix stood up and spoke, and as he spoke he shed many tears, for he was much afraid lest the ships of the Greeks should be burnt. "O Achilles," he said, "if you are indeed determined to go away, how can I stay here without you? Did not the old man Peleus, your father, make me your teacher, that I might show you both what you should say and what you should do, when he sent you from the land of Phthia to be with King Agamemnon? In those days, for all that you are now so strong and skilful in war, you were but a lad, knowing nothing of how warriors fight in battle, or of how they take counsel together. No: I cannot stay here without you; I would not leave you, no, not if the gods would make me young again as when I came to the land of Phthia, to be with Peleus your father. For at the first I lived in Hellas, and left it because the old man, my father, was angry with me. So angry was he that he cursed me, and prayed to Zeus and the other gods that no child of mine should ever sit upon his knees. And I, too, was very angry when I heard him say these words. Truly the thought came into my heart that I would fall upon him and slay him with the sword. But the gods were merciful to me and helped me to put away this wicked thought out of my heart. So I gave up my anger, for I could not bear that men should say of me: 'See, there is the man who killed his own father!' But I was determined to go away from my father's house and from the land of Hellas altogether. Then came my friends and my kinsmen, and made many prayers to me, beseeching me that I would not depart. But I would not listen to them. Then they would have kept me by force. Nine days and nine nights they watched my father's house, eating the flesh of sheep and oxen and swine, and drinking wine without stint from my father's stores. They took turns to watch, and they kept up two fires without ceasing, one in the cloister that was round the house, and one before the great door. But on the tenth night, when the watchmen were overcome with sleep and the fires were low, then I broke open the door of my chamber, for all that they had shut it fast with a knot that was hard to untie, and I leapt over the fence in the courtyard, and neither man nor maid saw me. So I escaped, and fled from Hellas, and came to Phthia to the old man Peleus your father. And your father was very kind to me, and was as a father to me. He gave me riches, and he gave me a kingdom which I might rule under him, and also he trusted you to me, O Achilles, when you were but a little child, that I might teach you and rear you. And this I did. And, indeed, you loved me much. With no one but me would you go into the hall or sit at the feast. I would hold you on my knees and carve the choicest bits for you from the dish, and put the wine-cup to your lips. Many a time have you spoilt my clothes sputtering out the wine from your lips, when I had put the cup to your lips. Yes, I suffered much, and toiled much for you, and you were as a child to me, for child of my own I never had. And now, I pray you, listen to me. Put away the anger in your heart even as I put the anger out of mine. It is not fit that a man should harden his heart in this way. Even the gods are turned from their purpose, and surely the gods are more honourable and more powerful than you. Yet men turn them by offering of incense and by drink-offerings and by burnt-offerings and by prayers. And if a man sins against them yet can he turn them from their anger. For, indeed, Prayers are the daughters of Zeus. They are weak and slow of foot, whereas Sin is swift and strong, and goes before, running over all the earth, and doing harm to men. But nevertheless they come after and heal the harm that Sin has done. If, therefore, a man will reverence these daughters of Zeus, and will do honour to them when they come near to him, and will listen to their voice, they will bless him and do good to him. But if a man hardens his heart against them and will not listen to their voice, then they curse him and bring him to ruin. Take heed, therefore, O Achilles, that thou do such honour to these daughters of Zeus as becomes a righteous man, for it will be well for you to do so. If, indeed, King Agamemnon had stood apart and given you no gifts, nor restored to you that which he took from you, then I would not have bidden you to cease from your anger, no, not to save the Greeks from their great trouble. But now he gives you many gifts, and promises you yet more, and has sent an embassy to you, the wisest and noblest that there are in the whole army, and also dear friends of yours. Refuse not, therefore, to listen to their words. Listen now to this tale that I will tell you, that you may see how foolish a thing it is for a man, however great he may be, to shut his ears when prayers are made to him.

"Once upon a time there was a great strife between the Ætolians and the men who dwelt near to Mount Curium. And the cause of the strife was this. There was a great wild boar which laid waste all the land of Calydon where the Ætolians dwelt. And Meleager, who was the King of the land, sent for hunters from all Greece, and they came from far and wide, bringing their dogs with them, for the beast was so great and fierce that it was not an easy thing to kill it, but there was need of many hunters. Now, among those that came was Atalanta, the fair maid of Arcadia. And when the beast was killed, then there was a great quarrel as to who should have the spoils, that is to say the head and the hide. For Meleager gave them to the fair Alalanta, and when the brethren of his mother took them from her, then he slew them. But when his mother, Althea by name, heard that her brethren were dead, then she cursed him, yea, even her own son. So it came to pass that there was war between the Ætolians and the men of Mount Curium, for Althea and her brethren were of that land. And also the curse began to work so that the quarrel became more fierce. Now, when in time past Meleager had fought among the Ætolians there was none that could stand up against him, so great a warrior was he. But now, being very angry with his mother, he stood aside from the war, and would not help, sitting in his chamber apart. The men of Mount Curium, therefore, prevailed in the battle, and the Ætolians were driven into the city of Calydon, and there was a din of war about the gates of the city, and great fear lest the enemy should break them down. Then first the elders of the city sent an embassy to him, priests of the gods, the holiest that there were in the land, to pray that he would come forth from his chamber and defend them. Also they promised him a noble gift, a great estate in the plain of Ætolia, half ploughland and half vineyard, such as he might choose for himself. So the priests came, beseeching him, and offering him the gift, but he would not listen to them. After them came his mother and sisters, and made their prayers to him, but them he refused even more fiercely. And the old man Œneus, his father, besought him, standing on the threshold of his chamber, and shak- ing the door; but he would not listen. Nor would he hear the voices of his friends and comrades, although they were very dear to him. But at the last, when the enemy had now begun to climb upon the towers, and to burn the fair city of Calydon with fire, aye and to batter on the doors of his palace, then his wife, the fair Cleopatra, arose and besought him with many prayers and tears. 'Think now,' she said, 'what woes will come upon your people if the enemy prevail against them, for the city will be burnt with fire, and the men will be slain, and the women will be carried into captivity.' Then at last his spirit was stirred within him, and he arose, and put on his arms, and went down into the street and drove the men of Mount Curium before him. So did he save the Ætolians, but the gifts which they promised, these he never had. This, O Achilles, is the story of Meleager. Let not your thoughts be like to his. It would be a foolish thing to put off saving of the ships till they are already on fire. Come, therefore, take the gifts which King Agamemnon gives you; so shall all the Greeks honour you even as they honour a god. But if you delay, then may you lose both honour and gifts, even though you save us from the Trojans."

Achilles answered: "Phœnix, my father, I have no need of this honour and these gifts. Riches I have as much as I need, and Zeus gives me honour. And listen to this: trouble me no more with prayers and tears, while you seek to help King Agamemnon. Take not his side, lest I, who love you now, come to hate you. It were better for you to vex him who has vexed me. Return now with me to the land of Phthia, and I will give you the half of my kingdom. And stay this night in my tent; to-morrow we will consult together whether we will depart or no."

Then Achilles nodded to Patroclus, and made signs that he should make a bed ready for the old man, so that the other two, seeing this, should depart without delay.

So Patroclus made the bed ready. And when Ajax saw this he said to Ulysses: "Let us go, Ulysses. We shall do nothing to-day. Let us depart at once, and carry back this message to them who sent us. As for Achilles, he cherishes his anger, and cares nought for his comrades or his people. What he desires, I know not. One man will take the price of blood from another, even though he has slain a brother or a son. He takes gold, and puts away his anger, and the shedder of blood dwells in peace in his own land. But this man keeps his anger, and all for the sake of a girl. And lo! the King offers him seven girls, yea seven for one, and he will not take them. Surely he seems to lack reason."

Achilles answered: "You speak well, great Ajax. Nevertheless the anger is yet hot in my heart, because Agamemnon put me to shame before all people, as if I were but a common man. But go, and take my message. I will not arise to do battle with the Trojans till Hector shall come to these tents and shall seek to set fire to my ships. But when he shall do this, then I will arise, and verily I will stop him, however eager he may be for the battle."

So Ajax and Ulysses departed, and gave the message of Achilles to King Agamemnon.

The Adventure of Diomed and Ulysses

While the other chiefs of the Greeks were sleeping that night, King Agamemnon was awake, for he had great trouble in his heart and many fears. When he looked towards Troy he saw the fires burning, and heard the sound of flutes and pipes, and the murmurs of many men, and he was astonished, for it seemed to him that the army of the Trojans was greater and stronger than it had ever been in times past. And when he looked towards the ships, he groaned and tore his hair, thinking what evils might come to his people. Then he thought to himself: "I will go and look for old Nestor; maybe he and I will think of something which may help us." So he rose from his bed, and put the sandals on his feet, and wrapped his coat about him, and put the skin of a lion round his shoulders, and a spear in his hand.

Now it so happened that Menelaüs could not sleep that same night, for he knew that it was on his account that the Greeks had come to Troy. So he arose from his bed, and wrapped the skin of a leopard about his shoulders and took a spear in his hand, and went to look for his brother. And when he found him, for, as has been said, he also had armed himself, he said: "What seek you? See you the Trojans there? Let us send a spy to find what they are doing, and how many there are of them, for I do not doubt that they are planning something against us. But is there any one who will dare to do such a thing, for, indeed, it is a great danger."

Agamemnon answered: "It is true, my brother, that we are in great trouble, and need good advice if we are to save the people. Surely Zeus has greatly changed his mind concerning us. There was a time when he favoured us, but now it is of his doing that Hector drives us before him in this fashion. Never did I see a man so manifestly strengthened by Zeus, and yet he is but a man, having neither a god for his father, nor goddess for his mother. But go now call the chiefs to counsel, and I will go to Nestor."

So the chiefs were called, and Nestor said: "First let us see whether the watch are sleeping or waking." So they went the round of the wall, and found the watchmen not sleeping but waking. As a dog that hears the sound of a wild beast in the wood, so they looked towards the plain, thinking to hear the feet of the Trojans. Old Nestor was glad to see them and said: "You do well, my children, lest we become a prey to our enemies."

After this they passed over the trench and sat down in an open place that was clear of dead bodies, for here it was that Hector had turned back from slaying the Greeks when darkness came over the earth. And Nestor rose up and said: "Is there now a man who will go among the Trojans and spy out what it is in their mind to do? Such a one will win great honour to himself, and the King will give him many gifts."

Diomed stood up in his place and said: "I will go, but it is well that I should have some one with me. For to have a companion gives a man courage and comfort; also two wits are better than one."

Many were willing to go with Diomed. And Agamemnon, fearing for his brother Menelaüs, for he offered himself among others, said: "Choose, O Diomed, the man whom you would most desire to have with you; think not of any man's birth or rank; choose only him whom you would best like for a companion."

Then Diomed said: "If I may have my choice, Ulysses shall go with me. He is brave, and he is prudent, and Athené loves him."

Ulysses answered: "Do not praise me too much, nor blame me too much. But let us go, for the night is far spent."

So the two armed themselves. Diomed took a two-edged sword and a shield, and a helmet without a crest, for such is not easy to be seen. Ulysses took a bow with a quiver full of arrows and a sword, and for a helmet a cap of hide, with the white teeth of a wild boar round it. Then they both prayed to Athené that she would help them. That being done, they set out and went through the night, like to two lions, and they trod on dead bodies and arms and blood.

Meanwhile Hector was thinking about the same thing, how that it would be well to find out what the Greeks were doing, and what they were planning for the next day. So he called the chiefs of the Trojans and the allies to a council and said: "Who now will go and spy among the Greeks, and see whether they are keeping a good watch, and find out, if he can overhear them talking together, what they mean to do to-morrow. Such a man shall have a great reward, a chariot, that is to say, with two horses, the best that there is in the whole camp of the Greeks."

Then there stood up a certain Dolon. He was the son of a herald, the only son of his father, but he had five sisters. He was an ill-favoured man, but a swift runner. Dolon said: "I will go, O Hector, but I want a great reward, even the horses of Achilles, for these are the best in the whole camp of the Greeks. Do you lift up your sceptre and swear that you will give me these, and none other."

It was a foolish thing, for who was Dolon that he should have the chariot and horses of the great Achilles? And Hector knew this in his heart;

nevertheless he lifted up his sceptre, and swore that he would give to Dolon these horses and none others. Then Dolon armed himself. He took his bow, and a cap of wolf's skin for a helmet, and a sharp spear, and went his way, nor did he try to go quickly, for he did not think that any one from the camp of the Greeks would be abroad. So Ulysses heard his steps and said to Diomed: "Here comes a man; maybe he is a spy, maybe he is come to spoil the dead bodies. Let him pass by, that we may take him, for we must not suffer him to go back to the city."

So the two lay down among the dead bodies on the plain, and Dolon passed by them, not knowing that they were there. And after he had gone fifty yards or so, then they rose up and ran after him. He heard the noise of running and stood still, thinking to himself: "Hector has sent men after me; perhaps he wishes me to go back." And this, indeed, he would gladly have done, for he was beginning to be afraid. But when they were but a spear's throw from him, he saw that they were Greeks, and fled. And the two ran after him, as two dogs follow a fawn or a hare; and though he was swift of foot he could not outrun them, nor could they come up to him, but they kept him from turning back to the city. But when they were near the trench, then Diomed called out to the man: "Stop, or I will slay you with my spear." And he threw his spear, not meaning to kill the man, but to frighten him, making it pass over his shoulder, so that it stood in the ground before him. When Dolon saw the spear he stood still, and his teeth chattered with fear. And the two came up to him, breathing hard, for they had been running fast. Then said Dolon, weeping as he spoke: "Do not kill me; my father will pay a great ransom for me, if he hears that you are keeping me at your ships; much gold and bronze and iron will he pay for my life."

Ulysses answered: "Be of good cheer. Tell us truly why you were coming through the darkness. Was it to spoil the dead, or did Hector send you to spy out what was going on at the ships, or was it on some private business of your own?"

Dolon answered: "Hector persuaded me to go, promising that he would give me the chariot and horses of Achilles. And I was to spy out what you had in your minds to do on the morrow and whether you were keeping watch."

Ulysses laughed when the man spoke of the chariot and horses of Achilles. "Truly," he said, "it was a grand reward that you deserved. The horses of Achilles are hard to manage except a man be the son of a god or a goddess. But tell me, where is Hector? and what watch does the Trojan keep?"

Dolon answered: "When I came away from the camp of the Trojans, Hector was holding council with the chiefs close to the tomb of Ilus. As for the watches, there are none set, except in that part of the camp where the Trojans are. As for the allies, they sleep without caring for watches, thinking that the Trojans will do this for them."

Then Ulysses asked again: "Do the allies then sleep among the Trojans or apart?"

Then Dolon told him about the camp, who were in this place and who were in that. "But," he went on, "if you would know where you may best make your way into the camp and not be seen, go to the furthest part upon the left. There are newcomers, men from Thrace, with Rhesus their king. Never have I seen horses so big and so fine as his. And they are whiter than snow, and swifter than the wind. But now send me to the ships, or, if you cannot do that, having no one to take me, bind me and leave me."

But Diomed said: "Think not, Dolon, that we will suffer you to live, though, indeed, you have told us that which we desired to know. For then you would come again to spy out our camp, or, maybe, would fight with us in battle. But if we kill you, then you will trouble us no more."

So they killed him, and stripped him of his arms. These they hung on a tamarisk tree that there was in the place, makig a mark with reeds and branches that they might know the place when they came back. Then they went on to the camp of the Trojans, and found the place of which Dolon had told them. There the men of Thrace lay asleep, each man with his arms at his side. And in the midst of the company lay King Rhesus, with his chariot at his side, and the horses tethered to the rail of the chariot. Then Diomed began to slay the men as they slept. He was like a lion in the middle of a fold full of sheep, so fierce and strong was he, and they so helpless. Twelve men he slew, and as he slew them, Ulysses dragged thir bodies out of the way, that there might be a clear road for the horses, for horses are wont to start aside when they see a dead body lying in the way. And "these maybe," so he thought to himself, "are not used to war." Twelve men did Diomed slay, and King Rhesus the thirteenth, as he lay and panted in his sleep, for he had a bad dream at the very time Diomed slew him. Meanwhile Ulysses had unbound the horses from the chariot and driven them out of the camp. With his bow he struck them, for he had not thought to take the whip from the chariot. And when he had got the horses clear, then he whistled, for a sign to Diomed that he should come without more delay, for well he knew that Diomed would not easily be satisfied with slaying. And truly, the man was lingering, doubting whether he might not kill yet more. But Athené whispered in his ear: "Think of your return; maybe some god will rouse the Trojans against you."

And indeed, Apollo was rousing them. The cousin of King Rhesus awoke and seeing the place of the horses empty, cried out, calling the King. So all the camp was roused. But Diomed and Ulysses mounted the horses and rode to the camp of the Greeks. Right glad were their comrades to see them and to hear the tale of what they had done.

The Wounding of the Chiefs

As soon as it was light Agamemnon called the Greeks, and Hector called the Trojans to battle, nor were either unwilling to obey. For a time the fighting was equal, but at noon, at the time when a man who is cutting down trees upon the hills grows weary of his work and longs for food, then the Greeks began to prevail. And the first man to break through the line of the Trojans was King Agamemnon. Never before had the King done such mighty deeds, for he drove the Trojans back to the very walls of the city. Hector himself did not dare to stand up before him, for Iris brought this message to him from Zeus: "So long as Agamemnon fights in the front, do you hold back, for this is the day on which it is his lot to win great honour for himself; but when he shall be wounded, then do you go forward, and you shall have strength to drive the Greeks before you till they come to the ships, and the sun shall set." So Hector held back, and after a while the King was wounded. There were two sons of Antenor in one chariot, and they came against him. First the King threw his spear at the younger of the two, but missed his aim. Then the Trojan thrust at Agamemnon with his spear, driving it against his breastplate. With all his strength he drove it, but the silver which was in the breastplate turned the spear, so that it bent as if it had been of lead. Then the King caught the spear in his hand, and drove it through the neck of his adversary, so that he fell dead from the chariot. But when the elder brother saw this he also thrust at the King with his spear, nor did he thrust in vain, but he pierced his arm beneath the elbow. But him also did the King slay, wounding him first with his spear and afterwards cutting off his head with his sword. For a time, while the wound was warm, the King still fought, but when it grew cold and stiff, then the pain was greater than he could bear, and he said to his charioteer, "Now carry me back to the ships, for I cannot fight any more."

The next of the chiefs that was wounded was Diomed. Him Paris wounded with an arrow as he was stripping the arms from a Trojan which he had slain. For Paris hid himself behind the pillar which stood on the tomb of Ilu, and shot his arrows from thence. On the ankle of the right foot did Paris hit him, and when he saw that he had not shot the arrow in vain, he cried out aloud: "I wish that I had wounded you in the loin, bold Diomed, then you would have troubled the men of Troy no more!"

But Diomed answered: "If I could but meet you face to face, you coward, your bow and your arrows would not help you. As for this graze on my foot, I care no more for it than if a woman or a child had struck me. Come near, and I will show you what are the wounds which I make with my spear."

Then he beckoned to Ulysses that he should stand before him while he drew the arrow from his foot. And Ulysses did so. But when he had drawn out the arrow, the pain was so great that he could not stand up, for all the brave words that he had spoken. And he bade his charioteer drive him back to the ships.

So Ulysses was left alone. Not one of the chiefs stood by him, for now that King Agamemnon and Diomed had departed, there was great fear upon all the Greeks. And Ulysses said to himself: "Now what shall I do? It would be a shameful thing to fly from these Trojans, though there are many of them, and I am alone; but it would be still worse, if I were to be taken here and slain. Surely it is the doing of Zeus, that this trouble is come upon the Greeks, and who am I that I should fight against Zeus? Yet why do I talk in this way? It is only the coward who draws back; a brave man stands in his place, whether he lives or dies." But while he was thinking these things many Trojans came about him, as dogs come about a wild boar in a wood, and the boar stands at bay, and gnashes his big white teeth. So Ulysses stood thrusting here and there with his long spear. Five chiefs he slew; but one of the five, before he was slain, wounded him in the side, scraping the flesh from the ribs. Then Ulysses cried out for help; three times he cried, and the third time Menelaüs heard him, and called to Ajax.

"O Ajax, I hear the voice of Ulysses, and it sounds like the voice of one who is in great trouble. Maybe the Trojans have surrounded him. Come, let us help him for it would be a great loss to the Greeks if he were to come to harm."

Then he led the way to the place from which the voice seemed to come, and Ajax followed him. And when they came to Ulysses, they found it was as Menelaüs had said; for the Trojans had beset Ulysses, as the jackals beset a deer with long horns among the hills. The beast cannot fly because the hunter has wounded it with an arrow from his bow, and the wound has become stiff, and he stands at bay. Then a lion comes, and the jackals are scattered in a moment. So the Trojans were scattered when Ajax came. Then Menelaüs took Ulysses by the hand, and led him out of the throng, while Ajax drove the Trojans before him.

And now yet another chief was wounded, for Paris from his hiding-place behind the pillar on the tomb of Ilus shot an arrow at Macha͞on, and wounded him on the right shoulder. And one of the chiefs cried to old Nestor, who was fighting close by: "Quick, Nestor, take Macha¯on in your chariot, and drive him to the ships, for the life of a physician is worth the lives of many men."

So Nestor took Macha¯on in his chariot, and touched his horses with the whip, and they galloped to the ships.

Now Hector was fighting on the other side of the plain, and his charioteer said to him: "See how Ajax is driving our people before him. Let us go and stop him." So they went, lashing the horses that they might go the faster, and the chariot rolled over many bodies of men, and the axle and the sides of it were red with blood. Then Zeus put fear into the heart of the great Ajax himself. He would not fly, but he turned round, throwing his great shield over his shoulder, and moved towards the ships slowly, step by step. It was as when an ass breaks into a field and eats the standing corn, and the children of the village beat him with sticks. Their arms are weak, and the sticks are broken on the beast's back, for he is slow in going, nor do they drive him out till he has eaten his fill. So the Trojans thrust at Ajax their lances. And now he would turn and face them, and now he would take a step backwards towards the ships.

Now Achilles was standing on the stern of his ship, looking at the battle, and Patroclus stood by him. And when old Nestor passed by taking Macha¯on to the ships, Achilles said to his friend: "Soon, I think, will the Greeks come and pray me to help them, for they are in great trouble. But go now and see who was this whom Nestor is taking to the ships. His shoulders, I thought were the shoulders of Macha¯on, but his face I could not see, for the horses went by very fast."

Then Patroclus ran to do his errand. Meanwhile Nestor took Macha¯on to his tent. And there the girl that waited on the old man mixed for them a bowl of drink. First she set a table, and laid on it a bronze charger, and on it she put a flask of wine, and a leek, with which to flavour it, and yellow honey, and barley meal. And she fetched from another part of the tent a great bowl with four handles. On each side of the bowl there was a pair of handles, and on each handle there was a dove, wrought in bronze, and the doves seemed to be pecking at each other. A very big bowl it was, and, when it was full, so heavy that a man could scarcely lift it from the table; but Nestor, though he was old, could lift it easily. Then the girl poured the wine from the flask into the bowl, and put honey into it, and shredded cheese made from goat's milk, and the leek to flavour it. And when the mess was ready, she bade them drink. So they drank, and talked together.

But while they talked, Patroclus stood in the door of the tent. And Nestor went to him, and took him by the hand, and said: "Come now and sit down with us, and drink from the bowl." But Patroclus would not. "Stay me not," he said; "I came to see who it was whom you have brought wounded out of the battle. And now I see that it is Macha‾on. Therefore I will go back without delay, for you know what kind of man is Achilles, how he quickly grows angry and is ready to blame."

Then said Nestor: "What does Achilles care about the Greeks? Why does he ask who are wounded? O Patroclus, do you remember the day when Ulysses and I came to the house of Peleus? Your father was there, and we feasted in the hall; and when the feast was finished, then we told Peleus why we had come, how we were gathering the chiefs of Greece to go and fight against Troy. And you and Achilles were eager to go. And old men gave you much advice. Old Peleus said to Achilles: 'You must always be the very first in battle.' But to you your father said: 'Achilles is of nobler birth than you, and he is stronger by far. But you are older, and years give wisdom. Therefore it will be your part to give him good counsel when there is need.' Why then do you not advise him to help us? And if he is still resolved not to go forth to the battle, then let him send you forth, and let him lend you his armour to wear. Then the Trojans will think that Achilles himself has come back to the battle, and they will be afraid, and we shall have a breathing space."

Then Patroclus turned and ran back to the tent of Achilles.

The Battle at the Wall

Now by this time the Trojans were close upon the trench; but there they stood, for the horses were afraid, the trench being deep, and having great stakes set in. Then Polydaˇmas, who was one of the wisest of the Trojans, said to Hector: "This is but a mad thing, O Hector, to try to cross the trench in our chariots, for it is wide, and has many stakes set in it. Look too at this: how will it be when we have crossed it? If, indeed, it is the pleasure of Zeus that the Greeks should perish utterly—well; but if, as has come to pass before, not once only, the Greeks take heart and turn upon us and drive us back, what shall we do? Nay; let us leave our chariots here, and if need be, we can come back and find them waiting for us. But we will go on foot against the wall."

So they jumped down from their chariots and went against the walls on foot. In five companies they went. The first, which was the largest and had the bravest of the Trojans, Hector himself led. And the next was commanded by Paris. The third was led by Heleˇnus the prophet, and with him was Deïphobus, who also was a son of King Priam; and Asius, one of the allies, who was King of Arisbé. Of the fourth Æneˉas was the leader, and of the fifth Sarpeˉdon of Lycia with Glaucus and others among the allies. They stood closely to each other, holding shield by shield, and so they went against the Greeks. All of them, also, left their chariots on this side of the trench, all except King Asius only. But he drove his chariot to a place where there was a road over the trench, and on the other side a gate. And this gate chanced to be open, for the keepers had set it open, so that any of the Greeks who were flying from the Trojans might find refuge inside it. When the keepers, who were two mighty men of valour, saw Asius and his company coming, they went forward and stood in front of the gate, for they had not time to shut it. There they stood, just as two wild boars might stand at bay against a crowd of men and dogs. And all the while the men who stood on the wall never ceased to throw down heavy stones on the Trojans. The stones fell as fast as the flakes of snow fall on a winter's day, and the helmets and shields of the Trojans rang out as the stones crashed upon them. Many fell to the ground, and King Asius, for all his fury, could not make his way through the gate.

At another of the gates, where Hector was leading his company, there was seen a very strange thing in the skies. An eagle had caught a great snake, and was carrying it in his claws to give to its young ones for food. But the snake fought fiercely for its life, and writhed itself about till it bit the bird upon the breast. And when the eagle felt that it had been bitten, it dropped the snake into the middle of the two armies, and flew away with a loud cry. Then Polyda˘mas, who was a wise man, and knew the meaning of all such signs, said to Hector: "O Hector, it will be well for us not to follow the Greeks to their ships. For this strange thing which we have just seen in the sky is a sign to us. The eagle signifies the Trojans, and the snake signifies the Greeks. Now, as the eagle caught the snake but could not hold it, so have we prevailed over the Greeks, but shall not be able to conquer them altogether. And as the snake turned upon the bird and bit it, so the Greeks turn upon us and do us great damage, so that we shall be driven back from the ships, and leave many of our comrades dead behind us."

But Hector was angry to hear such words, and said: "This is bad advice that you give me. Surely the gods have changed your wisdom into foolishness. Would you have me forget the commandment of Zeus, when he bade me to follow the Greeks even to their ships, and to take heed to birds, and do one thing or another because they fly this way or that? Little do I care whether they fly east or west or are seen on the right hand or on the left. Surely there is but one sign for a brave man, that he be fighting for his fatherland. Take heed, therefore, to yourself. Truly if you hold back from the war, or cause any other man to hold back, I will smite you with my spear."

Then he sprang forward, and the Trojans followed him with a great shout. And Zeus sent down from Mount Ida a great wind, and the wind carried the dust of the plain straight into the faces of the Greeks, troubling them not a little. But when the Trojans sought to drag down the battlements which were on the wall and to pull up the stakes which had been set to strengthen it, they could not, for the building was strong, and the Greeks stood firm in their place, with shield joining to shield, and fought for the wall.

After a while Sarpe¯don the Lycian came to the front, for Zeus put it into his heart so to do, that he might win great glory for himself. He came holding his shield before him and with a long spear in either hand. Just as a lion, when he is mad with hunger, goes against a stable in which oxen are kept, or against a sheepfold, and does not care though it is guarded by many men and dogs, so did Sarpe¯don go against the wall. And he spoke to Glaucus, his kinsman, saying: "Tell me, Glaucus, why is it that our people at home honour us with the chief places at feasts, and with fat portions of flesh, and with wine of the best, and that they have set apart for us a great domain of orchard and of ploughland by the banks of the Xanthus. Surely it is that we may fight in the front rank, and show to others how they should behave in the battle. For so some one who may see us will say, 'Of a truth these are honourable men, these princes of Lycia, and not without good do they eat the fat and drink the sweet, for they are always to be seen fighting in the front.' Maybe, if we could hope to live for ever and to escape from old age and death, I would not either fight myself in the front or bid you do so; but now, seeing that there are ten thousand chances of death about us, let us see whether we may not win glory from another, or haply another may win it from us."

When he had so spoken he leapt forward, and Glaucus went with him, and all the host of the Lycians followed close behind. Then the keeper of the gate—he was a man of Athens—was struck with great fear and looked about for help. All along the wall he looked, and he saw Ajax the Greater and Ajax the Less, and Teucer, for the hurt which Hector had given him was now healed. He would have shouted to them, but the din of arms, and the ringing of shields and helmets and the battering at the gates, would have drowned his voice. So he called a herald, and said: "Run now, and call Ajax hither—both the Greater and the Less, if it may be—for the danger is very great, and the chiefs of the Lycians press us hard. And if there is trouble there also, then let Ajax the Greater come at the least and Teucer with him, bringing his bow." So the herald ran with the message, and when Ajax the Greater heard it, he said to the other Ajax: "Stand here and keep off the enemy; and I will go yonder, and come again when I have done my work."

So Ajax, and Teucer his brother, ran as quickly as they could to the gate, and just as they got to it the Lycians came against it with a great rush, as if it had been a storm of wind and rain. But still the Greeks stood firm, and Ajax slew one of the Lycian chiefs and Teucer wounded Glaucus on the shoulder. Quietly he jumped down from the wall, for he did not wish that any one should see that he was wounded. But Sarpe‾don saw it and was sorry, because he was his kinsman and also a great help in the battle. Nevertheless he pressed on as bravely as before. First he slew one of the Greeks upon the wall, and then he laid hold of one of the battlements with his two hands and pulled it down, and a part of the wall with it. Thus there was a way made by which men might enter the camp. But Ajax and his brother stopped the Lycians for a time, aiming at Sarpe‾don, both of them together. Teucer struck at him with his spear, for the bow he could not use when the enemy was so near, and smote the strap of his shield, but did him no harm; Ajax drove his spear through the shield and pushed him back so that he was forced to leap from the wall to the ground. But his courage was not one whit abated. He cried out: "Help me now, ye men of Lycia. It is hard for me, however great my strength, to do this work alone, pulling down the wall and making a way for you to the ships." And all his people, when they heard his voice, came rushing up in a great crowd. But the Greeks, on the other hand, strengthened their line, others coming to the place where they saw the need to be the greatest, for indeed it was a matter of life and death. For a long time they fought with equal strength, for the Lycians could not break down the wall and make a way to the ships, and the Greeks could not drive the Lycians back.

But at the last Zeus gave the glory to Hector. Once again he sprang to the front, crying: "Now follow me, men of Troy, and we will burn the ships." In front of the gate there lay a great stone, broad at the bottom and sharp at the top. Scarcely could two men, the strongest that there are in these days, lift it on to a wagon; but Hector took it up as easily as a shepherd carries in one hand the fleece of a sheep. Now there were two folding doors in the middle of the gate, by which a man might enter without opening the gate. These doors were fastened by a bolt and a key. Then Hector lifted the great stone above his head, holding it with both his hands, and he put his feet apart, that his aim might be the surer and stronger, and threw with all his might at the doors. With a great crash did it come against them, and the bolts could not hold against it, and the hinges were broken, and the doors flew back. Then Hector leapt into the open space, holding a spear in either hand, and his eyes flashed with fire. And the Trojans followed him, some entering by the gate and some climbing over the wall.

The Battle at the Ships

Now Poseidon, the god of the sea, loved the Greeks, and when he saw from a distant mountain where he sat how they fled before the Trojans, he was greatly troubled; and he said to himself: "Now I will help these men." It happened, also that Zeus had turned his eyes from the battle, thinking that none of the gods would do the thing which he had forbidden, that is, bring help to the Greeks. So Poseidon left the mountain where he sat, and came to his palace under the sea. There he harnessed his horses to his chariot, and he passed over the waves, while the great beasts of the sea, whales, and porpoises and the like, gambolled round him as he went, because they knew that he was their king. And when he came to the land of Troy, he left his chariot in a cave, and went on foot into the camp of the Greeks, having made himself like to Calchas the herald. And he came to the place where Ajax the Greater and the other Ajax were standing, and said to them: "Stir yourselves, for it is for you, who are stronger than other men, to save the people. I do not fear for the rest of the wall, but only for the place where Hector is fighting. Go then and keep him back, and may some god give you strength and courage."

And as he spoke he touched them with his staff and filled them with fresh courage, and gave new strength to their hands and to their feet. And when he had done this, he passed out of their sight, as quickly as a hawk flies when he drops from a cliff, chasing a bird. Then the Lesser Ajax perceived that he was not Calchas the herald but a god; and he said to the other Ajax: "This is a god who sends us to the battle. I knew him as he went away; and truly I feel my heart in me eager for the fight." And Ajax the Greater answered: "So it is with me also. I am all on fire for the battle. I would go against this Hector, even should I go alone." Meanwhile Poseidon went through the army, stirring up the other chiefs in the same way. But still the Trojans came on, even fiercer than before. Then Teucer slew a famous chief, Imbrius by name, driving his spear point under the man's ear. Like to some tall poplar by a river-side which a woodman cuts down with his axe of bronze, so did Imbrius fall. Then Hector cast his spear at Teucer. Him he missed, but he struck the comrade who was standing next to him. And Hector, as the man lay upon the ground, seized his helmet, and would have dragged the body among his own people. But Ajax the Greater thrust with his spear, and struck the boss of Hector's shield so strongly that he was driven backward and loosed his hold of the helmet, and the Greeks carried the man to the ships.

Next there was slain a chief from the land of Caria who had come to Troy, desiring to have Cassandra, daughter of King Priam, for his wife. Loudly he had boasted, saying that he would drive the Greeks to the ships; and the King had promised him his daughter. But now he was slain. And the King of the Cretans, when he saw him lie dead, cried: "Truly this was a great thing which you promised to King Priam, so that he might give you his daughter. You should have come rather to us, and Agamemnon would have given you the fairest of his daughters, bringing her from Argos, that she might be married to you, if only you would take for us this city of Troy. But come now with me to the ships, that we may treat with you about this matter. Verily you will find that we Greeks are men of an open hand." Thus did the King speak, mocking the dead.

King Asius heard these words and was full of anger, and came at the Prince of Crete, lifting his spear to throw it. He was on foot, and his chariot followed close after him. But before he could cast the spear the Prince of Crete smote him full on the breast, and he fell as an oak or a pine tree falls before the axes of the wood-cutters on the hills. And when the driver of the chariot saw his master fall he was struck with fear, not knowing what to do. Then Antiloˇchus, who was the eldest son of old Nestor, struck him down with his spear, and jumped on to the chariot, and took it and the horses for his own. Many other of the Trojans did the Greeks slay, and many they wounded. Even the mighty Hector himself was struck down for a time. He cast his spear at the great Ajax but hurt him not, for the point was turned by the armour, so thick it was and strong. And when he saw that he had cast the spear in vain, then he turned, and sought to go back to the ranks of his comrades; but, as he went, Ajax took up from the ground a great stone, one of many that lay there, and served as props for the ships, and cast it at Hector, smiting him above the rim of his shield on the neck. He fell as an oak falls when the lightning has struck it, and the Greeks, when they saw him fall, rushed with a great cry, and would have caught hold of his body and dragged it away. But this the Trojans did not suffer, for many of the bravest of them stood before him, covering him with their shields. And when they had driven back the Greeks a space, they lifted him from the ground, and carried him to the river and poured water on him. After a while he sat up, and then his spirit left him again, for it was a grievous blow which Ajax had dealt him. But when the Greeks saw that Hector was carried out of the battle, they took fresh courage and charged the Trojans, and drove them back even beyond the walls and the trench. And when the Trojans came to the place where they had left their chariots and horses, they stood pale and trembling, not knowing what to do.

But now Zeus turned his eyes again to the land of Troy. Very angry was he when he saw what had happened, how the Trojans fled from the Greeks, and Hector lay upon the plain, like to one that has fallen in battle, and his friends stood round him in great fear lest he had been wounded to the death. So he said to Hera: "Is this then your doing, rebellious one? Tell me now the truth, or it will be worse for you." And Hera answered: "Nay, this is not my doing. It is Poseidon who gives to the Greeks strength and courage." Then said Zeus to Iris the messenger: "Go now to Poseidon and tell him that it is my will that he is not to meddle with these things any more. Let him go back to the sea, for there he is master; but the things that happen on the earth, these belong to me. And when you have given this message to Poseidon, then go to Apollo and bid him go to Hector where he lies like a dead man on the plain, and put new life and courage into him, and send him back with new strength to the battle."

So Iris went on her errand. First she came to Poseidon, and gave him the message of Zeus. He was very angry when he heard it, and said: "Am I not his equal in honour? By what right does he bid me do this thing and cease from doing that? We were three brothers, sons of Old Time, and to me was given the dominion of the sea, and to Pluto the dwellings of the dead, and to Zeus to reign over the heaven and the earth."

But Iris answered: "O Poseidon, is it well to speak thus of Zeus? Do you not know how the eldest born is ever the strongest?" And Poseidon answered: "These are words of wisdom, O Iris, yet truly, if Zeus is minded to save this city of Troy, there will be enmity without ceasing between him and me."

Then went Iris to Apollo and gave him the message of Zeus. So Apollo hastened to Hector where he sat by the river-side, for already his strength had begun to come back to him. And Apollo said to him: "Why is this, O Hector? Why do you sit and take no part in the battle?" Hector answered: "Is this a god that speaks to me? Did you not see how Ajax struck me down with a great stone, so that I could fight no more? Truly, I thought that I had gone down to the place of the dead." Apollo said: "Take courage, my friend. I am Apollo of the Golden Sword, and Zeus has sent me to stand by you and to help you. Come now, call the Trojans together again, and go before them, and lead them to the ships, and I will be with you and make the way easy for you." Then Hector stood up, and his strength came back to him as it had been before, and he called to the Trojans and went before them. The Greeks wondered when they saw him, for they thought that he had been wounded to death. They were like men who hunt a stag or a wild goat and find a lion. Nevertheless they kept up their courage, and stood close together with their faces towards the enemy; but though the chiefs stood firm, most of the Greeks turned their backs and fled. And Hector still came on and Apollo went before him, having a cloud of fire round his shoulders, holding the great shield of Zeus in his hand. Many of the Greeks were slain that day. And now the Trojans came again to the trench and crossed it, and neither the wall nor the gates stopped them, and they came as far as the ships, Hector being first of all. And close behind Hector was a chief who carried a torch in his hand, with which to set fire to a ship. Him Ajax smote on the breast with his sword and killed him. And Hector, when he saw it, cast his spear at Ajax. Him he missed, but he killed the comrade who was standing close by him. Then Ajax called to Teucer: "Where is your bow and arrows? Shoot." So Teucer shot. With the first arrow he slew a Trojan; but when he laid another arrow upon the string and aimed it at Hector, the string broke, and the arrow went far astray. When Teucer saw this he cried out: "Surely the gods are against us; see how the string of my bow is broken, and yet it was new this very day." And Ajax said to him: "Let your bow be, if the gods will not have you use it. Take your spear and fight. Truly, if the men of Troy prevail over us, yet they shall not take our ships for nothing." So Teucer threw away his bow, and took up spear and shield. When Hector saw it, he cried: "Come on, men of Troy, for Zeus is with us, and they whom Zeus favours are strong, and they whom he favours not are weak. See now how he has broken the bow of Teucer, the great archer. Come on, therefore, for the gods give us victory. And even if a man die, it is a noble thing to die fighting for his country. His wife and children shall dwell in peace, and he himself shall be famous for ever."

Thus did Hector urge on his people to the battle; and Ajax, on the other hand, called to the Greeks and bade them quit themselves like men. Many chiefs fell on either side, but still the Trojans prevailed more and more, and the Greeks fell back before them. And now Hector laid hold on one of the ships. Well did he know it, for it was the first that had touched the Trojan shore, and he had slain the chief whose ship it was with his own hand as he was leaping to shore. There the battle grew fiercer and fiercer; none fought with arrows or javelins, but close, man to man, with swords and battle-axes and spears, thrusting at each other. And Hector cried: "Bring me fire that we may burn the ships of these robbers, for Zeus has given us the victory to-day." And the Trojans came on more fiercely than before, so that Ajax himself was forced to give way, so much did the Trojans press him. For at first he stood on the stern deck, the ships being drawn up with the stern to the land and the forepart to the sea, and then being driven from the deck, in the middle of the ships, among the benches of the rowers. But still he fought bravely, thrusting at any one who came near to set fire to the ship. And he cried to the Greeks with a terrible voice, saying: "Now must you quit yourselves as men, O Greeks! Have you any to help you if you are conquered now? Have you any walls behind which you may seek for shelter? There is no city here with a wall and towers and battlements behind which you may hide yourselves. You are in the plain of Troy, and the sea is close behind us, and we are far from our own country. All our hope, therefore, is in courage, for there is no one to save if you will not save yourselves."

So did Ajax speak to the Greeks, and still as he spoke he thrust at the Trojans with his spear.

The Deeds and Death of Patroclus

Patroclus stood by Achilles, weeping bitterly. And Achilles said to him: "What is the matter, Patroclus, that you weep? You are like a girl-child that runs along by her mother's side, and holds her gown and cries till she takes her up in her arms. Have you heard bad news from Phthia? Yet your father still lives, I know, and so does the old man Peleus. Or are you weeping for the Greeks because they perish for their folly, or, maybe, for the folly of their King?"

Then Patroclus answered: "Be not angry with me, great Achilles. The Greeks are in great trouble, for all the bravest of their chiefs are wounded, and yet you still keep your anger, and will not help them. They say that Peleus was your father and Thetis your mother. Yet I should say, so hard are you, that a rock was your father and your mother the sea. If you will not go forth to the battle because you have had some warning from the gods, then let me go, and let your people, the Myrmidons, go with me. And let me put on your armour; the Trojans will think that you have come back to the battle, and the Greeks will have a breathing space."

So Patroclus spoke, entreating Achilles, but he did not know that it was for his own death that he asked. And Achilles answered: "It is no warning that I heed, and that keeps me from the battle. Such things trouble me not. But these men were not ashamed to stand by when their King took away from me the prize which I had won with my own hands. But let the past be past. I said that I would not fight again till the Trojans should bring the fire near to my own ships. But now, for I see that the people are in great need, you may put on my armour, and lead my people to the fight. And, indeed, it is time to give help, for I see that the Trojans are gathered about the ships, and that the Greeks have scarce standing ground between their enemies and the sea. And I do not see anywhere either Diomed with his spear, nor King Agamemnon; only I hear the voice of Hector, as he calls his people to the battle. Go, therefore, Patroclus, and keep the fire from the ships. But when you have done this, come back and fight no more with the Trojans, for it is my business to conquer them, and you must not take my glory from me. And mind this also: when you feel the joy of battle in your heart, be not over-bold; go not near the wall of Troy, lest one of the gods meet you and harm you. For these gods love the Trojans, and especially the great archer Apollo with his deadly bow."

So these two talked together in the tent. But at the ships Ajax could hold out no longer. For the javelins came thick upon him and clattered on his helmet and his breastplate, and his shoulder was weary with the weight of his great shield. Heavily and hard did he breathe, and the great drops of sweat fell upon the ground. Then, at the last, Hector came near and struck at him with his sword. Him he did not hit, but he cut off the head of his spear. Great fear came on Ajax and he gave way, and the Trojans put torches to the ship's stern, and a great flame rose up into the air. When Achilles saw the flames, he struck his thigh with his hand and said: "Make haste, Patroclus, for I see the fire rising from the ships."

Then Patroclus put on the armour—breastplate and shield and helmet—and bound the sword on his shoulder, and took a great spear in his hand. But the great Pelian spear he did not take, for that no man could wield but Achilles only. Then the charioteer yoked the horses to the chariot. Two of the horses, Bayard and Piebald, were immortal, but the third was of a mortal breed. And while he did this, Achilles called the Myrmidons to battle. Fifty ships he had brought to Troy, and fifty men in each. And when they were assembled he said: "Forget not, ye Myrmidons, what you said when first I kept you back from the battle, how angry you were, and how you blamed me, complaining that I kept you back against your will. Now you have the thing that you desired."

So the Myrmidons went forth to battle in close array, helmet to helmet and shield to shield, close together as are the stones which a builder builds into a wall. Patroclus went before them in the chariot of Achilles, with the charioteer by his side. And as they went, Achilles went to the chest which stood in his tent, and opened it, and took from it a great cup which Thetis his mother had given him. No man drank out of that cup but Achilles only. Nor did he pour libations out of it to any of the gods but to Zeus only. First he cleansed the cup with sulphur and then with water from the spring. After this he filled it with wine, and standing in the space before the tent he poured out from it to Zeus, saying: "O Zeus, this day I send my dear comrade to the battle. Be thou with him; make him strong and bold, and give him glory, and bring him home safe to the ships, and my people with him."

So he prayed; and Father Zeus heard his prayer: part he granted, but part he denied.

Meanwhile Patroclus with the Myrmidons had come to the place where the battle was so hot, namely the ship to which Hector had put the torch and set it on fire. And when the Trojans saw him and the armour he wore, they thought that it had been Achilles, who had put away his anger, and had come forth again to the battle. Nor was it long before they turned to flee. So the battle rolled back again to the trench, and many chariots of the Trojans were broken, for when they crossed it for the second time they took their chariots with them; but the horses of Achilles sprang across it in their stride, so nimble were they and so strong. And great was the fear of the Trojans; even the great Hector fled. The heart of Patroclus was set upon slaying him, for he had forgotten the command which Achilles had laid upon him, that when he had saved the ships from the fire he should not fight any more. But though he followed hard after him, he could not overtake him, so swift were the Trojan horses. Then he left following him and turned back, and caused the chariot to be driven backwards and forwards, so that he might slay the Trojans as they sought to fly to the city.

But there were some among the Trojans and their allies who would not flee. Among these was Sarpe̅don the Lycian; and he, when he saw his people flying before Patroclus, cried aloud to them: "Stand now and be of good courage: I myself will try this great warrior and see what he can do." So he leapt down from his chariot, and Patroclus also leapt down from his, and the two rushed at each other, fierce and swift as two eagles. Sarpe̅don carried a spear in either hand, and he threw both of them together. With the one he wounded to the death one of the horses of Achilles, that which was of a mortal strain, but the other missed its aim, flying over the left shoulder of Patroclus. But the spear of Patroclus missed not its aim. Full on the heart of Sarpe̅don it fell, and broke through his armour, and bore him to the earth. He fell, as a pine or a poplar falls on the hills before the woodman's axe. And as he fell, he called to Glaucus his kinsman: "Now show yourself a man, O Glaucus; suffer not the Greeks to spoil me of my arms." And when he had said so much, he died. Now Glaucus was still troubled by the wound which Teucer the archer had given him. But when he heard the voice of Sarpe̅don he prayed to Apollo, saying: "Give me now strength that I may save the body of my kinsman from the hands of the Greeks." And Apollo heard him and made him whole of his wound. Then he called first to the Lycians, saying, "Fight for the body of your king," and next to the Trojans, that they should honour the man who had come from his own land to help them, and lastly to Hector himself, who had now returned to the battle. "Little care you, O Hector," he said, "for your allies. Lo! Sarpe̅don is dead, slain by Patroclus. Will you suffer the Myrmidons to carry off his body and do dishonour to it?"

Hector was much troubled by these words, and so were all the men of Troy, for among the allies there were none braver than Sarpe̅don. So they charged and drove back the Greeks from the body; and the Greeks charged again in their turn. No one would have known the great Sarpe⁻don as he lay in the middle of the tumult, so covered was he with dust and blood. But at last the Greeks drove back the Trojans from the body, and stripped it of its arms; but the body itself they harmed not. For at the bidding of Zeus, Apollo came down and carried it out of the tumult, and gave it to Sleep and Death that they should carry it to the land of Lycia. Then again Patroclus forgot the commands of Achilles, for he thought in his heart, "Now shall I take the city of Troy," for, when he had driven the Trojans up to the very gates, he himself climbed on to an angle of the wall. Three times did he climb upon it, and three times did Apollo push him back, laying his hand upon the boss of his shield. And when Patroclus climbed for the fourth time, then Apollo cried to him in a dreadful voice: "Go back, Patroclus; it is not for you to take the great city of Troy, no, nor even for Achilles, who is a far better man than you." Then Patroclus went back, for he feared the anger of the god. But though he thought no more of taking the city, he raged no less against the Trojans. Then did Apollo put it into the heart of Hector to go against the man. So Hector said to his charioteer: "We will see whether we cannot drive back this Patroclus, for it must be he; Achilles he is not, though he wears his armour." When Patroclus saw them coming he took a great stone from the ground, and cast it at the pair. The stone struck the charioteer full on the helmet. And as the man fell head foremost from the chariot, Patroclus laughed aloud, and said: "See now, how nimble is this man! See how well he dives! He might get many oysters from the bottom of the sea, diving from the deck of a ship, even though it should be a stormy day. Who would have thought that there should be such skilful divers in Troy?"

Three times did Patroclus charge into the ranks of the Trojans, and each time he slew nine warriors. But when he charged the fourth time, then, for the hour of his doom was come, Apollo stood behind him, and gave him a great blow on his neck, so that he could not see out of his eyes. And the helmet fell from his head, so that the plumes were soiled with the dust. Never before had it touched the ground, from the first day when Achilles wore it. The spear also which he carried in his hand was broken, and the shield fell from his arm, and the breastplate on his body was loosened. Then, as he stood without defence and was confused, one of the Trojans wounded him in the back with his spear. And when he tried to hide himself behind his comrades, for the wound was not mortal, Hector thrust at him with his spear, and hit him above the hip, and he fell to the ground. And when the Greeks saw him fall they sent up a dreadful cry. Then Hector stood over him, and said: "Did you think, Patroclus, that you would take our city, and slay us with the sword, and carry away our wives and daughters in your ships? This you will not do, for, lo! I have overcome you with my spear, and the fowls of the air shall eat your flesh. And the great Achilles cannot help you at all. Did he not say to you, 'Strip the fellow's shirt from his back and bring it back to me'? and you, in your folly, thought that you would do it."

Patroclus answered: "You boast too much, O Hector. It is not by your hand that I am overcome; it has been Apollo who has brought me to my death. Had twenty such as you come against me, truly I had slain them all. And mark you this: death is very near to you, for the great Achilles will slay you."

Then said Hector: "Why do you prophesy my death? Who has shown you the things to come? Maybe, as I have slain you, so shall I slay the great Achilles." So Hector spoke, but Patroclus was dead already. Then he drew the spear from the wound, and went after the charioteer of Achilles, hoping to slay him and take the chariot for spoil, but the horses were so swift that he could not come up with them.

The Rousing of Achilles

Very fierce was the fight for the body of Patroclus, and many warriors fell both on this side and on that; and the first to be killed was the man who had wounded him in the back; for when he came near to strip the dead man of his arms, King Menelaüs thrust at him with his spear and slew him. He slew him, but he could not strip off his arms, because Hector came and stood over the body, and Menelaüs did not dare to stand up against him, knowing that he was not a match for him in fighting. Then Hector spoiled the body of Patroclus of the arms which the great Achilles had given him to wear. But when he laid hold of the body, and began to drag it away to the ranks of the Trojans, the Greater Ajax came forward, and put his big shield before it. As a lioness stands before its cubs and will not suffer the hunter to take them, so did Ajax stand before the body of Patroclus and defend it from the Trojans. And Hector drew back when he saw him. Then Glaucus the Lycian spoke to him in great anger: "Are you not ashamed, O Hector, that you dare not stand before Ajax? How will you and the other Trojans save your city? Truly your allies will not fight any more for you, for though they help you much, yet you help them little. Did not Sarpe⁻don fall fighting for you, and yet you left him to be a prey to the dogs? And now, had you only stood up against this Ajax, and dragged away the body of Patroclus, we might have made an exchange, giving him and his arms, and receiving Sarpe⁻don from the Greeks. But this may not be, because you are afraid of Ajax, and flee before him when he comes to meet you."

Hector answered: "I am not afraid of Ajax, nor of any man. But this I know, that Zeus gives victory now to one and now to another; this only do I fear, and this only, to go against the will of Zeus. But wait here, and see whether or no I am a coward."

Now he had sent the armour of Patroclus to the city; but when he heard Glaucus speak in this manner, he ran after the men who were carrying it and overtook them, and stripped off his own armour, and put on the armour of Achilles. And when Zeus saw him do this thing he was angry, and said to himself, "These arms will cost Hector dear." Nevertheless, when he came back to the battle, all men were astonished, for he seemed like to the great Achilles himself. Then the Trojans took heart again, and charged all together, and the battle grew fiercer and fiercer. For the Greeks said to themselves: "It were better that the earth should open her mouth and swallow us up alive than that we let the Trojans carry off the body of Patroclus." And the Trojans said to themselves: "Now if we must all be slain fighting for the body of this man, be it so; but we will not yield." Now while they fought the horses of Achilles stood apart from the battle, and the tears rushed down from their eyes, for they loved Patroclus, they knew that he was dead. Still they stood in the same place; they would not enter into the battle, neither would they turn back to the ships. And the charioteer could not move them with the lash, or with threats, or with gentle words. As a pillar stands by the grave of some dead man, so they stood; their heads drooped to the ground, and the tears trickled down from their eyes, and their long manes were trailed in the dust.

When Zeus saw them he pitied them in his heart. And he said: "It was not well that I gave you, immortal as you are, to a mortal man, for of all things that live and move upon the earth, surely man is the most miserable. But Hector shall not have you. It is enough for him, yea, it is too much that he should have the arms of Achilles."

Then the horses moved from their place, and obeyed the driver as before; and Hector could not take them, though he greatly desired so to do.

All this time the battle raged yet more and more fiercely about the body of Patroclus. At the last, when the Greeks were growing weary, and the Trojans pressed them more and more, Ajax said to Menelaüs, for these two had borne themselves more bravely in the battle than all the others: "See now if you can find Antilo˘chus, Nestor's son, and bid him run and carry the news to Achilles that Patroclus is dead, and that the Greeks and Trojans are fighting over his body." So Menelaüs went, and found Antilo˘chus on the left side of the battle. And he said to him: "I have bad news for you. You see that the Trojans prevail in the battle, to-day. And now Patroclus lies dead. Run, therefore, to Achilles and tell him; maybe he can yet save the body; as for the arms, Hector has them."

Antilo˘chus was greatly troubled to hear the news; his eyes filled with tears, and he could not speak for grief. But he gave heed to the words of Menelaüs, and ran to tell Achilles what had happened.

And Menelaüs went back to Ajax, where he had left him standing close by the body of Patroclus. And he said to him: "I have found Antilo˘chus, and he is carrying the news to Achilles. Yet I doubt whether he will come to the battle, however great his anger may be and his grief, for he has no armour to cover him. Let us think, therefore, how we may best save the body of Patroclus from the Trojans."

Ajax said: "Do you and Merioˇnes run forward and lift up the body and carry it away." So Menelaüs and Merioˇnes ran forward and lifted up the body. But when they would have carried it away, then the Trojans ran fiercely at them. So the battle raged; neither could the Greeks save the body, nor could the Trojans carry it away. Meanwhile Antiloˇchus came to Achilles where he sat by the door of his tent. With a great fear in his heart he sat, for he saw that the Greeks fled and the Trojans pursued after them. Then said Nestor's son: "I bring bad news. Patroclus is dead, and Hector has his arms, but the Greeks and Trojans are fighting for his body."

Then Achilles threw himself upon the ground, and took the dust in his hands, and poured it on his head, and tore his hair. And all the women wailed aloud. And Antiloˇchus sat weeping; but while he wept he held the hands of Achilles, for he was afraid that in his anger he would do himself a mischief. But his mother heard his cry, where she sat in the depths of the sea, and came to him and laid her hand upon his head, and said: "Why do you weep, my son? Tell me; hide not the matter from me." Achilles answered: "All that you asked from Zeus, and that he promised to do, he has done: but what is the good? The man whom I loved above all others is dead, and Hector has my arms, for Patroclus was wearing them. As for me, I do not wish to live except to avenge myself upon him."

Then said Thetis: "My son, do not speak so: do you not know that when Hector dies, the hour is near when you also must die?"

Then Achilles cried in great anger: "I would that I could die this hour, for I sent my friend to his death; and I, who am better in battle than all the Greeks, could not help him. Cursed be the anger that sets men to strive with one another, as it made me strive with King Agamemnon. And as for my fate—what matters it? Let it come when it may, so that I may first have vengeance on Hector. Seek not, therefore, my mother, to keep me back from the battle."

Thetis answered: "Be it so, my son: only you cannot go without arms, and these Hector has. But to-morrow I will go to Hephæstus, that he may make new arms for you."

But while they talked, the Trojans pressed the Greeks still more and more, so that Ajax himself could no longer stand against them. Then truly they would have taken the body of Patroclus, had not Zeus sent Iris to Achilles with this message: "Rouse yourself, son of Peleus, or, surely, Patroclus will be a prey to the dogs of Troy." But Achilles said: "How shall I go? For I have no arms, nor do I know of any whose arms I could wear. I might shift with the shield of great Ajax; but this he is carrying, as is his custom, in the front of the battle.

Then said Iris: "Go only to the trench and show yourself, for the Trojans will be swift and draw back, and the Greeks will have a breathing-space."

So Achilles ran to the trench. And Athené put her great shield about his shoulders, and set as it were a circle of gold about his head, so that it shone like to a flame of fire. To the trench he went, but he obeyed the word of his mother, and did not mix in the battle. Only he shouted aloud, and his voice was as the voice of a trumpet. It was a terrible sound to hear, and the hearts of the men of Troy were filled with fear. The very horses were frightened, and started aside, so that the chariots clashed together. Three times did Achilles shout across the trench, and three times did the Trojans fall back. Twelve chiefs perished that hour; some were wounded by their own spears, and some were trodden down by their own horses; for the whole army was overcome with fear, from the front ranks to the hindermost. Then the Greeks took up the body of Patroclus from the place where it lay, and put it on the bier, and carried it to the tent of Achilles, and Achilles himself walked by its side weeping. This had been a sad day, and to bring it sooner to an end Hera commanded the sun to set before his time. So did the Greeks rest from their labours.

On the other side of the field, the Trojans held an assembly. And one of the elders stood up and said: "Let us not wait here for the morning. It was well for us to fight at the ships so long as Achilles was angry with King Agamemnon. But now this has ceased to be. To-morrow will he come back to the battle, the fiercer on account of his great grief, Patroclus being slain. Surely it will be an evil day for us, if we wait for his coming. Let us go back to the city, for its walls are high and its gates are strong, and the man who seeks to pass them will perish."

But Hector said: "This is bad counsel. Shall we shut ourselves up in the city? Are not our goods wasted? Have we enough wherewith to feed the people? Nay; we will watch to-night and to-morrow we will fight. And if Achilles comes to the battle, I will meet him, for the gods give victory now to one man and now to another."

And the people clapped their hands, for they were foolish, and knew not what the morrow would bring forth.

The Making of the Arms

Meanwhile there was a great mourning for Patroclus in the camp of the Greeks. And Achilles stood up in the midst of the people and said: "Truly the gods do not fulfil the thoughts of men. Did I not say to the father of Patroclus that I would return with him, bringing back our portion of the spoils of Troy? And now he is dead; nor shall I return to the house of Peleus my father, for I too must die in this land. But I care not, if only I may have vengeance upon Hector. Truly I will not bury Patroclus till I can bring the head and the arms of Hector with which to honour him." So they washed the body of Patroclus, and put ointment into the wounds, and laid it on a bed, and covered with a linen cloth from the head to the feet, putting over the linen cloth a white robe. And all night the Myrmidons made lamentations for him.

Thetis went to the house of Hephæstus, who was the god of all who worked in gold and silver and iron. She found him busy at his work, for he was making cauldrons for the palace of the gods. They had golden wheels underneath them with which they could run of themselves into the chambers of the palace, and come back of themselves as might be wanted. The Lady Grace who was wife to Hephæstus saw Thetis, and caught her by the hand, and said: "O Goddess, whom we love and honour, what business brings you here? Gladly will we serve you." And she led her into the house, and set her on a chair that was adorned with silver studs, and put a stool under her feet. Then she called to her husband, saying: "Thetis is here, and wants something from you. Come quickly." He answered: "Truly there could be no guest more welcome than Thetis. When my mother cast me out from her house because I was lame, then Thetis and her sister received me in their house under the sea. Nine years I dwelt with them, yes, and hammered many a trinket for them in a hollow cave that was close by. Truly I would give the price of my life to serve Thetis." Then he put away his tools, and washed himself, and took a staff in his hands and came into the house, and sat down upon a chair, and said: "Tell me all that is in your mind, for I will do all that you desire if only it can be done." Then Thetis told him of how her son Achilles had been put to shame by King Agamemnon, and of his anger, and of all that came to pass afterwards, and of how Patroclus had been slain in battle, and how the arms were lost. And having told this story, she said: "Make for my son Achilles, I pray you, a shield, and a helmet, and greaves for his legs, and a breastplate."

"That will I do," answered Hephaestus, "I will make for him such arms as men will wonder at when they see them. Would that I could keep from him as easily the doom of death!"

So he went to his forge and turned the bellows to the fire, and bade them work, for they did not need a hand to work them. And he put copper and tin and gold and silver into the fire to make them soft, and set the anvil, and took the hammer in one hand and the tongs in the other.

First he made a shield, great and strong, with a silver belt by which a man might hold it. On it he made an image of the earth and the sky and the sea, with the sun and the moon and all the stars. Also he made images of two cities; in one city there was peace, and in the other city there was war. In the city of peace they led a bride to the house of her husband with music and dancing, and the women stood in the door to see the show. And in another part of the same city the judges sat, to judge the case of a man who had been slain. One man said that he had paid the price of blood, for if one man slays another he must pay a price for him, and the other man said the price was not paid. Round about the city of war there was an army of besiegers and on the wall stood men defending it. Also the men of this same city had set an ambush by a river, at a place where the cattle came down to drink. And when the cattle came down the men that lay in ambush rose up quickly, and took them, and slew the herdsmen. And the army of the besiegers heard the cry, and rode on horses, and came quickly to the river and fought with the men who had taken the cattle. Also he made the image of one field in which men were ploughing, and of another in which reapers reaped the corn, and behind the reapers came boys who gathered the corn in their arms and bound it in sheaves; at the top of the field stood the master, glad at heart because the harvest was good. Also he made a vineyard, and through the vineyard there was a path, and along the path went young men and maids bearing baskets of grapes, and in the midst stood a boy holding a harp of gold, who sang a pleasant song. Also he made a herd of oxen going from the stalls to the pasture; and close by two lions had laid hold of a great bull and were devouring it, and the dogs stood far off and barked. A sheep-fold also he made, and a dance of men and maids; the men wore daggers of gold hanging from silver belts, and the maids had gold crowns round their heads. And round about the shield he made ocean like to a great river. Also he made a breastplate, and a great helmet with a ridge of gold, in which the plumes should be set, and greaves of tin for the legs. When he had finished all his work, he gave the shield and the other things to Thetis. And she flew, swift as a hawk, to where her son abode by the ships. She found him lying on the ground, holding in his arms the body of Patroclus, weeping aloud, while his men lamented.

The goddess stood in the midst, and caught her son by the hand and said: "Come now, let us leave the dead man; it was the will of the gods that he should die. But you must think about other things. Come now and take this gift from Hephæstus, armour beautiful exceedingly, such as man has never yet worn."

And as she spoke, she cast the armour down at the feet of Achilles. It rattled loud as it fell, and shone so brightly that the eyes of the Myrmidons were dazzled by it. But Achilles took up the arms from the ground, glad at heart to see them, and said: "Mother, these indeed are such arms as can be made in heaven only. Gladly will I put them on for the battle. Yet one thing troubles me. I fear lest decay should come on the body of Patroclus, before I can do it such honour as I desire."

But Thetis answered: "Let this not trouble you. I will keep the body from decay. But do you make peace with the king and prepare yourself for the battle." And she put precious things such as are known only in heaven into the nostrils of the dead man to keep him from decay.

The Quarrel Ended

Achilles went along by the ships, shouting with a loud voice to the Greeks that they should come to the battle. And they all came; there was not a man left, even those who had been used to stay behind, the men who looked after the ships, and they who had the care of the food. They all followed when Achilles came back to the war. And the chiefs came to the assembly, some of them, as Diomed and Ulysses and King Agamemnon himself, leaning on their spears because their wounds were fresh.

Achilles stood up and spoke: "It was a foolish thing, King Agamemnon, that we quarrelled about a girl. Many a Greek who is now dead had still been alive but for this, and the Trojans would not have profited by our loss. But let bygones be bygones. Here I make an end of my anger. Make haste, then, and call the Greeks to battle, and we will see whether the Trojans will fight by the ships or by their own walls."

Then King Agamemnon answered from the place where he sat: "Listen, ye Greeks. You have blamed me for this quarrel; yet it was not I, but the Fury who turns the thoughts of men to madness, that brought it about. Nevertheless it is for me to make amends. And this I will do, giving thee all the gifts which Ulysses promised in my name. Stay here till my people bring them from the ships." Achilles said: "Give the gifts, O King, if you are pleased so to do, or keep them for yourself. There is one thing only I care for, to get to the battle without delay."

Then said the wise Ulysses: "Achilles, do not make the Greeks fight before they have eaten, for the battle will be long, because the gods have put courage into the hearts of the Trojans. A man who has not eaten cannot fight from morning to sunset, for his limbs grow weary, and he thinks about food and drink. Let us bid the people therefore disperse, and make ready a meal, and let King Agamemnon first send the gifts to your tent, and then let him make a feast, as is right when friends who have quarrelled make peace again." King Agamemnon answered: "You speak well, Ulysses. Do you yourself fetch the gifts, and my people shall make ready a feast." Achilles said: "How can I think of feasting when Patroclus lies dead? Let there be no delay, and let the Greeks sup well when they have driven the Trojans into their city. As for me, neither food nor drink shall pass my lips."

But Ulysses answered: "You are by far stronger than I am, O son of Peleus, but I am older, and have seen many things. Ask not the Greeks to fast because of the dead. For men die every day, and every day would be a day of fasting. Rather let us bury our dead out of our sight, and mourn for them for a day, and then harden our hearts to forget. And let them who are left strengthen themselves with meat and drink, that they may fight the better."

Then Ulysses went to the ships of King Agamemnon and fetched thence the gifts, and the cauldrons and the horses and the gold, and the women slaves, and chief of all the girl Briseïs, and he took them to the tent of Achilles. And when Briseïs saw Patroclus lying dead upon the couch, she beat her breast and her face and wailed aloud, for he had been gentle and good. And the other women wept with her, thinking each of her own troubles.

When the King and the chiefs would have had Achilles feast with them he refused. "I will not eat or drink," he said, "till I have had vengeance. Often, O Patroclus, have you made ready the meal when we were going to battle, and now you lie dead. I had not grieved so much if my old father or my only son had died. Often have I said to myself: 'I, indeed shall die in this place, but Patroclus will go back and show my son all that was mine, goods and servants and palace.' "

And as he wept the old men wept with him, thinking each of those whom he had left at home.

Then the Greeks took their meal, the chiefs with King Agamemnon, and the others each with his own company. But Achilles sat fasting. Then Zeus said to Athené: "Do you not care for your dear Achilles? See how the other Greeks eat and drink, but he sits fasting." So Athené flew down from heaven, and poured heavenly food into the breast of Achilles that his strength might not fail for hunger. But he did not know what she did; only he felt the new strength in him. Then he armed himself with the arms which Thetis brought to him from Hephæstus, and took from its case the great Pelian spear which no man but he could wield. After this he climbed into his chariot, and he said to his horses: "Take care now, Bayard and Piebald, that you do not leave your master to-day, as you left Patroclus yesterday, dead on the field." Then Hera gave a voice to the horse Bayard, and he said: "It was not our fault, O Achilles, that Patroclus died. It was Apollo who slew him, but Hector had the glory. You too, some day, shall be slain by a god and a man." Achilles answered: "I know my doom, but I care not so that I may have vengeance on the Trojans."

The Battle at the River

When the two armies were set in order against each other, Apollo said to Æne͞as: "Æne͞as, where are now your boastings that you would stand up against Achilles and fight with him?"

Æne͞as answered: "That, indeed, I said long ago in days that are past. Once I stood up against him; it was when he took the town of Lyrnessus. But he overcame me, and I fled before him, and but for my nimble feet I had been slain that day. Surely a god is with him, and makes his spear to fly so strongly and so straight."

But Apollo answered: "But if he is the son of a goddess, so also are you; and, indeed, your mother is greater than his, for she is the child of Zeus, and Thetis is but a daughter of the Sea. Drive straight at him with your spear, and do not fear his fierce words and looks."

So Æne͞as came forth out of the press to meet Achilles. And Achilles said to him: "What mean you, Æne͞as? do you think to slay me? Have the Trojans promised that they will have you for their king, or that they will give you a choice portion of land, ploughland and orchard, if only you can prevail over me? You will not find it an easy thing. Have you forgotten the day when you fled before me at Lyrnessus?"

Æne͞as said: "Son of Peleus, you will not frighten me with words, for I also am the son of a goddess. Come, let us try who is the better of us two."

So he cast his spear, and it struck full on the shield of Achilles, and made so dreadful a sound that the hero himself was frightened. But the shield that a god had made was not to be broken by the spear of a mortal man. It pierced, indeed the first fold and the second, which were of bronze, but it was stopped by the third, which was of gold, and there were two more folds, and these of tin. Now Achilles threw his spear. Easily it pierced the shield of the Trojan, and though it did not wound him it came so near that he was deadly frightened. Yet he did not fly, for when Achilles drew his sword and rushed at him, he took up a great stone from the ground to throw at him. Nevertheless he would have been most certainly slain but for the help of the gods. For it was decreed that he and his children after him should reign in the time to come over the men of Troy. Therefore Poseidon himself, though for the most part he had no love for the Trojans, caught him up and carried him out of the battle; but first he took Achilles' spear out of the shield and laid it at the hero's feet. Much did he marvel to see it. "Here is a great wonder," he cried, "that I see with my eyes. My spear that I threw I see lying at my feet, but the man at whom I threw it I see not. Truly this Æne¯as is dear to the gods."

Then he rushed into the battle, slaying as he went. Hector would have met him, but Apollo said: "Fight not with Achilles, for he is stronger than you and will slay you." So Hector stood aside. Yet when he saw the youngest of his brothers slain before his eyes, he could bear it no longer and rushed to meet Achilles. Right glad was Achilles to see him, saying to himself: "The time is come; this is the man who killed Patroclus." And to Hector he said: "Come and taste of death." But Hector answered: "You will not frighten me with words, son of Peleus, for though one man be stronger than another, yet it is Zeus who gives the victory."

Then he cast his spear, but Athené turned it aside with a breath. And when Achilles leapt upon him with a shout, then Apollo snatched him away. Three times did he leap at him, and three times he struck only the mist. The fourth time he cried with a terrible voice: "Dog, these four times you have escaped from death, but I shall meet you again when Apollo is not at hand to help you."

And now as the Trojans fled before Achilles, they came to the river Xanthus, and they leapt into it till it was full of horses and men. Achilles left his spear upon the bank and rushed into the water, having only his sword. And the Trojans were like to fishes in the sea when they fly from a dolphin—in rocks and shallows they hide themselves, but the great beast devours them apace. There was but one man of them all who dared to stand up against him. When Achilles saw him he said, "And who are you that dare to stand up against me?" And the man said, "I am the son of Axius, the river god, and I come from the land of Pæonia." And as he spoke he cast two spears, one with each hand, for he could use both hands alike. The one struck on the shield and pierced two folds, but was stayed in the third, as the spear of Æne¯as had been; with the other he grazed the right hand of Achilles, so that the blood gushed forth. Then Achilles cast his spear but missed his aim, and the spear stood fast in the river bank. Then the other laid hold of it and tried to drag it forth. Three times he tried, but could not move it; the fourth time he tried to break it. But as he tried Achilles slew him. Yet he had this glory that he alone wounded the great Achilles.

But Achilles had to fight not only with mortal men, but with the god of the river also. For when the god of the river saw that Achilles was slaying many both of the Trojans and of the allies, he took upon himself the form of a man, and said to Achilles: "Without doubt, O Achilles, you are the greatest warrior among all the sons of men; for not only are you stronger than all others, but the gods themselves help you and protect you. It may be that they have given you to destroy all the sons of Troy; nevertheless I require of you that you depart from me, and do that which you have to do upon the plain, for my streams are choked with the multitude of those whom you have slain, and I cannot pass to the sea."

Achilles answered: "I would not do anything that displeases you. Nevertheless I will make no end of slaying the Trojans till they have made their way into the city, or till I have come face to face with Hector, and either slay him or be slain, as the gods may please."

Then Achilles turned again to the Trojans and slew still more of them. Then the river rose up against Achilles with all his might, and beat upon his shield, so that he could not stand upon his feet. He caught hold, therefore, of a lime tree that grew upon the bank; but the tree broke away from its place with all its roots, and lay across the river and stopped it from flowing, for it had many branches. Then Achilles was afraid, and climbed out of the water, and ran across the plain; but the River still followed him, for it wished to hinder him from destroying the men of Troy. For the Trojans were dear to the River because they honoured him with sacrifices. And though he was very swift of foot, yet it overtook him, for, indeed, the gods are mightier than men; and when he tried to stand up against it, it rushed upon him with a great wave upon his shoulders, and bowed his knees under him. Then Achilles lifted up his hands to heaven and cried: "Will no one of the gods have pity upon me and help me? Surely it would be better that Hector should slay me, for he is the bravest of men. This were better than that I should perish miserably as a boy whom a storm sweeps away when he is herding his cattle on the plain."

But the River raged yet more and more and he called to another river his brother, for there were two that flowed across the plains of Troy, saying: "Brother, let us two stay the fury of this man, or he will surely destroy the city of Priam, which is dear to us. Fill your stream to the highest, and bring against him a great wave, with trunks of trees and bodies of men whom he has slain. So we will sweep him away, and his people will have no need to heap up a mound of earth over his bones, for we will cover him with sand."

But when Hera saw this, she cried to the Fire-god, her son: "Come near and help us, and bring much fire with you, and burn the trees upon the bank of the river, yea, and the river itself."

So the Fire-god lit a great fire. First it burnt all the dead bodies on the plain; next it burnt all the trees that were on the banks of the river, the limes and the willows and the tamarisks; also it burnt the water-plants that were in the river; the very fishes and eels it scorched, so that they twisted hither and thither in their pain. Then the River cried to the Fire-god: "Cease now from burning me; Achilles may do what he will with the Trojans. What do I care for mortal men?" So the Fire-god ceased from burning him, and the river troubled Achilles no more.

The Slaying of Hector

King Priam stood on a tower of the wall and saw how Achilles was driving the men of Troy before him, and his heart was much troubled within him, thinking how he could help his people. So he went down and spoke to those who kept the gates: "Keep now the wicket-gates open, holding them in your hand, that the people may enter by them, for they are flying before Achilles." So the keepers held the wicket-gates in their hands, and the people made haste to come in; they were wearied with toil and consumed with thirst, and Achilles followed close after them. And the Greeks would have taken the city of Troy that hour but that Apollo saved it, for the gates being open they could enter with the Trojans, whereas the gates being shut, the people were left to perish. And the way in which he saved the city was this. He put courage into the heart of Age‾nor, son to Antenor, standing also by him that he should not be slain. Age‾nor, therefore, stood thinking to himself: "Shall I flee with these others? Not so: for Achilles will overtake me, so swift of foot is he, and shall slay me, and I shall die the death of a coward. Or shall I flee across the plain to Mount Ida, and hide myself in the thicket, and come back to the city when it is dark? But if he see me, he will pursue me and overtake me. Shall I not rather stand here and meet him before the gates? For he too is a mortal man, and may be slain by the spear."

Therefore he stood by the gates waiting for Achilles, for Apollo had given him courage. And when Achilles came near Age‾nor cast his spear, and struck his leg beneath the knee, but the greave turned the spear, so strong was it, having been made by a god. But when Achilles rushed at him to slay him, Apollo lifted him up from the ground and set him safe within the walls. And that the men of Troy might have time to enter, the god took Age‾nor's shape and fled before Achilles, and Achilles pursued him. Meanwhile the Trojans flocked into the city through the wicket-gates, nor did they stay to ask who was safe and who was dead, so great was their fear and such their haste. Only Hector remained outside the city, in front of the great gates which were called the Scæan Gates. All the while Achilles was fiercely pursuing the false Age‾nor, till at last Apollo turned and spoke to him: "Why do you pursue me, swift-footed Achilles? Have you not yet found out that I am a god, and that all your fury is in vain? And now the Trojans are safe in the city, and you are here, far out of the way, seeking to kill one who cannot die."

Achilles answered him in great anger: "You have done me a great wrong in this. Surely of all the gods you are the one who loves mischief most. If it had not been for this many Trojans more would have fallen; but you have saved your favourites and robbed me of great glory. Oh that I could take vengeance on you! truly you would have paid dearly for your cheat."

Then he turned and ran towards the city, swift as a racehorse when it whirls a chariot across the plains. And his armour shone upon him as bright as Orion, which men call also the Dog, shines in the autumn, when the vintage is gathered, an evil light, bringing fevers to men. Old Priam saw him and groaned aloud, and stretched out his hands crying to Hector his son, where he stood before the gates waiting to fight with this terrible warrior:

"O my son, wait not for this man, lest he kill you, for indeed he is stronger than you. I would that the gods had such love for him as I have. Soon would he be food for dogs and vultures. Of many sons has he bereaved me, but if he should bereave me of you, then would not I only and the mother who bore you mourn, but every man and woman in Troy. Come within the walls, my dear son, come, for you are the hope of the city. Come, lest an evil fate come upon me in my old age, that I should see my sons slain with the sword and my daughters carried into captivity, and the babes dashed upon the ground."

So spoke old Priam, but he could not move the heart of his son. Then from the other side of the wall his mother, Queen Hecuba, cried to him. She wept aloud, and hoping that she might so persuade him, she laid bare her bosom, saying: "O Hector, my son, have pity on me. Think of the breast which in old days I gave you, when you were hungry, and stilled your crying. Come, I beseech you, inside the walls, and do not wait for him, or stand up in battle against him. For if he conquers you, then not only will you die, but dogs and vultures will eat your flesh far from here, by the ships of the Greeks."

But all her prayers were in vain, for he was still minded to await the coming of Achilles, and stand up to him in battle. And as he waited many thoughts passed through his mind: "Woe is me, if I go within the walls! Will not they reproach me who gave me good advice which I would not hear, saying that I should bring the people within the walls, when the great Achilles roused himself to the battle? Would that I had done this thing! it had been far better for us; but now I have destroyed the people. I fear the sons and daughters of Troy, lest they should say: 'Hector trusted in his strength, and he has brought the people whom he should have saved to harm.' It would be far better for me to stay here and meet the great Achilles, and either slay him, or, if it must be so, be slain by him. Or shall I lay down my shield and take off my helmet and lean my spear against the wall, and go meet him and say: 'We will give back the Fair Helen and all the riches which Paris carried off with her; also we will give all the precious things that there are in the city that the Greeks may divide them among themselves, taking an oath that we are keeping nothing back, if only you will leave us in peace'? But this is idle talk. He will have neither shame nor pity, and will slay me as I stand without defence before him. No: it is better far to meet in arms and see whether Zeus will give the victory to him or to me."

These were the things which Hector thought in his heart. And Achilles came near, shaking over his right shoulder the great Pelian spear, and the flashing of his arms was like to fire or to the sun when it rises. But Hector trembled when he saw him, and his heart failed him so that he turned his back and fled. Fast he fled from the place where he stood by the great Scæan Gate, and fast did Achilles pursue him, just as a hawk, which is more swift than all other birds, pursues a dove among the hills. The two ran past the watch-tower, and past the wild fig tree, along the wagon-road which ran round the walls, till they came to the springs from which the river rises. Two springs there were, one hot as though it had been heated with fire, and the other cold, cold as ice or snow, even in the summer. There were two basins of stone in which the daughters of Troy had been used to wash their garments; but that was in the old days, when there was peace, before the Greeks came to the land. Past the springs they ran; it was no race which men run for some prize, a sheep, maybe, or an ox-hide shield. Rather the prize was the life of Hector. So they ran round the city, and the Trojans on the wall and the Greeks upon the plain looked on. And the gods looked on as they sat in their palace on the top of Olympus. And Zeus said:

"Now this is a piteous thing which I see. My heart is grieved for Hector—Hector, who has never failed to honour me and the other gods with sacrifice. See how the great Achilles is pursuing him! Come, let us take counsel together. Shall we save him from death, or shall we let him fall by the spear of Achilles?"

Athené said: "What is this that you purpose? Will you save a man whom the fates appoint to die? Do this, if you will, but the other gods do not approve."

Then said Zeus: "This is a thing that I hate; but be it as you will." All this time Hector still fled, and Achilles still pursued. Hector sought for shelter in the walls, and Achilles ever drove him towards the plain. Just as in a dream, when one seems to fly and another seems to pursue, and the first cannot escape, neither can the second overtake, so these two ran. Yet Apollo helped Hector, giving strength to his knees, else he had not held out against

Achilles, than whom there was no faster runner among the sons of men. Three times did they run round the city, but when they came for the fourth time to the springs Athené lighted from the air close to Achilles and said: "This is your day of glory, for you shall slay Hector, though he be a mighty warrior. It is his doom to die, and Apollo's self shall not save him. Stand here and take a breath, and I will make him meet you."

So Achilles stood leaning on his spear. And Athené took the shape of Deïphobus, and came near to Hector and said to him: "My brother, Achilles presses you hard; but come, we two will stand up against him." Hector answered, "O Deïphobus, I have always loved you above all my brothers, and now I love you still more, for you only have come to my help, while they remain within the walls." Then said Deïphobus: "Much did my father and my mother and my comrades entreat me to stay within the walls, but I would not, for I could not bear to leave you alone. Come, therefore, let us fight this man together, and see whether he will carry our spoils to the ships or we shall slay him here."

Then Hector said to Achilles: "Three times have you pursued me round the walls, and I dared not stand against you, but now I fear you no more. Only let us make this covenant. If Zeus gives me the victory to-day, I will give back your body to the Greeks, only I will keep your arms: do you, therefore, promise to do the same with me?"

Achilles frowned at him and said: "Hector, talk not of covenants to me. Men and lions make no oaths to each other, neither is there any agreement between wolves and sheep. Make no delay; let us fight together, that I may have vengeance for the blood of all my comrades whom thou hast slain, and especially of Patroclus, the man whom I loved beyond all others."

Then he threw the great spear, but Hector saw it coming and avoided it, crouching down so that the spear flew over his head and fixed itself in the ground. But Athené snatched it up and gave it back to Achilles; but this Hector did not see. Then said Hector to Achilles: "You have missed your aim, Achilles. Now see whether I have not a truer aim." Then he cast his spear, and the aim, indeed, was true, for it struck upon the shield; it struck, but it bounded far away. Then he cried to Deïphobus: "Give me another spear;" but lo! Deïphobus was gone. Then he knew that his end was come, and he said to himself: "The gods have brought my doom upon me. I thought that Deïphobus was with me; but he is behind the walls, and this was but a cheat with which Athené cheated me. Nevertheless, if I must die, let me at least die in the doing of such a deed as men shall remember in the years to come."

So he spoke, and drew his great sword, and rushed upon Achilles as an eagle rushes down from the clouds upon its prey. But never a blow did he deal; for Achilles ran to meet him, holding his shield before him and the plumes of his helmet streamed behind him as he ran, and the point of his spear was as bright as the evening star. For a moment he doubted where he should drive it home, for the armour of Patroclus which Hector wore guarded him well. But a spot there was, where the stroke of spear or sword is deadliest, by the collar-bone where the neck joins the shoulder. There he drove in the spear, and the point stood out behind the neck, and Hector fell in the dust. Then Achilles cried aloud: "Hector, you thought not of me when you slew Patroclus and spoiled him of his arms. But now you have fallen, and the dogs and vultures shall eat your flesh, but to him the Greeks will give honourable burial."

But Hector said, his voice now growing faint: "O Achilles, I entreat you, by all that you hold dear, to give my body to my father and mother that they may duly bury it. Large ransoms will they pay of gold and silver and bronze."

"Speak not to me of ransom," said Achilles. "Priam shall not buy thee back, no, not for your weight in gold."

Then Hector said: "I know you well, what manner of man you are, and that the heart in your breast is of iron. Only beware lest the anger of the gods come upon you for such deeds in the days when Paris and Apollo shall slay you hard by these very gates."

So speaking, he died. And Achilles said: "Die, dog that you are; but my doom I will meet when it shall please the gods to send it."

Then did Achilles devise a cruel thing. He pierced the ankle-bones of the dead man, and fastened the body with thongs of ox-hide to the chariot, and so dragged it to the ships.

Now Andromaché knew nothing of what had come to pass. She sat in her house weaving a great mantle, embroidered with flowers. And she bade her maidens make ready the bath for Hector, when he should come back from the battle, knowing not that he would never need it any more. Then there rose a great wailing from the walls, and she rose up from her weaving in great haste, and dropped the shuttle from her hands and said to the maids: "Come now, I must see what has happened, for I fear that some evil has come to the men of Troy. Maybe Hector is in danger, for he is always bold, and will fight in the front."

Then she ran along the street to the walls like a madwoman. And when she came to the walls she looked, and lo! the horses of Achilles were dragging the body of Hector to the ships. Then a sudden darkness came upon her, and she fell to the ground as though she were dead.

The Ransoming of Hector

The Greeks made a great mourning for Patroclus, and paid due honours to him, the body of Hector was shamefully treated, for Achilles caused it to be dragged daily about the tomb of his friend. Then Zeus sent for Thetis and said to her: "Go to the camp, and bid your son give up the body of Hector for ransom; it angers me to see him do dishonour to the dead."

So Thetis went to the tent of Achilles and found him weeping softly for his friend, for the strength of his sorrow was now spent. And she said to him: "It is the will of Zeus that you give up the body of Hector for ransom." And he said: "Let it be so, if the gods will have it."

Then, again, Zeus sent Iris his messenger to King Priam, where he sat in his palace with his face wrapped in his mantle, and his sons weeping round him, and his daughter and his daughters-in-law wailing in their chambers of the palace. Iris said to him: "Be of good cheer; I come from Zeus. He bids you take precious gifts wherewith to buy back the body of Hector from Achilles. Nor will Achilles refuse to give it up."

So Priam rose from his place with gladness in his heart. Nor would he listen to the Queen when she would have kept him back.

"I have heard the voice of the messenger of Zeus, and I will go. And if I die, what do I care? Let Achilles slay me, so that I hold the body of my son once more in my arms."

Then he caused precious things to be put into a wagon, mantles which had never been washed, and rugs, and cloaks, twelve of each, and ten talents of gold, and cauldrons and basins, and a great cup of gold which the Thracians had given him. Nothing of his treasures did he spare if only he might buy back his son. Then he bade his sons yoke the mules to the wagon. With many bitter words did he speak to them; they were cowards, he said, an evil brood, speakers of lying words, and mighty only to drink wine. But they did not answer him. Then Priam himself yoked the horses to the chariot, the herald helping. But before he went he poured out wine to Zeus, and prayed, saying: "Hear me, O Father, and cause Achilles to pity me; give me also a lucky sign that I may go on this business with a good heart."

So Zeus sent an eagle, a mighty bird, and it flew with wings outstretched over the city, on the right hand of the King.

Then the King passed out of the gates. Before him the mules drew the wagon; these the herald drove. But Priam himself drove his horses. Then said

Zeus to Hermes: "Go, guide the King, so that none of the Greeks may see him before he comes to the tent of Achilles." So Hermes fastened on his feet the winged sandals with which he flies, and he flew till he came to the plain of Troy. And when the wagon and the chariot were close to the tomb of Ilus, the herald spied a man (for Hermes had taken the shape of a man), and said to the King: "What shall we do? I see a man. Shall we flee, or shall we beg him to have mercy on us?" And the King was greatly troubled. But Hermes came near and said: "Whither do you go in the darkness with these horses and mules? Have you no fear of the Greeks? If any one should spy all this wealth, what then? You are old, and could scarcely defend yourselves. But be of good cheer; I will protect you, for you are like to my own dear father."

Priam answered: "Happy is he to have such a son. Surely the gods are with me, that I have met such a one as you."

Then said Hermes: "Tell me true; are you sending away these treasures for safe keeping, fearing that the city will be taken now that Hector is dead?"

Priam answered: "Who are you that you speak of Hector?"

Hermes said: "I am a Myrmidon, one of the people of Achilles, and often have I seen your son in the front of the battle."

Then the King asked him: "Is the body of Hector yet whole, or have the dogs and the vultures devoured it?"

Hermes answered: "It is whole, and without blemish, as fresh as when he died. Surely the gods love him, even though he be dead."

Then King Priam would have had the young man take a gift; but Hermes said: "I will take no gift unknown to my master. So to do would be wrong to him. But I will guide you to his tent, if you would go thither."

So he leapt into the chariot and took the reins. And when they came to the trench, where the sentinels were at their meal, Hermes caused a deep sleep to fall on them, and he opened the gate, and brought in the King with his treasures. And when they were at the tent of Achilles, the young man said: "I am Hermes, whom Father Zeus sent to be your guide. Go in and clasp him about the knees, and entreat him to have pity upon you." And he vanished out of his sight.

Then Priam went to the tent, where Achilles, who had just ended his meal, sat at the table, and caught his knees and kissed his hands, yea, the very hands which had slain so many of his sons. He said: "Have pity on me, O Achilles, thinking of your own father. He is old as I am, yet it goes well with him, so long as he knows that you are alive, for he hopes to see you coming back from the land of Troy. But as for me, I am altogether miserable. Many sons have I lost, and now the best of them all is dead, and lo! I kiss the hands which slew him."

Then the heart of Achilles was moved with pity and he wept, thinking now of his own father and now of the dead Patroclus. At last he stood up from his seat and said: "How did you dare to come to my tent, old man? Surely you must have a heart of iron. But come, sit and eat and drink; for this a man must do, for all the sorrows that come upon him."

But the King said: "Ask me not to eat and drink while my son lies unburied and without honour. Rather take the gifts which I have brought, with which to ransom him."

But Achilles frowned and said: "Vex me not; I am minded to give back the body of Hector, but let me go my own way." Then Priam held his peace, for he feared to rouse the anger of Achilles. Then Achilles went forth from the tent, and two companions with him. First they took the gifts from the wagon; only they left two cloaks and a tunic wherewith to cover the dead. And Achilles bade the women wash and anoint the body, only that they should do this apart from the tent, lest Priam should see his son, and lament aloud when the body was washed and anointed, Achilles himself lifted it in his arms, and put it on a litter, and his comrades put the litter in the wagon.

When all was finished, Achilles groaned and cried to his dead friend, saying: "Be not angry, O Patroclus, that I have given the body of Hector to his father. He has given a noble ransom, and of this you shall have your share as is meet."

Then he went back to his tent and said: "Your son, old man, is ransomed, and to-morrow shall you see him and take him back to Troy. But now let us eat and drink." And this they did. But when this had ended, they sat and looked at each other, and Achilles wondered at King Priam, so noble was he to behold, and Priam wondered to see how strong and how fair was Achilles.

Then Priam said: "Let me sleep, Achilles, for I have not slept since my son was slain." So they made up for him a bed, but not in the tent, lest, perhaps, one of the chiefs should come in and see him. But before he slept the King said: "Let there be a truce for nine days between the Greeks and the Trojans, that we may bury Hector." And Achilles said: "It shall be so; I will stay the war for so long."

But when the King slept, Hermes came again to him and said: "Do you sleep among your enemies, O Priam? Awake and depart, for although Achilles has taken ransom for Hector, what would not your sons have to pay for you if the Greeks should find you in the camp?"

Then the old man rose up. And the wise herald yoked the mules to the wagon and the horses to the chariot. And they passed through the camp of the Greeks, no man knowing, and came safe to the city of Troy.

On the ninth day the King and his people made a great burying for Hector, such as had never been seen in the land of Troy.

The End of Troy

After these things came Memnon, a black warrior, who men said was the son of Morning. He slew Antiloˇchus, son of Nestor, and was himself slain by Achilles. Not many days afterwards Achilles himself was slain near the Scæan Gates. It was by an arrow from the bow of Paris that he was killed, but the arrow was guided by Apollo.

Yet Troy was not taken. Then Heleˇnus, the seer, having been taken prisoner by Ulysses, said: "You cannot take the city till you bring the man who has the arrows of Hercules." So they fetched the man, and he killed many Trojans with the arrows, and among them Paris, who was the cause of all this trouble.

Last of all the Greeks devised this plan. Some of the bravest of the chiefs hid themselves in a great horse of wood, and the rest made a pretence of going away, but went no further than to an island hard by. And when the Trojans had dragged the horse into the city, thinking it was an offering to the gods of the city, the chiefs let themselves out of it by night, and the other Greeks having come back, took the city in the tenth year from the beginning of the siege.

The Odyssey for
Boys and Girls

The Cyclops

A great many years ago there was a very famous siege of a city called Troy. The eldest son of the king who reigned in this city carried off the wife of one of the Greek kings, and with her a great quantity of gold and silver. She was the most beautiful woman in the world, and all the princes of Greece had come to her father's court wishing to marry her. Her father had made them all swear, that if any one should steal her away from the man whom she would choose for her husband, they would help him to get her back. This promise they had now to keep. So they all went to besiege Troy, each taking a number of his subjects with him. On the other hand, the Trojans were helped by many of the nations that lived near them. The siege lasted for a long time, but in the tenth year the city was taken. Then the Greeks began to think about going home. The story that you are now going to hear is about one of these Greek princes, Ulysses by name, who was the King of Ithaca. (This was an island on the west coast of Greece, and you can find it now marked on the map.) Ulysses was, according to one story, very unwilling to go. He had married, you see, a very good and beautiful wife, and had a little son. So he pretended to be mad, and took a plough down to the sea-shore and began to plough the sand. But some one took his little son and laid him in front of the plough. And when Ulysses stopped lest he should hurt him, people said: "This man is not really mad." So he had to go. And this is the story of how, at last, he came back.

When Troy had been taken, Ulysses and his men set sail for his home, the Island of Ithaca. He had twelve ships with him, and fifty men or thereabouts in each ship. The first place they came to was a city called Isma˘rus. This they took and plundered. Ulysses said to his men: "Let us sail away with what we have got." They would not listen to him, but sat on the sea-shore, and feasted, for they had found plenty of wine in the city, and many sheep and oxen in the fields round it. Meanwhile the people who had escaped out of the city fetched their countrymen who dwelt in the mountains, and brought an army to fight with the Greeks. The battle began early in the morning of the next day, and lasted nearly till sunset. At first the Greeks had the better of it, but in the afternoon the people of the country prevailed, and drove them to their ships. Very glad were they to get away; but when they came to count, they found that they had lost six men out of each ship.

After this a great storm fell upon the ships, and carried them far to the south, past the very island to which they were bound. It was very hard on Ulysses. He was close to his home, if he could only have stopped; but he could not, and though he saw it again soon after, it was ten years before he reached it, having gone through many adventures in the meantime.

The first of these was in the country of the Cyclopes or Round-eyed People. Late on a certain day Ulysses came with his ships to an island, and found in it a beautiful harbour, with a stream falling into it, and a flat beach on which to draw up the ships. That night he and his men slept by the ships, and the next day they made a great feast. The island was full of wild goats. These the men hunted and killed, using their spears and bows. They had been on shipboard for many days, and had had but little food. Now they had plenty, eight goats to every ship, and nine for the ship of Ulysses, because he was the chief. So they ate till they were satisfied, and drank wine which they had carried away from Isma˘rus.

Now there was another island about a mile away, and they could see that it was larger, and it seemed as if there might be people living in it. The island where they were was not inhabited. So on the second morning Ulysses said to his men: "Stay here, my dear friends; I with my own ship and my own company will go to yonder island, and find out who dwells there, whether they are good people or no." So he and his men took their ship, and rowed over to the other island. Then Ulysses took twelve men, the bravest that there were in the ship, and went to search out the country. He took with him a goat-skin of wine, very strong and sweet, which the priest of Apollo at Isma˘rus had given him for saving him and his house and family, when the city was taken. There never was a more precious wine; one measure of it could be mixed with twenty measures of water, and the smell of it was wondrously sweet. Also he took with him some parched corn, for he felt in his heart that he might need some food.

After a while they came to a cave which seemed to be the dwelling of some rich and skilful shepherd. Inside there were pens for the young sheep and the young goats, and baskets full of cheeses, and milk-pans ranged against the walls. Then Ulysses' men said to him: "Let us go away before the master comes back. We can take some of the cheeses, and some of the kids and lambs." But Ulysses would not listen to them. He wanted to see what kind of man this shepherd might be, and he hoped to get something from him.

In the evening the Cyclops, the Round-eye, came home. He was a great giant, with one big eye in the middle of his forehead, and an eyebrow above it. He bore on his shoulder a huge bundle of pine logs for his fire. This he threw down outside the cave with a great crash, and drove the flocks inside, and then closed up the mouth with a big rock so big that twenty waggons could not carry it. After this he milked the ewes and the she-goats. Half the milk he curdled for cheese, and half he set aside for his own supper. This done, he threw some logs on the fire, which burnt up with a great flame, showing the Greeks, who had fled into the depths of the cave, when they saw the giant come in.

"Who are you?" said the giant, "traders or pirates?"

"We are no pirates, mighty sir," said Ulysses, "but Greeks sailing home from Troy, where we have been fighting for Agamemnon, the great king, whose fame is spread abroad from one end of heaven to the other. And we beg you to show hospitality to us, for the gods love them who are hospitable."

"Nay," said the giant, "talk not to me about the gods. We care not for them, for we are better and stronger than they. But tell me, where have you left your ship?"

But Ulysses saw what he was thinking of when he asked about the ship, namely, that he meant to break it up so as to leave them no hope of getting away. So he said, "Oh, sir, we have no ship; that which we had was driven by the wind upon a rock and broken, and we whom you see here are all that escaped from the wreck."

The giant said nothing, but without more ado caught up two of the men, as a man might catch up two puppies, and dashed them on the ground, and tore them limb from limb, and devoured them, with huge draughts of milk between, leaving not a morsel, not even the bones. And when he had filled himself with this horrible food and with the milk of the flocks, he lay down among his sheep, and slept.

Then Ulysses thought: "Shall I slay this monster as he sleeps, for I do not doubt that with my good sword I can pierce him to the heart. But no; if I do this, then shall I and my comrades here perish miserably, for who shall be able to roll away the great rock that is laid against the mouth of the cave?"

So he waited till the morning, very sad at heart. And when the giant awoke, he milked his flocks, and afterward seized two of the men, and devoured them as before. This done, he went forth to the pastures, his flocks following him, but first he put the rock on the mouth of the cave, just as a man shuts down the lid of his quiver.

All day Ulysses thought how he might save himself and his companions, and the end of his thinking was this. There was a great pole in the cave, the trunk of an olive tree, green wood which the giant was going to use as a staff for walking when it should have been dried by the smoke. Ulysses cut off this a piece some six feet long, and his companions hardened it in the fire, and hid it away. In the evening the giant came back and did as before, seizing two of the prisoners and devouring them. When he had finished his meal, Ulysses came to him with the skin of wine in his hand and said, "Drink, Cyclops, now that you have supped. Drink this wine, and see what good things we had in our ship. But no one will bring the like to you in your island here if you are so cruel to strangers."

The Cyclops took the skin and drank, and was mightily pleased with the wine.

"Give me more," he said, "and tell me your name, and I will give you a gift such as a host should. Truly this is a fine drink, like, I take it, to that which the gods have in heaven."

Then Ulysses said: "My name is No Man. And now give me your gift."

And the giant said: "My gift is this: you shall be eaten last." And as he said this, he fell back in a drunken sleep.

Then Ulysses said to his companions, "Be brave, my friends, for the time is come for us to be delivered from this prison."

So they put the stake into the fire, and kept it there till it was ready, green as it was, to burst into flame. Then they thrust it into his eye, for, as has been told, he had but one, and Ulysses leant with all his force upon the stake, and turned it about, just as a man turns a drill about when he would make a hole in a ship timber. And the wood hissed in the eye as the red-hot iron hisses in the water when a smith would temper it to make a sword.

Then the giant leapt up, and tore away the stake, and cried out so loudly that the Round-eyed people in the island came to see what had happened.

"What ails you," they asked, "that you make so great an uproar, waking us all out of our sleep? Is any one stealing your sheep, or seeking to hurt you?"

And the giant bellowed, "No Man is hurting me."

"Well," said the Round-eyed people, "if no man is hurting you, then it must be the gods that do it, and we cannot help you against them."

But Ulysses laughed when he thought how he had beguiled them by his name. But he was still in doubt how he and his companions should escape, for the giant sat in the mouth of the cave, and felt to see whether the men were trying to get out among the sheep. And Ulysses, after long thinking, made a plan by which he and his companions might escape. By great good luck the giant had driven the rams into the cave, for he commonly left them outside. These rams were very big and strong, and Ulysses took six of the biggest, and tied the six men that were left out of the twelve underneath their bellies with osier twigs. And on each side of the six rams to which a man was tied, he put another ram. So he himself was left, for there was no one who could do the same for him. Yet this also he managed. There was a very big ram, much bigger than all the others, and to this he clung, grasping the fleece with both his hands. So, when the morning came, the flocks went out of the cave as they were wont, and the giant felt them as they passed by him, and did not perceive the men. And when he felt the biggest ram, he said—

"How is this? You are not used to lag behind; you are always the first to run to the pasture in the morning and to come back to the fold at night. Perhaps you are troubled about thy master's eye which this villain No Man has destroyed. First he overcame me with wine, and then he put out my eye. Oh! that you could speak and tell me where he is. I would dash out his brains upon the ground." And then he let the big ram go.

When they were out of the giant's reach, Ulysses let go his hold of the ram, and loosed his companions, and they all made as much haste as they could to get to the place where they had left their ship, looking back to see whether the giant was following them. The crew at the ship were very glad to see them, but wondered that there should be only six. Ulysses made signs to them to say nothing, for he was afraid that the giant might know where they were if he heard their voices. So they all got on board and rowed with all their might. But when they were a hundred yards from the shore, Ulysses stood up in the ship and shouted: "You are an evil beast, Cyclops, to devour strangers in your cave, and are rightly served in losing your eye. May the gods make you suffer worse things than this!"

The Cyclops, when he heard Ulysses speak, broke off the top of a rock and threw it to the place from which the voice seemed to come. The rock fell just in front of the ship, and the wave which it made washed it back to the shore. But Ulysses caught up a long pole and pushed the ship off, and he nodded with his head, being afraid to speak, to his companions to row with all their might. So they rowed; and when they were twice as far off as before, Ulysses stood up again in the ship, as if he were going to speak again. And his comrades begged him to be silent.

"Do not make the giant angry," they said; "we were almost lost just now when the wave washed us back to the shore. The monster throws a mighty bolt, and throws it far."

But Ulysses would not listen, but cried out: "Hear, Cyclops, if any man ask you who put out your eye, say that it was Ulysses of Ithaca."

Then the giant took up another great rock and threw it. This time it almost touched the end of the rudder, but missed by a hand's breadth. This time, therefore, the wave helped them on. So big was it that it carried the ship to the other shore.

Now Ulysses had not forgotten to carry off sheep from the island for his companions. These he divided among the crews of all the ships. The great ram he had for his own share. So that day the whole company feasted, and they lay down on the sea-shore and slept.

Of the Home of the Winds and of Circe

The next day Ulysses and his companions set sail. After a while they came to the floating island where the King of the Winds had his home. Ulysses told the king all his story, how he had fought against Troy, and what had happened to him afterwards. For a whole month the king made him welcome, and when he wished to go home, he did what he could to help him. He took the hide of an ox, very thick and strong, and put in it all the winds that would hinder him in getting to his home, and fastened it to the deck of his ship. Then he made a gentle wind blow from the west. For nine days it blew, till the ships were very near to the island of Ithaca—so near that they could see the lights on the cliffs. But just before dawn on the tenth day, Ulysses, who had kept awake all the time, for he would not let any one else take the rudder, fell asleep. And the crew of his ship said to each other: "See that great bag of ox hide. It must have something very precious inside it—silver and gold and jewels. Why should the chief have all these good things to himself?" So they cut the bag open, and all the winds rushed out and blew the ship away from Ithaca. Ulysses woke up at the noise, and at first thought that he would throw himself into the sea and die. Then he said to himself, "No! it is better to live," and he covered his face and lay still, without saying a word to his men. And the ships were driven back to the island of the King of the Winds.

Ulysses went to the king's palace with one of his companions, and sat down outside the door. The king came out to see him, and said, "How is this? Why did you not get to your home?" Ulysses said, "I fell asleep, and my men opened the bag. I pray you to help me again." "Nay," answered the king, "it is of no use to help the man whom the gods hate. Go away!"

So Ulysses and his men launched their ships again and rowed for six days and nights. On the seventh day they came to a certain city named Lamos, a country where the night is as light as the day. Here there was a fine harbour, with a very narrow mouth, and high rocks all round it, so that it was always calm. It seemed so pleasant a place that all the ships were taken inside by their crews, only Ulysses thought it safer to keep his ship outside. He sent two of his men to see the king of the place. These met a very tall and strong girl as they went, and asked her the way to the palace. She told them—and, indeed, she was the king's daughter. So they knocked at the door; but when it was opened, and they saw the queen, they were terribly frightened, for she was as big as a mountain, and dreadful to look at. They ran away, but the queen called to her husband the king, and the king shouted to the people of the city. They were cannibals all of them, and when they saw the ships they threw great rocks at them and broke them in pieces; and when the men tried to swim to shore, they speared them as if they had been fishes, and devoured them. So all the ships inside the harbour were destroyed; only the ship of Ulysses was left. He cut the cable with his sword, and cried to his men to row away with all their might, and so they escaped. But Ulysses had now only one ship left with its crew out of the twelve which he had at first.

After a while they came to a strange island, and drew up their ship upon the beach, and sat beside it weeping and lamenting, for now there were but some thirty or so left out of six hundred. This they did for two days. On the third day Ulysses took his spear and sword, and climbed up a hill that was near, to see what kind of a place they had come to. From the top of the hill he saw a great wood, and a smoke rising up out of the midst of it, showing that there was a house there. Then he thought to himself: "I will go back to the ship, and when we have dined, some of us will go and see who lives in the island." But as he went towards the shore, he saw a great stag coming down to a spring to drink, and it crossed the path almost in front of him. Then he threw his spear at the beast, and killed it; and he tied its feet together, and put it on his neck, and carried it leaning on his spear, for, indeed, it was a very heavy load for a man to bear. When he came to the ship, he threw down the stag on the shore, and the men looked up, and were glad to see the great beast. So they feasted on deer's flesh and wine, and Ulysses put off the searching of the island till the next day.

In the morning he told them what he had seen, but the searching of the island did not please, for they thought of what they had suffered already. Then Ulysses said: "We shall divide the crew into two companies; one shall be mine, and of the other Eurylo˘chus shall be chief; and we will cast lots to see who shall search the island." So they cast lots, and the lot of Eurylo˘chus came out first. So he went, and twenty men or so with him, and in the middle of the wood they found an open space, and in the space a palace, and all about it wolves and lions were wandering. The men were very much afraid of the beasts, but they did them no harm. Only they got up on their hind legs and fawned on them, as dogs fawn upon their master, hoping to get some scraps of food from him. And they heard the voice of some one who sat inside the palace and sang as she worked a loom, and a very sweet voice it was. Then said one of the men: "Let us call to this singer, and see whether she is a woman or a goddess." So they called, and a certain Circé, who was said to be a daughter of the Sun, came out, and asked them to go in. This they did, and also they drank out of a cup which she gave them. A cup of wine it seemed to be, mixed with barley-meal and honey, but she had put in it some strange drug, which makes a man forget all that he loves. And when they had drunk, lo! they were turned into pigs. They had snouts and bristles, and they grunted like pigs, but they had the hearts of men. And Circé shut them in sties, and gave them acorns and beech-mast to eat.

But Eurylo˘chus had stayed outside when the others went in, and he ran back to the ship and told Ulysses what had happened. Then Ulysses armed himself, and said: "I will go and save these men." Nor would he listen when the others begged him not to go. "Thou wilt not do them any good," they said, "but wilt perish thyself." "Nay," he answered; "stay here if you will, and eat and drink; but I must go and rescue my men, for I am their chief."

So he went; and when he came near to the house, he saw a very beautiful youth, who had a golden stick in his hand. The youth said: "Ulysses, art thou come to rescue thy comrades? That thou canst not do. Thou wilt rather perish thyself. But stay; you are one that fears the gods, therefore they will help you. I will give you such a drug as shall make all Circé's drugs of no power. Drink the cup that she gives you, but first put into it this drug." So he showed Ulysses a certain herb which had a black root and a flower as white as milk. It was called Moly.

So Ulysses took the herb moly in his hand, and went and stood in the porch of Circé's palace, and called to her. And when Circé heard him she opened the door, and said, "Come in." Then he went in, and she made him sit on a great chair of carved oak, and gave him wine to drink in a gold cup. But she had mixed a deadly drug in the wine. So Ulysses took up the cup and drank, but before he drank he put the moly into it. Then Circé struck him with her wand, and said, "Go now to the sty, and lie there with thy fellows." But Ulysses drew his sword, and rushed at her, as if he would have killed her. She caught him by the knees and prayed him not to hurt her. And she said: "How is this, that my drugs do thee no harm? I did not think that there was any man on earth who could do so. Surely thou must be Ulysses, for Hermes told me that he would come to this island when he was on his way back to his home from Troy. Come now, let us be friends." But Ulysses said: "How can we be friends when thou hast turned my companions into swine? And now I am afraid that thou wilt do me some great harm if thou canst take me unawares. Swear to me then, by a great oath, that thou wilt not hurt me." So Circé sware.

Then her handmaids, very lovely women born in the springs and streams and woods, prepared a feast. One set purple rugs on the chairs, and another set silver tables by the chairs, and others put on the tables baskets of gold. Also they made ready a bath of hot water for Ulysses, and put some wonderful thing into the water, so that when he had bathed he did not feel tired any more. Then one of the women, who was the housekeeper, and whom they all obeyed, brought Ulysses some very fine wheaten bread, and set many dainty dishes on the tables. Then Circé said: "Eat and drink, Ulysses." But he sat and ate and drank nothing. "How is this?" she said. "Dost thou think that I will harm thee? Did I not swear a great oath that I would not?" And Ulysses said: "How can I eat and drink when my companions have been changed into brute beasts?"

Then Circé arose from her chair, and took her wand in her hand, and went to the sties where she had put the men that had been turned into swine. And she opened the doors of the sties, and rubbed a wonderful drug on each beast as he came out. And, lo! in a moment the bristles fell from their bodies, and they became men again, only they looked to be younger and more handsome than they were before. And when they saw their chief, they clung to him, weeping for joy. Even Circé herself felt a little pity.

After this they all went into the palace, and ate and drank. And when they had finished their meal, Circé said to Ulysses: "Go now to thy ship, and put away all the goods that are in it and all the tackle in the caves that are on the sea-shore, and then come back here, and bring the rest of your comrades with you."

So Ulysses went. And when his companions saw him, they were very glad, for they had thought that he was lost. They were as glad as calves which have been penned in the yard all day when their mothers come back from the fields in the evening. But when Ulysses said to them: "Come back with me to the great house in the wood," Euryloˇchus said to them, "Don't go, my friends; if you do, you will be turned into lions or bears or pigs, and will be kept shut up for the rest of your lives. This foolhardy Ulysses is always leading us into trouble. Was it not he who took us to the cave of the Cyclops?" Ulysses was very angry when he heard this, and was ready to kill the man. But the others stopped him from doing it. "We will go with you," they said, "and if this man is afraid, let him stay by the ship." So they went with Ulysses, and Euryloˇchus himself, when he saw them go, went with them.

For a whole year Ulysses and his companions stayed with Circé. She feasted them royally, and they were well content to be her guests. But at the end of the year the men said to their chief: "Should we not be thinking of going home?" And he knew that they were right. So he said to Circé: "It is time for us to go home. Pray do what you can to help us on our way." Circé said: "I would not keep a guest against his will."

So they made their ship ready, and Circé and her handmaids brought down to the shore flesh and bread and wine in plenty, and they stored them away as provision for their voyage, and then they departed. But first Circé told Ulysses what things would happen to them by the way, and what he and his companions ought to do, and what they ought to avoid, if they wished to get safely home.

Of the Sirens and Other Wonders

The first place they came to was the Island of Sirens. The Sirens were women of the sea, such as mermaids are, who sang so sweetly, and with such lovely voices, that no one who heard them could pass on his way, but was forced to go to them. But when he came near the Sirens flew upon him and tore him to pieces, and devoured him. So they sat there on their island, with the bones of dead men all round them, and sang. Now Circé had warned Ulysses about these dreadful creatures, and told him what he ought to do. So he closed the ears of his companions with wax so tightly that they could hear nothing. As for himself, he made his men tie him with ropes to the mast of the ship. "And see," he said, "that you don't loose me, however much I may beg and pray." As soon as the ship came near to the island the wind ceased to blow, and there was a great calm, and the men took down the sails, and put out their oars, and began to row. Then the Sirens saw the ship, and began to sing. And Ulysses, where he stood bound to the mast, heard them. And when he understood what they said he forgot all his prudence, for they promised just the thing that he wanted. For he was a man who never could know enough, he thought, about other countries and the people who dwelt in them, what they think and how they spend their days. And the Sirens said that they could tell him all this. Then he made signs with his head to his men, for his hands and feet were bound, that they should loose him. But they remembered what he had told them, and rowed on. And two of them even put new bonds upon him lest he should break the old ones. So they got safely past the Island of the Sirens.

And now Ulysses had to choose between two ways. One of them was through the Wandering Rocks. Circé had told him of these; that they were rocks which floated about in the sea, and that when any ship came near them they moved very fast through the water, and caught the ship between them and broke it up. So fast did they move that they caught even the birds as they flew. And Circé told him that only one ship had ever escaped them, and that this was the Argo, when the heroes went in it to fetch back the Golden Fleece. "This," said Circé, "was by the special favour of the gods, and because there were many children of the gods among the crew." So Ulysses thought it better not to try that way, though the other way was dreadful also.

After a while they saw what looked like smoke going up from the sea, and heard a great roar of the waves dashing upon the rocks, for they were coming near to another dangerous place which Circé had warned them about. This was a narrow place between the mainland and an island. On the one side there was a cave, in which there dwelt a terrible monster, Scylla by name, and on the other side there was a dreadful whirlpool. If a ship ever got into that, it was sucked down to the bottom of the sea and never came up again. Now, Circé had told Ulysses all about this place, and had told him what he should do. "It will be better," she had said, "to go near Scylla than to go near Charybdis; one or other of these two thou must do, for there is no room in the middle. It is true that Scylla will pounce down upon your ship when it comes within her reach, and will take out of it six men, one for each of the six heads which she has. But if you go too near to Charybdis then will your whole ship be swallowed up; and it is better to lose six men than that all should be drowned." And when Ulysses had said, "May I not take shield and spear and fight with this monster?" Circé had answered, "Thou art wonderfully bold; thou wouldst fight with the gods themselves. But be sure that thou canst not fight with Scylla; she is too strong for any man. And while you linger she will take six other men. No: fly from the place as fast as you can." So had Circé spoken to Ulysses, and he remembered what she had said; but he did not tell it to his companions, lest they should lose heart.

So now he bade the steersman steer the ship as near as he could to that side of the strait on which was Scylla's cave. Nevertheless, they went very close to the whirlpool. And a wonderful sight it was, for at one time you could see to the very bottom of the sea, and at another the water seemed to boil up almost to the top of the cliffs. Now, Ulysses had said nothing to his men about the monster on the other side, for he was afraid that if they knew about her they would not go on with their voyage. So they all stood and watched the whirlpool, and while they were doing this there came down upon the ship Scylla's dreadful hands, and caught up six of the crew, the bravest and strongest of them all. Ulysses heard them cry to him to help them, but he could do nothing to help them. And this, he used to say afterwards, was the very saddest thing that happened to him in all his troubles.

After this the ship came to the Island of the Three Capes, which is now called Sicily. And while they were still a long way off, Ulysses heard the bleating of sheep and the lowing of cattle. As soon as he heard these sounds he remembered what Circé had told him about the last of the dangers which he and his companions would meet on their way home. What Circé had said was this: "You will come, last of all, to a beautiful island, where the Sun keeps his herds and flocks. There are seven herds of cattle and fifty in each, and seven flocks of sheep of fifty also; and each has a nymph to look after it. Now,

I advise you to sail by this island without landing. If you do, you will get safe home; but if you land, perhaps your men will kill some of the Sun's cattle and sheep for food. And if they do this, something dreadful is sure to happen to them." So Ulysses said to his men: "Listen to me. Circé told me that this island was a very dangerous place, and that we had better sail by it without landing, and that if we did we should get safe home. Think, now, how many of our companions have been lost, and that we only remain. Take my advice, I pray you, for some of us at least will be saved." But Eurylo˘chus said: "Truly, Ulysses, you seem to be made of iron, for you are never tired, and now you would have us pass by this beautiful island without landing, though we have been working for days and nights without rest. And, besides, it is not safe to sail at night. Perhaps some storm will fall upon us, or a strong wind will spring up from the south or west, as it often does in these parts, and break our ship to pieces. No; let us stay for the night, and sleep on land, and to-morrow we will sail again on the sea till we get to our home." And all the others agreed with what he said. Then Ulysses knew that he was going to suffer some terrible thing. And he said: "You are many and I am one; so I cannot stop you from doing what you will. But swear all of you an oath, that if you find here any flock of sheep or herd of cattle, you will not touch them; no, however hungry you may be, but that you will be content with the food that Circé gave us."

So they all swore an oath that they would not touch sheep or cattle. Then they moored the ship in a creek, where there were little streams falling into the sea. And they took their meal upon the shore. After the meal they mourned for their companions whom Scylla had carried off from the ship, and when they had done this, they slept.

The next morning Ulysses told them again that they must not touch the sheep or cattle, but must be content with the food that they had. And he told them also the reason: "These creatures," he said, "belong to the Sun, and the Sun is a mighty god, and he sees everything that men do over all the earth."

But now the wind blew from the south for a whole month, day after day, except some days when it blew from the east. Now, neither the south wind nor the east wind was good for their voyage, so that they could not help staying on the island. As long as any of the food that Circé had given them remained, they were content. And when this was eaten up they wandered about the island, searching for food. They snared birds and caught fishes, but they never had enough, and their hunger was very hard to bear. And Ulysses prayed to the gods that they would help him, but it seemed that they took no heed of him.

At last Eurylo˘chus said to his companions: "Listen, my friends, to me, for we are all in a very evil case. Death is a dreadful thing, but nothing is so dreadful as to die of hunger, and this we are likely to do. Let us take some of these oxen and make a sacrifice to the gods, and when we have given them their portion we will eat the rest ourselves. And after the sacrifice we will pray to them that they will send us a favourable wind. Also we will promise to build a great and fair temple to the Sun when we get to our home. And if the Sun is angry on account of the oxen, and is minded to sink our ship, let it be so; it is better to be drowned than to die of hunger."

To this they all agreed; and Eurylo˘chus drove some of the fattest of the kine down to the shore, and the men killed them, and made sacrifice according to custom. They had no meal to sprinkle over the flesh, so they used leaves instead; and they had no wine, so they used water. And when they had done this, and were now beginning their feast, Ulysses, who had been asleep, awoke, and he smelt the smell of roast flesh, and knew that his companions had broken their oath, and had killed some of the beasts of the Sun.

In the meantime, two of the nymphs that kept the cattle had flown up to the sky, and had told the Sun what had been done. And when the Sun heard it, he was very angry, and said to the other gods: "See now what these wicked companions of Ulysses have done. They have killed the cattle which it is my delight to see, both when I climb up the sky and when I come down from it. Now, if they are not punished for this evil deed, I will not shine any more upon the earth, but will give my light to the place of darkness that is underneath it." And the king of the gods answered, "Shine, O Sun, upon the earth as thou art wont to do. I will break the ship of these sinners with my thunderbolt while they are sailing on the sea."

Ulysses was very angry with his companions, and rebuked them for their folly, and because they had broken their oath. But he could not undo what had been done, for the kine were dead. And the men were greatly frightened by what they saw and heard; for the skins of the cattle that had been killed crept along the ground, and the flesh bellowed on the spits as if the beasts had been still alive. Nevertheless they did not leave off feasting on them. For six days they feasted, and on the seventh day they set sail.

For a time all seemed to go well, for the wind blew as they desired. But when they were now out of sight of land, suddenly all the sky was covered with a dark cloud, and a great wind came down upon the ship, and snapped the shrouds on either side of the mast. Then the mast fell backwards and broke the skull of the man that held the rudder and steered the ship, so that he fell into the sea. Next there came down a great thunderbolt from the sky, and the ship was filled with fire and smoke from one end of it to the other. And all the men were blown out of the ship, some on one side and some on the other. Only Ulysses was left. He stayed on the ship till the ribs were broken away from the keel by the waves. And when only the mast and the keel were left together, Ulysses bound himself by a thong of leather to them, and sat on them, and was driven by the wind over the waves. All night long was he driven, and when the day dawned he came to the passage where there was Scylla's cave on one side and the great whirlpool on the other. Now, there was a fig-tree that grew at the top of the cliff that was above the whirlpool. Circé had told Ulysses of this same tree, for she knew all things, and Ulysses remembered her words; and when the keel and the mast were carried up to the top, he caught hold of the branches. But he found that he could not climb any higher, so he waited till the keel and the mast should come again, for they had been swallowed up. For four hours or so he waited, and when he saw them again, he loosed his hold on the fig-tree, and caught hold of them, and sat upon them as he had done before. Now after the water had risen to the top, there was calm for a little time before it began to sink again, and Ulysses paddled with his hands as hard as he could, and so got away. By good luck Scylla did not see him, for if she had, he would most certainly have perished.

For eight days and nights Ulysses was carried by the winds and waves over the sea, and on the ninth day he came to a beautiful island where there dwelt a goddess, by name Calypso. There he lived for seven long years. Long they seemed, for though he had all that a man could wish for, yet he would gladly have gone home. "Oh!" he would say to himself, "if I could but see the smoke rising up from the chimneys of my own home!" But the island was far away in the midst of the sea, and no ship came near to it. So he could do nothing but wait.

Of What Happened in Ithaca

Now we must leave Ulysses in the island of Calypso, and see what was gong on at his home in Ithaca. You have been already told that before he went to Troy he had married a wife, Penelopé by name, and had a son who was called Telemaˇchus. When this son was still only a baby, Ulysses had to go to Troy with the other chiefs of the Greeks to fight with the Trojans. And now nearly twenty years had passed, and he had not come home: and no one knew what had become of him. What had happened to the other chiefs every one knew. Some had died during the siege, and others had perished on the way home, and the leader of them all had come back and been wickedly killed by his wife, and another had had to fly from his home and build a city in a distant country, and others had got back safely, sooner or later; but Ulysses was still absent, and, as has been said, no one knew where he was, or whether he was alive or dead. But it seemed most likely that he was dead. It is no wonder, then, that many of the young men among the nobles of Ithaca, and of the islands round about, came and tried to persuade his wife Penelopé to marry again. "It is of no use," they said, "for you to wait any longer for your husband. By this time he must be dead. And you ought to have some one to look after your property and your kingdom, for your son is too young to do this properly."

Now Penelopé believed in her heart that her husband was alive, and that he would come back; but she knew that hardly any one else believed it. And she felt very helpless. The people of Ithaca thought that she ought to marry again. They were very badly governed when there was no king. Even if the man whom she chose—for, of course, her husband would be king—was not very good, this would be better than to have a whole crowd of men coming day after day to the palace, eating and drinking and gambling, and wasting the king's goods. So she tried to gain time. She thought to herself: "If I can put off these people"—suitors they were called—"for a while, perhaps my husband will come back in the meanwhile." So she said to them: "You know that my husband's father is an old man, and that it would be a great disgrace to me if he were to die and there were no proper grave clothes to bury him in; for you know that he has been a king, and should be buried with honour. Let me weave a shroud for him, and when this is finished, then I will choose one from among you to be my husband." The Suitors were glad to hear this, for they said to themselves: "This weaving cannot take a very long time; and when it is finished, then one of us, at least, will get what he wants." So they waited, but somehow the weaving was not finished. The truth was that the queen undid every night what she had done in the day. How long this would have gone on no one knows, but at last one of the women that waited on the queen told the secret to a friend of hers among the Suitors. That night three or four of them were taken by the woman to the queen's own room, and found her undoing what she had done in the day. So the queen could not put the Suitors off any longer in this way; the shroud was finished, and she did not know what to do.

Now there was one among the gods and goddesses who more than all the others cared for Ulysses. This was Athené, the goddess of Wisdom, and she loved Ulysses because he was so wise. And Athené thought to herself: "Now there are two things to be done: we must bring Ulysses back to his home; he has been away for twenty years, and that is enough, and too much. And we must not let Telemaˇchus, his son, sit still any longer and do nothing, as if he did not care at all what has happened to his father, and whether he is alive or dead. It would be a bad thing if Ulysses were to come home and find out that Telemaˇchus had never taken any pains to look for him or ask about him. For Telemaˇchus is now a young man, and able to think and act." And Athené, being wise, saw that this was the first thing to do, for nothing could be worse than that, for any reason, father and son should not be good friends. And the way in which she stirred up Telemaˇchus was this.

One day he sat among the Suitors, who were feasting and playing draughts in his father's house. Every day did they come thither, and they made a sad waste of the things which belonged to Ulysses. The sheep and oxen and swine were killed for their meat, and they drank the wines from his cellars. And Telemaˇchus could do nothing, for he was but one against many. As he sat very sad at heart, there came a stranger to the door. Now this stranger was Athené, who had come down to the earth and taken a man's shape. When Telemaˇchus saw him, he got up from his place and brought him in, and commanded his servants to set food and drink before him.

When he had ended his meal, Telemaˇchus asked him his business. The stranger said: "I am Mentes; I am king of the Taphians, and I am on my way to Cyprus with a cargo of iron, which I am going to exchange for copper. And I have come wishing to see your father, for I knew him and his father also. But now they tell me that he is not here. Something has hindered him from coming home, for I am sure that he is alive. But who are these? what are they doing here? Is this a wedding feast? A wise man would not like to see such doings in his house."

And Telemăchus answered: "Oh, sir, while my father was yet alive, this house was rich and prosperous. But now that he is gone, things go very ill with me. It had been far better if he had fallen in battle fighting against the Trojans, but now the sea has swallowed him up. And these men are the princes of Ithaca and of the islands round about, and they come, they say, seeking my mother in marriage. She will neither say Yes nor No to them. Meanwhile they sit and waste my substance."

Then said Mentes: "It is indeed time that Ulysses should come back and put an end to such doings. But it is time also that you should do something for yourself. Now listen to me. First call the people of Ithaca to an Assembly. It is well to have the people on your side. Then bid the Suitors depart, each man to his house. And if your mother be minded to take another husband, let her go back to her father's house, and let her own people make ready a wedding feast and other things such as a daughter should have. When these things are done, make ready a ship with twenty oars, and go inquire after your father; perhaps some man may have seen him or heard of him; perhaps the gods themselves will give you an answer if you ask them. Go first to Pylos, where the old man Nestor lives. After that go to Sparta, and see King Menelaüs, for he was the last of all the Greeks to get back to his home. And if you should find out that your father is dead, then raise a mound for him, and give him such honours as are due to the dead. And if these Suitors still trouble you, then devise some way of slaying them. It is time for you to behave yourself as a man."

Telemăchus said: "You speak to me as a father might speak to his son, nor will I ever forget what you have said. But come now, stay awhile, that I may give you some goodly gift such as a friend should give to a friend."

"Nay," said Mentes, "I cannot stay. Keep your gift, I pray you, till I come again."

So he rose from his seat, and went out at the door. And lo! of a sudden he seemed to change his shape. It was as if he were changed into a sea-eagle. And Telemăchus knew that this stranger was not Mentes, but the goddess Athené. And he went back to the hall of the palace, where a minstrel, Phemius by name, was telling the tale of how the Greeks came back from Troy, and of the many things which they suffered because they had sinned against the gods. And lo! in the midst of his telling, Penelopé came down from the upper chamber where she sat, having two handmaids with her. She stood in the door of the hall, having drawn her veil over her face, and said to the minstrel: "Phemius, you know many tales about the deeds of gods and men. Tell one of these, and let the guests hear it while they drink their wine.

But tell this tale no more, for it breaks my heart to hear it. Surely I am the most unhappy of women, for of all the chiefs that went to Troy, and never came back to their homes, my husband was the most famous."

Then said Telemaˇchus: "Mother, why do you forbid the minstrel to make us glad in the way that he thinks best? Why do you forbid him to sing of the coming back of the Greeks? 'Tis a new tale, and men always like to hear that which is new. Go back, then, to your chamber, and mind the business of the house, and see that your maids do their work, their spinning and the like. But here I am master."

And Penelopé went back to her chamber without answering a word, for never had Telemaˇchus spoken in such a way before. But she wept for Ulysses her husband, till sleep came down upon her eyes.

And when she was gone, Telemaˇchus said to the Suitors: "Let us now feast and be merry, and let there be no quarrelling among us. And let us listen to the minstrel's tale. What could we do better, for his voice is as the voice of a god. But mark this. To-morrow we will have an Assembly of the people, and there I will declare my purpose. And my purpose is this—that you go away from this place, and eat and drink in your own homes at your own cost."

And they were astonished at his boldness, just as his mother had been astonished, for he had never so spoken before. And one of them, whose name was Antinoüs, said: "Surely it is some god that makes you speak so boldly. I hope that you will never be king here in Ithaca, though it is but right that you should have that which belonged to your father."

Telemaˇchus said: "I know that it is a good thing to be a king, for a king has riches and honour. But there are many here in Ithaca, young men and old, who may have the kingdom now that Ulysses is dead. Only this I know, that I will be master in my own house."

Then stood up another of the Suitors, and said: "It is for the gods to settle who shall be king in Ithaca; but that you ought to be master in your own house, and keep your own goods, no man will deny. But tell me, who was this stranger that came just now to the palace? Did he bring news of your father, or did he come on business of his own? Why did he not stay to greet us? He was no common man, I take it."

Telemaˇchus answered: "As for tidings of my father, I do not make any count of them, whoever it is that brings them; Ulysses will come back no more. And as for the soothsayers whom my mother loves to entertain, that find out for her what has befallen her husband, I think nothing of them. They are makers of lies. As for this stranger about whom you ask: he was Mentes, king of the Taphians." So he said, but he knew in his heart that the stranger was Athené.

Then the Suitors feasted, and made merry with singing and dancing, till the night was far spent; and they went each man to his own home to sleep. But Telemachus went to his chamber, and Eurycleia, who had been his nurse when he was but a baby, led the way, holding a torch in either hand, to light him. And when he came to the chamber, he took off his doublet and gave it to the nurse, and she folded it and smoothed it, and hung it on a pin. This done, she went out and pushed to the door and made it fast. But Telemachus lay long awake, thinking of the journey which he was about to take.

How Telema˘chus Went to Look for His Father

The next day, as soon as it was light, Telema˘chus sent the officers to call the people to the Assembly. And when the people heard the call, they came quickly, for such a thing had not happened now for many years. And, when they were all gathered together, Telema˘chus himself went, holding a spear in his hand, and with two dogs at his heels. And when he sat down in his father's place all who were there wondered to see him, for he looked not like the boy but like a man.

The first that stood up in the Assembly was a certain old man, Aegyptus by name—very old he was, so that he was almost bent double, and he was very wise. He had four sons, but one was dead, for he had gone with Ulysses to Troy, and had died, with the rest of Ulysses' companions, on his way back, as has been told. Another son was one of the Suitors; and two were with their father, working on the farm. Aegyptus said: "Listen to me, men of Ithaca! who has called us together to-day? Is it Telema˘chus who has done this? If it is he, what does he want? Has he heard anything of his father, and of the men who went with him to fight against Troy?"

Then Telema˘chus stood up in his place and said: "Men of Ithaca, I am in great trouble. First, I fear that my father is dead, and you, who all loved him, feel for me. And then there have come men from all the islands round about, making suit to my mother, and while they wait they devour my substance. But my mother will not listen to any one of them, for she still believes that her husband will come back. Yes; they waste all that I have, and I cannot hinder them from doing it."

And he dashed his spear on the ground, and sat down weeping. Then one of the Suitors, Antinoüs by name, stood up and said: "Telema˘chus, do not blame us, but blame your mother. Surely there never was so crafty a woman." And he told the people the story of the web, how she wove it by day and unwove it by night. "Do not let her put us off any longer. Make her choose one of us and marry him. But till you do this, we will not leave your house."

Then said Telema˘chus: "How could I do this to my own mother? It would be against my duty as a son. And besides, I should have to pay a great sum of money to her father, all the dowry that she brought with her. No; I cannot do this thing."

And when he had ended his speech there happened a strange thing. Two eagles were seen high up in the air, which flew along till they came to the place where the Assembly was. Then they fought together, and tore from each other many feathers.

Then said a certain man who knew what such things meant: "Beware, ye Suitors; great trouble is coming to you and to others. As for Ulysses, he said that he should come back to Ithaca in the twentieth year after his going, and that, I verily believe, he will do."

Then Telemăchus spake again: "Give me a ship with twenty rowers, and I will go to the mainland, to certain kings who went to Troy with my father, as Nestor and Menelaüs. And if I hear that he is dead, I will come back, and make a great mound for him that will keep his name in remembrance, and I will also make my mother choose another husband."

Then stood up one Mentor, whom Ulysses had made steward of his house when he went away, and said: "I am ashamed of this people of Ithaca. There is not one of them who remembers Ulysses, and yet he was as gentle as a father with them. Let no king henceforth be gentle and kind. Let him rather be a hard man and unrighteous, for then his people will remember him. See, now, these Suitors, how they are bent on doing evil. Well, I will not hinder them. They will have to suffer for what they do. But the people I blame. See, now, how they sit without saying a word, when they ought to cry shame upon the Suitors; and yet they are many in number and the Suitors are few."

Then stood up one of the Suitors, and said: "Surely, Mentor, your wits are wandering, when you bid the people put us down by force. They could not do it. And if Ulysses himself came back, he could not do it. He would come to a bad end if he fought with us, for we are many in number. And as for the ship and the twenty rowers that Telemăchus asks for, let Mentor find them for him. As for me, I do not think that he will be able to do it."

Then the Assembly was dismissed. And Telemăchus went down to the sea-shore; and after he had washed his hands in the sea, he prayed to Athené, saying: "Hear me, O goddess, thou didst bid me yesterday take a ship and rowers and ask about my father—yes, it was thou, though it seemed as if King Mentes was speaking to me—but the Suitors hinder me, and the people will not help. I pray thee, therefore, to put it into my heart what I should do."

And while he was yet speaking, Athené stood before him, and she had taken the shape of Mentor the steward. She said: "Be brave; you have spirit and wit; and are, I take it, a true son of your father and mother. Go now on this journey, for I trust that it will turn out to your profit. As for the Suitors, take no thought about them; they speak folly, and do not know the doom that is coming upon them. Make ready provisions for a journey, wine and meat; meanwhile I will collect men who will offer of their own free will to go with you, and I will also find a ship, the best in all Ithaca."

So Telemaˇchus went back to the palace, and he found the Suitors flaying goats and singeing swine for their dinner. And Antinoüs caught him by the hand, and said: "Come now, Telemaˇchus; eat and drink with us, and we will find a ship and rowers for you, that you may be able to go whither you will, and ask after your father." But Telemaˇchus said: "Do you think that I will eat and drink with you, who are wasting my substance in this shameful fashion? Be sure that I will have my revenge on you. And if you will not let me have a ship of my own, then I will sail in another man's." And another of the Suitors said: "What now will Telemaˇchus do? Will he get men from Pylos, where old Nestor lives, or from Sparta, where King Menelaüs is, to fight against us? Or, maybe, he will put poison in our wine, and so destroy us."

And another said: "What if he should perish himself as his father has perished? It would be a great business dividing his property. As for his house, we would give it to his mother and the man whom she may choose for her husband?"

So they made sport of him. But he went to the store-room of the palace, where there were laid up casks of old wine, and olive oil, and clothing, and plates of gold and silver and copper. All these things were in the charge of his nurse Eurycleia. Telemaˇchus said to her: "Look out for me twelve jars of wine, not the best, but the second best, and twenty measures of barley meal. I will come for them to-night when my mother is asleep, for I am going to Pylos and to Sparta, to see whether I can hear anything about my father."

But the old woman cried out: "Oh, my son, why will you travel abroad, you an only son? Your father has perished; will you perish also? These wicked men, the Suitors, will plot against you and kill you. Surely it would be better to sit quietly at home."

Telemaˇchus said: "Mother, I must go, for it is the gods that bid me. Swear now that you will say nothing to my mother about it for ten or twelve days, unless, indeed, she should ask you about me: then you must say for what I am gone."

So the old woman sware that she would say nothing. And Telemaˇchus went among the Suitors, and behaved as if he had nothing on his mind. Meanwhile Athené, in Mentor's shape, had got a crew of sailors together, persuading them to go as no man could have persuaded them. And she borrowed a ship, for no man could refuse to lend her what she asked for. And lest the Suitors should come to know of what was going on, she caused a deep sleep to fall upon them. They slept each man in his chair. And then she came to the palace, and she still had the shape of Mentor, and called Telemaˇchus out, saying to him, "The rowers are ready: let us go."

So the two went down to the shore, and found the ship, and the ship's crew ready to go on board. And Telemaˇchus said: "Come now, my friends, to my room at the palace, for there I have stored away the meat and the drink that we want for the voyage. One woman only knows about the matter; not my mother, nor any of her maids, but only my old nurse."

So they went up to the palace, and carried all the provisions themselves to the shore, and stowed it away in the ship. And Telemaˇchus went on board, and sat down on the stern, and Mentor, that was really Athené, sat down by him. And he told the sailors to make ready to start.

First, they pushed off the ship from the shore. Then they raised the mast, which was made of a pine tree, and lay along the deck in a kind of crutch that was made for it. A hole was ready in which to put the end. So the men raised it, and made it fast with ropes on both sides. And they hauled up the sail with ropes made of ox hide. And the wind filled the sail, and the ship went quickly through the water, the sea bubbling and foaming about it as it went, and Telemaˇchus poured wine out of a bowl, praying to the god of the sea, and to Zeus that he might have a prosperous voyage. So all the night the ship sped along till the dawn began to show in the east.

How Telemachus Saw Nestor

At sunrise the ship came to Pylos, which was on the west coast of the Island of Pelops. Here Nestor was king. He was the oldest man in the world. He had ruled over three generations of men, that is, for ninety years and more, and he was still hearty and strong. Now it so happened that on this day the people were offering a sacrifice to the god of the sea, whose name was Poseidon. There were nine companies of men, and in each there were five hundred, and each five hundred sacrificed nine bulls. They had finished the sacrifice, and were beginning the feast, for there was always a feast after the sacrifice, when Telemaˇchus and his men moored the ship on the shore and landed. Then said Athené to the young man: "Go, and speak to the old King Nestor. There is no need for you to be ashamed. You have come to get news of your father, if such can be got. Go boldly, therefore, and ask him if he can tell you anything."

But Telemaˇchus said: "How can I speak to him, for I am young and ignorant?"

"Nay," said the goddess, "think of something yourself, and the gods will put what may be wanting into your mouth."

So she led the way, being, as before in the shape of Mentor, to where Nestor sat with his sons and a great company about him, ready to begin the feast. And when the men of Pylos saw the strangers they shook their hands, and made them sit down on soft fleeces of wool that had been laid down on the shore for seats. And Nestor's youngest son brought them some of the best of the flesh, and wine in a golden cup. The cup he gave first to Mentor, judging him to be the elder of the two, saying to him: "Pray now to the god of the sea, and pour out some of the wine as an offering, and when you have done so, give the cup to your friend, that he may do the same."

So Mentor took the cup and prayed to the god of the sea, saying: "Give renown to Nestor and his sons, and make such a return to the men of Pylos as is their due for this great sacrifice, and grant to us that we may accomplish that for which we have come hither."

And when he had said these words he poured out some of the wine on the sand. Then he passed the cup to Telemaˇchus, and he also said the same words and poured out some of the wine.

When they had eaten and drunk as much as they desired, Nestor said to them: "Strangers, who are you, and what is your business? Are you traders that sail over the seas to buy and sell in foreign lands, or are you pirates?"

Telemaˇchus answered, Athené putting into his heart what he should say: "We come from Ithaca, and we are neither traders nor pirates. I seek for news of my father, who in time past fought by your side, and helped you to take the city of Troy. Now we know about all the other chiefs who fought against Troy, how some came back safe to their homes, and some perished. But of Ulysses, my father, no man knows anything, whether he be alive or dead. For this reason I am come to you. It may be that you saw his death with your own eyes, or that you have heard of it from another that saw it. Speak no smooth words, I pray you, for pity's sake, but tell me plainly what you have seen or heard."

Nestor answered: "Ah me! you bring back to my mind old things, old troubles that we bore when we fought against the great city of Priam. There the best of us were slain. There lies the mighty Ajax—Ajax of the great shield which no one but he could carry. There also lies Achilles, the greatest of all the Greeks. No one was so swift of foot as he, and he had a spear which no one but he could throw. There, also, lies my own dear son, Antilochus. But who could tell the tale of all that we suffered? For nine years we fought against the city, and your father was always the wisest of us; no man gave such counsel as did he, and truly you are like him; when you speak I seem to be hearing him. But now I will tell you what I know. When at last, in the tenth year, Troy was taken, then there came fresh trouble upon us. For there were some who were not just or prudent, and they made the gods angry by their evil doings. First, there was a quarrel between Agamemnon and his brother Menelaüs. Menelaüs was for going back home without delay, but Agamemnon thought that the Greeks should stay awhile and make a great sacrifice to Athené, for he feared that she was angry with the people. So they called the people to an Assembly, and there was much talking and disputing, some crying out one thing and some another. The next day I and the others that held with Menelaüs launched our ships, and put into them all our goods, and all the spoil that we had taken out of Troy, and so set sail. With us there was one half of the people, and the other half stayed behind with King Agamemnon. But when we had gone but a little there was another division, for your father, Ulysses, went back to Troy, and others went with him. But I knew in my heart that the gods were angry with us, for it was they who had caused this strife and division among us. So I went on my way; so did the brave Diomed, and so did Menelaüs; straight across the sea we sailed. And on the fourth day Diomed came safely to his city of Argos, and I went on to my own city of Pylos here, and reached it without suffering loss or harm. You see, therefore, that I cannot speak of my own knowledge as to what happened to other chiefs. But I will tell you all the news that I have heard here since then. The people of Achilles came safe to their home, his son leading them, and Philoctetes came safe, and Agamemnon came safe—but, alas! a wicked woman slew him. But as for Ulysses, I have told you all I know."

Then said Telemaͮchus: "Tell me now about Menelaüs. Did he also come safely to his home?"

Nestor answered: "Yes, he, too, came safely, but after a long time. He and I sailed together across the sea, and came without loss to a certain cape which is near to the city of Athens. There his pilot died, and he could not but stay awhile, though he greatly wished to get home, for the man was dear to him, and he must needs give him an honourable burial. But when he had done this and had set sail again, a great storm arose, and his fleet was divided. Some of the ships were driven ashore at the Island of Crete and were wrecked, the men barely escaping with their lives. As for Menelaüs, he was driven eastward by the wind to Egypt, he and five ships with him—five ships out of sixty, you must know, for he had sixty ships when he came to Troy. For seven years he wandered about in those parts, and in the beginning of the eighth year he came back, bringing much gold and other precious things with him in his ship. And now, my son, my advice to you is this: do not wander about looking for your father. You will only waste your goods by so doing. But go to Menelaüs, where he lives in his own city of Sparta, and ask him to tell whether he has seen or heard anything about your father. You see that he has but lately come back after many wanderings, and if there is anything to be heard about your father, it has doubtless come to his ears. You can go in your ship, if you will. But there are many miles between Sparta and the sea, so that you would do better to go in a chariot. This I will provide for you, and horses to draw it, and one of my sons to be your guide."

By this time it was near to sunset, and Mentor said to Telemaͮchus: "Come now, let us go back to our ship that we may sleep there." But Nestor, when he heard this, said: "Not so, my friends; the gods forbid that you should sleep in your ship when my house is near at hand. I am no needy man who cannot find rugs and mats and clothing enough for my guests that they may lie soft and warm. No, no! I have enough of these. Never shall the son of my old friend Ulysses sleep on the deck of his ship while I have my hall, or while my son after me shall have a hall in which to shelter him."

Then Mentor spoke: "This is well said, my father. Telemaˇchus shall sleep in your house, and I will go back to the ship and cheer the men, for they will wish to know how their young master has fared. Besides, I have business on hand which I must do a debt, among other things, which I must needs collect, for it is large and has been a long time owing."

When he had finished speaking, the man Mentor, for such they thought him to be, was changed into the shape of an eagle of the sea in the sight of all the company, and they were astonished to see it. And old Nestor took Telemaˇchus by the hand and said: "Truly you are no weakling, for I see that young as you are the gods have a favour for you. This is none other than Athené; she was always helping your father when he was at Troy."

Then the old man led the company to his house, and bade them sit down. And he mixed for them a bowl of old wine. The wine was eleven years old, and he shredded on it goats' milk cheese, and sprinkled also barley meal, and when they had drunk as much as they desired, they lay down to sleep. Telemaˇchus slept on a bed beneath the gallery of the house, and Nestor's youngest son slept on a bed close by; to take care that he should not suffer any harm.

The next day, as soon as it was light, Nestor rose and called his sons. One he sent to fetch a heifer from the plain, and another he told to go to the ship and bring all the crew up to the palace, leaving two only to take care of it. And a third fetched the goldsmith that he might gild the horns of the heifer. Meanwhile the maids made everything ready for a feast. So Nestor sacrificed the heifer, and the company feasted on the flesh. As for Telemaˇchus, he sat by Nestor's side, and he had put on a handsome tunic and a mantle over the tunic, which Nestor's youngest daughter had made ready for him.

When they had finished their meal, Nestor said: "Harness the horses to the chariot, and let Telemaˇchus start on his journey."

So they harnessed the horses, and the housekeeper put food and wine, such as princes eat and drink, into the chariot, and Nestor's youngest son took the reins in his hand, and Telemaˇchus rode with him. That day they travelled as far as the town of Pherae. There they stopped for the night with the king of the place. And the next day they came to Sparta, where Menelaüs lived.

How Telemachus Came to Sparta

It happened that on the very day when Telemaˇchus and Nestor's son came to Sparta, King Menelaüs had a double wedding in his house. His daughter Hermioné was married to the son of Achilles, and he had found a wife in one of the noble families of the country for his son, whose name was Megapenthes. So when the two young men drove the chariot up to the door of the palace, the king's steward was a little vexed, and he said to himself: "We have quite enough to do already, and here are two strangers whom we shall have to entertain." So he went to the king and said: "Here are two strangers at the door. Shall we keep them here, or shall we send them on to another house?"

Menelaüs was very angry, and answered: "What? shall we, who have been guests in so many houses, turn away guests from our door? Not so; unharness their horses, and bid them sit down and eat."

So the steward gave orders to the grooms that they should unharness the horses, and take them to the stables, and give them corn to eat. And to the young men he said: "Will you please to get down from your chariot and come in?" So the two got down, and he led them into the king's hall. A wonderful place it was, as bright as if the sun or the moon was shining in it. And when they had looked about them, the steward took them to the baths, which were of polished marble. And when they had bathed they came back to the hall, and the king himself told them to sit down by him. So they sat down, and first a maid brought silver basins, and poured water into them from a golden jug, that they might wash their hands. After this the old housekeeper came and put a polished table before them, and on the table she set dainty dishes and plates and golden bowls of wine and cups. And the king told a servant to bring a chine of beef, which was his own portion, and bade them eat. When they had had enough, Telemaˇchus said to his friend: "See the gold and the silver and the amber and the ivory. This must be as fine as the hall of the gods."

This he said with his face close to his friend's ear, but the king heard it, and said: "Nay, my son, nothing upon earth can be compared with the hall of the gods; and, it may be, there are other men who have things as fine as these. Yet fine they are; I have wandered far to get them. But alas! while I was getting them, my own dear brother was wickedly slain in his own home. I would give them all if he were alive again, he and other good friends of mine. Many are gone; but there is none whom I miss more than Ulysses. And no man knows whether he is alive or dead." And when Telemaˇchus heard his father's name, he held up his cloak before his eyes and wept. Menelaüs saw him, and knew who he was, for, indeed, as has been said, he was very like his father. Then he thought to himself, "Shall I speak to him about his father, or shall I wait till he speaks himself?"

Just then Helen herself came into the hall, and three maids with her. One set a couch for her to sit on, and another spread a carpet for her feet, and the third had a basket of purple wool for her to spin. And she had a distaff of gold in her hands. When she saw the strangers she said:—

"Who are these, Menelaüs? Never have I seen any one so like to Ulysses as is this young man. Surely this must be Telemaˇchus, whom he left a baby in his home when he went to Troy."

And the king said: "It is true, lady. These are the hands and feet of Ulysses; and he has the same look in his eyes, and his hair is of the same colour."

Then all shed tears; Helen and the king and Telemaˇchus, and also Nestor's son. How could he help it when his friends were so sad? And, besides, he thought how his own dear brother had gone to Troy and had never come back. But he was the first to stop his tears, for he said to the king: "Is it well to weep in this way while we sit at meat? There is a time to mourn for the dead, to weep and to crop close the hair; but there is also a time to rejoice."

"You are right," said the king. "You are the wise son of a wise father. Yes, we will weep no more. As for Telemaˇchus, he and I have much to say to each other. Let that be to-morrow; but now we will eat and drink."

Then the fair Helen took a certain medicine, and mixed it in the wine that they were about to drink. It was an herb, and it grew in the land of Egypt, and the wife of the king of Egypt had given it her. It was called Painless, and it was a wonderful medicine; for if any one drank the wine in which it was mixed, he could feel no pain or grief—no, not though his father and mother should die, or his son or his brother should be killed before his eyes. So they sat and drank wine and talked together. And one of the matters about which they talked was the wisdom of Ulysses. Then Helen told this story:—

"While the Greeks were besieging the city of Troy, Ulysses disguised himself as a beggar man and came to the gate of the city, and desired to speak with some of the chief men. It could be seen that he had many weals and bruises upon his body, as if he had been cruelly beaten; and, indeed, he had beaten himself. So they brought him to me, knowing that he was a Greek. And when I saw him I knew who he was, and I asked him many questions.

Very cunningly did he answer them. But I promised him that I would not make him known. So he sent about the city, and found out many things that the Greeks desired to know. Also he killed some of the Trojans stealthily. Other women in Troy mourned and lamented, but I was glad; for I desired to go again to my home."

Then Menelaüs said: "You speak truly, lady. Ulysses is indeed the wisest of men. I have travelled over many lands, but never have I seen any one who could be matched with him. Well do I remember how, when I and other chiefs of the Greeks were hidden in the Wooden Horse, you came with one of the princes of Troy and walked round the horse. Some one of the gods who loved the Trojans had put it into your heart to do this. Three times you walked round, and you called to each of us by name, and when you called you imitated the voice of the man's wife. And so well you did it that we could not believe but that our wives were truly calling to us. Then Diomed would have answered, and I too, but Ulysses would not let us speak, for he knew what it really was. Thus he saved the Greeks that day."

Then Telemaˇchus said: "Yet all his wisdom has not kept him from perishing."

After that they went to their beds and slept.

Menelaus's Story

The next day Menelaüs said to Telema˘chus: "Tell me now on what business you have come. Is it on some affair of your own, or is it something that concerns the State?"

Telema˘chus answered: "I have come to see whether you can tell me anything about my father. No one knows whether he is alive or dead. And I am in great trouble at home, because certain nobles of Ithaca and of the islands round about would have my mother choose a husband from among them, and meanwhile they devour my substance."

Menelaüs said: "They will certainly be punished for their wrong-doing. So a hind lays her young in a lion's den, but when the lion comes back, he slays both her and her fawn. So will Ulysses slay these Suitors, for he will most certainly come back. But now I will tell you all that I know. In my travels I went to the land of Egypt, and when I wished to sail homeward, I could not, for the winds were against me. There is an island opposite the mouth of the Nile, which is the great river of Egypt. There I stayed, not of my own choice, for twenty days, till all our food was eaten up. Truly we had all perished, I and my men, but that one of the goddesses of the sea had pity on us. She was the daughter of a sea god, and one day as I sat alone, for my men were wandering about fishing with hooks for anything that they might catch, she stood by me and said: 'Surely this is a foolish thing that you do, sitting here till you and your men die of hunger.' I answered: 'I know not who you are, but I will tell you the truth. It is not of my own choice that I stay; the winds are against me, and I cannot go. Tell me, now, whether I have offended the gods, and tell me also how I can return to my home.' Then she said: 'I cannot tell you these things, but there is one who can, and that is my father Proteus. He comes here with the sea-beasts which he herds. But you must lay hold on him, for he will not tell you these things except by force.' Then I asked her to tell me how this could be done. Then she said: 'The old man comes here at noon to a certain cave that there is by the sea, and he brings his sea-beasts with him. Then he lies down in the cave to sleep, and the beasts lie all round him. That is the time for you to lay hold of him. Choose now out of your men the three that are bravest and strongest, and I will take them and you at daybreak and hide you in the cave. The old man will come at noon. First, he will count the beasts, as a shepherd counts his sheep, and then he will lie down to sleep in the middle of them. Then you must rush upon him, and lay your hands upon him and hold him fast. Remember that he will take all kind of shapes, beasts and creeping things, and water and fire. But when he shall come back to his proper shape, then let him go, and ask him what you want to know, and he will tell you.' When the goddess had said this, she dived into the sea. So I chose three of my men, the bravest and the strongest that there were, and we waited at the place where the goddess had spoken to me. Just before dawn she came out of the sea, bringing four skins of sea-beasts with her. And she took us into the cave, and dug out hiding places for us in the sand, and wrapped the skin of a sea-beast about each of us, and made us lie down in the places which she had dug out. She wrapped the skins about us in order that the old man might take us for sea-beasts. Now the beasts had been just killed, and the smell of them was such as could scarcely be borne; so she took portions of ambrosia, which is the food of the gods, and very sweet smelling. She put a portion under the nose of each one of us, and so we were able to endure the smell of the beasts. So we waited all the morning. At noon the old man came from the sea, and the beasts came with him, and went into the cave and lay down on the sand. And the old man went along the line, and counted the beasts, counting us with the rest, and he did not perceive our device. This done, he lay down to sleep in the midst of the herd. Then we rushed upon him, and held him fast. He took many shapes, a lion, and a snake, and a panther, and a wild boar, yes, and running water, and a tree covered with flowers. All the while we held him fast. But when he was come back to his proper shape, we let him go. Then he said: 'Who told you how to beguile me?' To this I made no answer, for why should I make mischief between him and his daughter? But I said: 'Tell me now the things that I desire to know. I am kept fast in this island; tell me how I can escape.' He said: 'You are kept here by the gods; if you had done proper sacrifice to them before you set sail, you had been near to your home by this time. But now go back to Egypt, and do sacrifices, as is proper, and the gods will give you your desire.' It troubled me to hear this, for I desired to go homeward and not back to Egypt. But I said: 'There is yet another thing which I would hear. Tell me about the chiefs whom Nestor and I left behind us in Troy; have they returned safely to their homes or no?' The old man said: 'Why did you ask this question, for the answer will make you sorry? Two only of the chiefs perished. Ajax the Lesser was shipwrecked. He had offended Athené, and she brake his ship with a thunderbolt. And yet he might have escaped with his life, for the gods of the sea helped him so that he got to the rocks. But he boasted foolishly that he had saved himself in spite of the gods; and when the god of the sea heard this, he was angry, and smote the rock on which Ajax sat, so that it was broken into two pieces, and Ajax fell into the sea, and was drowned. And the other chief who perished was thy own brother Agamemnon. He came safely indeed to his own land; but there Aegisthus wickedly killed him.' Then I said: 'There is yet one chief of whom I wish to hear something.' But before I could tell his name, the old man said: 'I know of whom you are speaking. It is Ulysses of Ithaca. Him I saw in the island of Calypso. He was weeping, because Calypso keeps him there against his will, and he has no companions and no ship.' And when he had said this he plunged into the sea. Then I went back to Egypt, and offered sacrifice to the gods, and so came safely home, for the gods gave me a favourable wind. And now, my son, tarry with me as long as you will. And when you wish to depart, I will give you a chariot and horses, and also a goodly cup."

But Telemaˇchus said: "Keep me not, for I would go home as soon as may be. But as for the horses I thank you, but I desire them not. Here you have corn, land, and pasture, but we have none such in Ithaca. There is no feeding land save for goats; and yet I love it."

Menelaüs answered: "You speak well and warily, as becomes your father's son. I will therefore change the gift. You shall have the finest cup that I have in my house, the one that the king of Sidon gave me. It is of silver, but the rim is finished with gold."

Then Telemaˇchus departed and went to his ship where it lay at Pylos. And the crew came from Nestor's palace, when they heard of his return, and in due course they started for their home. Now Antinoüs had taken a ship with twenty men, and lay in wait in the Strait between Ithaca and Samé. But Telemaˇchus was warned by Athené that he should go home by another way, and this he did, and so escaped the danger.

How Ulysses Came to the Phaeacians

Now the time was come when Ulysses was to be set free from his prison in Calypso's island. Athené said in the council of the gods: "It seems to me that a good king is not in the least better off than a bad one. Look at Ulysses; he was as a father to his people, and see how he is shut up in Calypso's island. For seven years and more he has been there."

Then said Zeus to Hermes, who was the messenger of the gods: "Go now to Calypso in her island, and tell her that it is my will that Ulysses should go back to his own country."

So Hermes tied his golden sandals on his feet, and took his wand in his hand, and flew from Olympus to Calypso's island, and to the cave in which she dwelt. It was a very fair place. All about the mouth of the cave there was a vine with clusters of purple grapes; and round about the cave there was a wood of alder-trees, and poplars, and cypresses, in which many birds used to roost; also there were four fountains from which four streams of the clearest water that could be flowed down through meadows of parsley and violets. In the cave itself there was burning a fire of sweet-smelling woods. Calypso sat at her loom, and sang in a very lovely voice. Hermes looked about on the vine, and the grove, and the fountains, and the meadows, and thought to himself that it was a lovely place. Then he went into the cave, and when Calypso saw him she knew who he was, and why he had come. Nevertheless she pretended not to know. "You are welcome, Hermes," she said, "and all the more because you have never been here to see me before. Now you must tell me why you have come; but first, come, eat and drink."

So she set a table before him, and on the table she put ambrosia, which is the food of the gods; and she mixed a bowl of nectar for him, for this is what the gods drink. And when he had eaten and drunk enough, he said to Calypso: "You ask me why I have come; so I will tell you. Zeus bade me come, and we must all do what Zeus tells us. You have a man in your island here—yes, and have had him for seven years and more, and he is very unhappy, because he wishes to go home. He fought against Troy for nine years and more, and in the tenth year he set out to return. But many misfortunes happened to him, and he lost all his companions, and somehow he was brought to this island. Now send him back to his home as quickly as you can, for this is his fate that he should live the rest of his life among his friends."

This was just what Calypso expected to hear; but she was very angry and said: "Did I not save this man's life when Zeus broke his ship with a thunderbolt, and he was carried by the waves to this island? Yes, if Zeus so wishes, he shall go, but I cannot send him, for I have no ship and no rowers."

And Hermes said: "Send him nevertheless, lest Zeus should be angry with you." And when he had said this he spread his wings, for he had wings on his shoulders and on his feet, and flew away.

Then Calypso went down to the sea-shore—for it was there that Ulysses used to sit looking at the waves, and longing to go over them that he might see his own dear country again. There she found him weeping and lamenting, for he was weary of his life. And she stood by him and said: "Weep no more. You shall have your wish: I will do what I can to help you on your way home. Take an axe and cut down trees and make a raft, tying the beams together with ropes, and putting planks on them for a deck. And I will give you bread, and water, and wine; yes, and clothes too, that you may go to your own country, if you will have it so." Ulysses said: "What is this plan of yours? Shall I go on a raft across the great sea which the ships with oars and sail can hardly pass? Now swear by the great oath which the gods dare not break, that you mean to do me no harm." Calypso smiled, and said: "These are strange words. Why should I do you harm? But if you will so have it, then I will swear by the great oath of the gods that I have no thought of doing you harm."

The next day Calypso gave him an axe, and took him to a part of the island where there were trees fit for making the raft—alder, and poplar, and pine. Twenty of these he cut down, and he hewed them to one shape. And the goddess gave him a tool by which he bored holes in the logs, so that he could fasten them together; also he cut planks for a deck, and for the sides. He made a mast, too, and a rudder by which to steer the raft; also he made a bulwark of skin which was to keep out the waves. The sails Calypso wove, and Ulysses fitted them with ropes. Last of all, he pushed the raft down to the sea with levers. All these things were finished by the end of the fourth day, and on the fifth day he departed. But first Calypso gave him a store of food, and water, and wine, and also clothes. And being a goddess and able to do such things, she sent a fair wind blowing behind him. So he set his sails, and went gladly on his way. In the day time he steered by the sun, and in the night by the stars, for Calypso had said to him: "Keep the Great Bear always on your left." So he sailed for seventeen days, and during this time he never slept. On the eighteenth day he saw the island of the Phaeacians.

Now the god of the sea was very angry with Ulysses, because he had blinded the Cyclops, who was his son. It so happened that he had been for many days feasting with the Ethiopians, and was coming back to Olympus, where the gods dwell, on this very day. And when he saw Ulysses on his left, he said to himself: "Truly this is a new thing. Here is Ulysses close to the island of the Phaeacians; if once he gets there he will soon be at home. But I will give him some trouble yet."

Then he took his trident, which he carried in his hand—it was a great fork with three prongs—and struck the sea with it, and immediately the waves rose high all round the raft, and he made the winds blow. Ulysses was much troubled and frightened, for a man who does not feel fear in battle may feel it in a storm. He said to himself: "I would that I had been killed on that day when we fought with the Trojans for the dead body of Achilles. Then I should have been buried with honour by my own people; but now I shall perish miserably." While he was speaking thus to himself a great wave struck the raft, and made him leave hold of the rudder, and tossed him far away into the sea. Deep did he sink into the water, and hard was it for him to rise again to the top, for the fine clothes which Calypso had given him were very heavy, and dragged him down. But at last he rose, and spat the salt water out of his mouth and sprang at the raft, for he was a brave man, and never lost heart, and caught it, and clambered on to it and sat on it.

While he was being carried hither and thither by the waves, a goddess of the sea saw him and pitied him, for she had once been a woman, and very unhappy. She rose out of the sea in the shape of a gull, and perched upon the raft, and said to him: "Why does the god of the sea hate you so, unlucky man? He would willingly drown you, but it shall not be. Take off these heavy clothes that you are wearing, and put this veil under you"—and she gave him a veil—"and so swim to the island that you see yonder. And when you have got to the shore, throw the veil into the sea, and mind that you do not look behind you when you throw it." And when she had said this, she plunged into the sea.

But Ulysses thought to himself: "Is this a snare for my life, or is it a help? I will wait awhile. The land I see, but it is a long way off, and it would be hard to swim so far. As long as the raft shall hold together I will stay upon it; but if the waves break it, then I will swim; and, indeed, there will be nothing else for me to do. Maybe the veil will help me."

While he was speaking there came another great wave against the raft and broke it up altogether; but Ulysses kept hold of one of the planks of which it was made with his arms and legs, and got astride of it. Then he stripped off the clothes that Calypso had given him, and jumped into the sea with the veil under him, and spread out his hands to swim. And the god of the sea laughed when he saw him, and said: "Swim away; you will have trouble enough before you get safely home." But the goddess Athené did not forget him. She stopped the other winds from blowing, but left the north wind, for that would keep him on his way. And so he swam for two days and two nights. On the third day there was a calm, though there was still a great swell in the sea, as there always is when the wind has been high. And Ulysses saw the land from the top of a great wave, and it was close at hand. Very glad was he to see it, as glad as children to see their father when he has been ill a long time and is now well again. But when he looked again he saw that there was no place where he could land, for the cliffs rose straight out of the sea, and the waves dashed high against them. And Ulysses thought: "Now what shall I do? I see the land, indeed, but I cannot set my foot upon it. If I swim to it, then a wave may dash me on the rocks and kill me. And if I swim along the shore till I find a place where I may land, then some monster of the sea may lay hold of me."

But while he was thinking, a great wave caught him and carried him on towards the cliffs. He caught hold of a jutting rock that was there, and clung to it with all his might till the wave had spent its force, so that he was not dashed against the face of the cliff. Nevertheless, when the water flowed back, he could not keep his hold on the rock, but was carried out to the deep. After this he swam along outside the breakers looking for a place where it was calm, or for a harbour, if such there might be. At last he came to where a river ran into the sea. The place was free from rocks, and sheltered from the winds, and Ulysses felt the stream of the river, for it was fresh, in the salt water of the river. And he prayed to the god of the river, saying: "Hear me, O king, and help, for I am flying from the anger of the god of the sea." And the river god heard him, and stayed his stream, and made the water smooth before him. So, at last, he won his way to land. His knees were bent under him, and he could not lift his arms, and the salt water ran out of his mouth and his nose. He was breathless and speechless, very near, indeed, to death. But, after a while, he came to himself. Then he loosed the veil from under him, and threw it into the stream of the river, and did not look behind him when he threw it.

This done, he lay down on the rushes by the river side. And first he kissed the earth, so glad was he to feel it again under him; yet he doubted what he should do. If he slept there by the river, the dew and the heat might kill him, for it was cold in the morning; and if he went into the wood and lay down there to sleep, then some wild beast might devour him. It seemed better to go to the wood. So he went. And in the wood he found two olive trees growing together. So thickly did they grow that neither wind, nor sun, nor rain made its way through the shade. Ulysses crept underneath them, and found a great quantity of dead leaves, enough to shelter a man, or even two men. Right glad was Ulysses to see the place, and he crept under the trees and covered himself with leaves; and sleep came down upon him, and he forgot all his troubles.

Nausicaa

While Ulysses was still asleep, Athené thought how she might make friends for him in this new country to which he had come. So she went to the palace of the king of the country, and to that room of the palace in which the king's daughter slept. This daughter was called Nausicaa, and she was as beautiful a girl as there was in the whole world. And Athené made Nausicaa dream a dream, and the dream was this. She thought that a very dear friend of hers, a girl of the same age, daughter of a famous sailor called Dymas, stood by her bed-side and spoke to her. And what the girl seemed to say in the dream was this:—

"Nausicaa, how is it that your good mother has such a careless child? All your clothes lie unwashed, and this though your wedding day will soon be here, when you must have clean clothing for yourself and for your bridesmaids. The bride who is prepared with these things is well spoken of by everybody. As soon as it is morning, rise from your bed and go and wash the clothes, and I will come with you to help you. But first go to the king, your father, and ask him to give you a waggon and mules to draw it, that you may take the clothes to the washing places near the sea."

When Nausicaa woke in the morning, she remembered her dream, and all the words that her friend had said came back to her. So she went to look for her father and mother. Her mother she found spinning with her maids; the yarn that they were spinning was dyed with a lovely purple, of the colour of the sea. And her mother said that the clothes certainly should be washed. Then Nausicaa went to look for her father. Him she found, just as he was going to hold a council with his chiefs. She said to him: "Father, let me have the waggon with the mules, that I may take the clothes to the river to wash them. You like to have clean robes when you go to the council, and there are my five brothers, too, who like to be nicely dressed for the dance."

But she said nothing about her wedding day, for she was a little shy. But her father knew what she was thinking about, and said:

"Dear child, I don't grudge you the mules, nor the waggon, nor anything else. The men shall get them ready for you."

So he called to his men, and they made the waggon ready, and harnessed the mules. And Nausicaa brought down the clothes that had to be washed from her chamber, and put them in the waggon. And her mother filled a basket with good things for her daughter and her maids to eat, and she gave them a skin bottle of wine, and a flask of olive oil, to be used after they had bathed. So Nausicaa and her maids got into the waggon, and she took the reins in her hands, and touched the mules with her whip. The mules started off at a trot, and did not halt till they reached the places by the river where the clothes were to be washed.

The girls undid the harness from the mules, and let them feed on the sweet clover that grew by the river side. And they took the clothes from the waggon, and put them into trenches that had been dug out for washing places. If they had tried to wash them in the river itself, they would have been carried away by the stream. The trenches were filled with water, but it was quite still. So they laid the clothes in them, and trod on them and washed them till all were quite clean. Then they took them out of the trenches, and laid them to dry on the shingle by the sea. After this they all bathed in the sea, and anointed themselves with the olive oil. Then they sat down to eat and drink by the river side. And when they had had enough, they got up to have a game at ball. As they played, they sang, and Nausicaa led the singing. They were tall and beautiful, all of them, but the princess was taller than all the others.

So when they had ended their play, and had taken up the dry clothes from the shingle where they had been laid, and had folded them up, and put them in the waggon, and were about to harness the mules, this thing happened. Athené put it into the mind of the princess to take up the ball, and throw it for sport to one of the maids, though, as has been said, the play was ended. So wide did she throw it that it fell into the river, and all the maids cried out, fearing that it might be lost. So loudly did they cry, that they woke Ulysses. And he said to himself: "What land is this to which I have come? I wonder whether the people who live in it are savage or kind to strangers? And what was this cry that I heard? It sounded to me like the voice of nymphs." Then he looked out from the place where he was lying, and saw the princess and her maids. They were not far from him, for they had come down to the river to look for the ball. So he broke a bough full of leaves from off a tree which stood by, and twisted it round his middle, and came out of his hiding place, and went towards the maids. They were very much afraid when they saw him, and ran away; and indeed he looked very wild and fierce. But Nausicaa did not run, but stood where she was. Then Ulysses said to himself: "Shall I go up to her and clasp her knees?" (This was what people used to do in those days, when they wanted to ask a great favour.) "But perhaps this will make her angry. Would it not be better to stand where I am, and speak?"

This he did, saying: "O queen, I beg you to be kind to me. Maybe you are a goddess. But if you are a woman, then your father is a happy man, and happy your brothers, and happiest of all he who is to be your husband. Never did I see man or woman so fair. You are like a young palm-tree that I once saw springing up by a temple in the island of Delos. Have pity on me, for I have been cast up here by the sea, and have nothing. Give me something to put on—a wrapper of linen, maybe, and show me the way to the city."

Nausicaa said: "You do not look like a bad or foolish man; as for the sad plight in which you are, the gods give good luck to some, and bad luck to others. You shall have clothing and food, and everything that you need. And I will take you to the city, for I am daughter to the king of this country. And the name of the country, if you wish to know it, is the Island of Phaeacia."

Then the princess turned to the maids, and said: "Why do you run away when you see a man? No one comes here to do us harm, for the gods love us and take care of us. And besides, we live in an island, and so are safe. But if some one upon whom trouble has fallen comes here, we ought to help him. Give this man, therefore, food and drink, and let him wash in the river in some place that is out of the wind."

So the maids led him down to the river, and gave him clothes: a tunic to wear next to his skin, and a cloak to put over the tunic. Also they gave him a flask of olive oil, to use after he had his bath. Then they left him to himself, and he bathed in the river, and washed the salt from his skin, and out of his hair, and rubbed the oil on his body, and put on the tunic and the cloak. And Athené made him look taller and fairer than he was, and caused the hair to grow thicker and darker on his head. So he sat down on the sea-shore, and waited. And when the princess saw him, she said: "Surely it is the gods who have brought this man here. When I saw him first, I thought that he was not uncomely, but now he seems more like a god than a man. I should be well contented to have such a man for my husband, and perhaps he may be willing to stay in this country." Then she turned to the maids, and said: "Give the stranger food and drink." So they gave him, and he ate ravenously, for he had had a long fast, for it was now the third day since the raft had been broken by the sea, and all the store of food and drink which Calypso had given him had been lost.

Then Nausicaa told the maids to harness the mules, and she said to Ulysses: "Come stranger, with me, and I will take you to my father's house. But now listen, and do as I shall tell you; as long as we are in the country, follow with the maids, and keep close to the waggon. But when we come to the city, then drop behind. This is how you will know the place. There is a narrow passage leading to the city gate, and on each side of the passage there is a harbour. Then you will see a grove of poplar trees, and a spring in the midst of the grove, with grass round it. Stay there till I shall have had time to reach my father's house. Now the reason why I would have you do so is this. I do not wish the common people to gossip about me. If they were to see you following close after the chariot, one of them might say: 'Who is this tall and handsome stranger that comes with Nausicaa? Will he be her husband? Is he a god come down from heaven, or is he a man from some place over the sea? The princess is too proud, it seems, to marry one of us.' I would not have such words spoken about me. Stay, then, in the grove till you think that I have got to my home. Then come out, and pass through the gate, and ask for the king's palace. Any one, even a child, can tell you the way, for there is not another house in the city like it. And when you have come to it, pass quickly through the hall to the place where my mother sits. It is on one side of the hearth, and my father's is on the other. Do not speak to him, but lay hold of my mother's knees, and beg of her that she will send you safely home."

Then she touched the mules with the whip, and they set off. But the princess was careful not to drive so fast but that Ulysses and the maids could easily keep up with the waggon. And when the sun was about to set, they came to the city, and Ulysses stayed behind the grove, but Nausicaa with the maids went on to the palace. When she came thither, her brothers unyoked the mules from the waggon and carried the linen into the house, and she went to her room, where her maid lit a fire for her and prepared a meal.

Alcinous

After a while Ulysses rose to go into the city, and Athené spread a mist about him so that the passers-by might not see him as he went. Also she took upon her the shape of a young girl who was carrying a pitcher, and met him.

Ulysses asked her: "My child, can you tell me where King Alcinoüs lives? I am a stranger here."

She answered: "I will show you his abode; it is close to the home of my father." So she led the way, and Ulysses followed her. Much did he wonder, as he went, at all he saw—the harbour, and the ships, and the place of assembly, and the walls, till they came to the palace. Athené said: "This is the king's house." Further, she said—and now Ulysses knew that it was Athené and not a girl that was speaking—"Go in, fear nothing; the fearless man always fares best. And look first for the queen. Her name is Areté. Never was there a wife more loved by her husband, or a queen more honoured by her people. Be sure that if she favours you, you have come to the end of your troubles, and will see your dear land of Ithaca again."

When she had said this, Athené vanished out of sight, and Ulysses went into the palace. A wonderful place it was, as bright as if the sun had been shining in it. The walls were of brass, and the doors were of gold, and the posts on which the doors were hung were of silver, and along the sides of the hall were golden chairs on which the chiefs were used to sit when they were invited to a feast. By each seat was the golden statue of a man, holding a torch in his hand, so that the hall might be lighted when it was night. There were fifty maid-servants in the house; half of them were grinding corn, and half of them were weaving robes. All round the house were beautiful gardens, full of fig-trees and apples, and pears, and pomegranates, and olives. They never are harmed by frost or by drought, and there is never a time when some fruit is not ripe. Also there was a vineyard, and this bore grapes all the year round. Some of them were hanging dried in the sun, and some were being gathered, and some were just turning red. Also there were beds of beautiful flowers, and in the middle were two fountains which never grew dry.

Ulysses could not help looking for a short time at all these wonderful and beautiful things. There were many people in the hall, but no one saw him, for, as we know, there was a mist all around him which hid him from them. So he went on to where the queen was sitting, and knelt down before her, and put his hands on her knees. And as he did this, the mist cleared away from round him, and all the people in the hall saw him quite plainly.

He said: "O queen, I beg a favour of you. I pray you, and your husband, and your children to help me. Send me to my home, for I know that you help strangers to travel across the sea."

And when he had said this, he sat down among the ashes on the hearth. Then said one of the nobles that were in the hall—he was the very oldest man that there was in all the land: "King Alcinoüs, do not let this stranger sit there among the ashes. Tell him to sit upon a chair, and give him something to eat and drink."

Then the king told his eldest son to take the stranger by the hand and raise him up, and make him sit down on his own seat. This the young man did. And a servant brought a basin and poured water over Ulysses' hands, and the housekeeper brought him something to eat and to drink. The king said: "This man begs a favour of us, that we may take him to his home. To-morrow we will have an Assembly, and will consider how we may best do this. And now you can go all of you to your homes." But before they went, Ulysses said: "I could tell you, my friends, of many troubles that I have suffered. But first I must eat and drink; that a man must do, however unhappy he may be. I will say only this, when you come together to-morrow, do your best to help me in this matter. I should be content to die if I could only see my home again."

This they all promised to do, and so departed.

When Ulysses was left alone, the queen looked at him somewhat more closely, and she saw that the clothes which he wore had been made by herself and her maids, and she said: "From what country have you come, and who gave you these clothes?"

Then Ulysses told her how he had travelled many miles across the sea on the raft, and how the raft had been broken, and how he had got to the shore after swimming for two days and two nights and more, and how Nausicaa had found him, and had had pity on him, and brought him to the city. The queen said: "I blame my daughter that she did not bring you with her. That was what she should have done." "Nay, lady," said Ulysses, "she would have brought me, but I would not come, for I did not like that the girl should be blamed."

Then said the king: "Eat and drink in peace, stranger. We will do what you wish, and take you to your home. There are no men in all the world who can row better than the Phaeacian youths. You will lie down to sleep, and before you wake they will have carried you to your own country. They can go to the farthest part of the world, and can come back the same day, and not be tired."

Ulysses was glad to hear what the king said, and he prayed in his heart: "May the king do what he promises, and may I come in peace to my own land."

Then the queen told the maids to make a bed ready for the stranger. And they went with torches in their hands and made it ready, and came again and said to Ulysses: "Stranger, your bed is ready." So he followed them. Right glad was he to sleep after all that he had suffered.

Ulysses among the Phaeacians

The next day the Assembly of the people was held. Many came to it, so that the king's hall was filled from one end to the other. For Athené had taken upon her the shape of the king's herald, and gone through the city, saying: "Come, captains and counsellors of the Phaeacians, and hear about this stranger who has lately come to the king's palace." So they came, and they marvelled much when they saw Ulysses, for Athené had made him fairer and fatter and stronger.

The king rose in his place, and said: "This stranger has come to my hall. I do not know who he is, or whence he comes, whether from the east or the west. And he begs us to convey him safely to his home. Now this, as you know, is a thing that we have been used from old time to do for strangers. Go, then, and choose out a ship. Let it be new—one that never has been on the sea before. And pick out fifty and two rowers. Let them be the best and strongest that there are in the country. When you have done this, come to my hall and feast. And let the minstrel come also, for the gods have given him the gift of song, and there is nothing better than song to make glad the hearts of men." So the chiefs of the people went and did as the king commanded. They chose a ship, and they chose rowers, and moored the ship by the shore. This done, they went back to the king's hall. And he had bidden his servants prepare a great feast for them, eight swine and twelve sheep and two oxen.

And when the people were ready to begin, there came two servants of the king leading the singer by the hand, for he was blind. They made him sit down in a silver chair in the middle of the hall; they hung his harp on a rail that there was above his head where he could easily reach it. And by his side they put a table, and on the table a basket full of good things, and a cup of wine so that he might drink when he pleased.

Then the people began to eat and drink, and when they had had enough, the singer sang. And what he sang was this: how there had been a fierce quarrel at a great sacrifice between Achilles, who was the bravest man among the Greeks, and Ulysses, who was the wisest, and how Agamemnon was glad to see it, because a prophet had told him that when wisdom and valour should fall out the end of Troy would soon come. As he sang, Ulysses held his cloak before his face to hide his tears, for he was ashamed that the people should see them. When the song was at an end, he wiped them away, and sat like the others; but when the chief called out that it should be sung again, for indeed it pleased them much, then he wept again. But the king was the only man to see it.

After this the king said: "Now, let us go and have games as is our custom, boxing and wrestling and running, so that this stranger may see what we can do." The best of the boxers was the king's eldest son, and he said to Ulysses: "Stranger, why do you sit there so sad and silent? Why do you not try your skill in some game?"

Ulysses answered: "I am in no mind for sport and games. I can think of nothing but how I can get back to my home."

Then another of the young men, who had won the prize for wrestling, said: "Well, stranger, you have not the look of one who is skilful in boxing and wrestling. I should say that you were one who travels about to buy and sell."

Then Ulysses was angry, and said: "That is a foolish speech. Some men have good looks, and some can speak wisely. I find no fault with your looks, but your words are idle. I know these games right well, and in old time was skilful in them, but I have suffered much, both in war and in many journeys over land and sea. Yet I will show you what I can do."

And he took up a quoit, heavier than any of those which the Phaeacians had used, and sent it with a whirl through the air. And one of the company—so it seemed, but it was really Athené in the shape of a man—marked the place where it fell, and said: "Stranger, even a blind man could see that there is no one here to match you in strength."

Ulysses was glad to hear these words, for he thought: "Now I have a friend here;" and he said aloud: "Now let any one match this throw. Ay, and if any one will box with me, or wrestle with me, let him stand up. I will even run a race, though in this I can hardly be the winner, so much have I suffered on the sea."

Then said the king: "Stranger, you speak well: we Phaeacians are not good at boxing and wrestling. Swift of foot we are, and we love feasts and dances, and music and gay clothing. Of these things no man knows more than do we."

This the king said, wishing to make peace. Also he said: "Now let each one of the princes give to this stranger two coats, an inner and an outer, and a talent of gold. And let the prince whose words made him angry, give a double gift."

To this they all agreed; and the prince who had given him offence gave him also a sword, which had a silver hilt and an ivory scabbard. And as he gave it, he said: "Father, I wish you well; if there was any offence in my words, let the winds carry it away. The gods grant that you may see again your wife, and your friends, and your own country!"

And Ulysses answered: "And I also wish you well! May you live happily, and never miss this handsome sword which you have given me!"

Then the other princes gave him their gifts. And the king said to the queen: "Now let them fetch a chest, the best you have, and do you put in it two coats, an outer and an inner. And I will give this stranger a beautiful cup of gold that is my own. So will he remember me all the days of his life, when he sits at the feast and drinks out of the cup."

So they brought a chest from the queen's chamber, and all the gifts that the princes had given to Ulysses were put in it, and she herself with her own hands put in it the outer coat and the inner. And when the chest was filled with these things, she said to Ulysses: "Now look to the lid, and fasten it so that no man may rob you as you sleep, while the ship takes you back to your native country."

So Ulysses fixed the lid, tying it with a very cunning knot that Circé had taught him. After this he went to the bath. And as he came from the bath, Nausicaa met him, and wondered to see how handsome he was, and she said: "Farewell, stranger. When you come to your own country, think of me, for indeed you owe me your life."

And Ulysses said: "Surely, Nausicaa; I will honour you as I would honour one of the goddesses, all the days of my life, for indeed I owe you my life."

Then he went into the hall, and sat down by the side of the king, and there came in a steward leading the blind singer by the hand. Now there had been set before Ulysses the chine of a wild boar, for this is the dish which was served to a guest whom his host wished to honour above all others. And he took his knife, and cut from it a great helping, and said to a servant: "Now carry this to the singer, for there is no one whom men should more honour than him who sings of the great deeds of famous men." So the servant bore the dish to the singer, and laid it upon his knees. After a while, when the company had had enough of meat and drink, Ulysses said to the singer: "You sing right well of the toil and trouble which the Greeks had before the great city of Troy. Truly you could not have done this thing better if you had been there yourself. Come now, sing to us of the Wooden Horse which was made after the device of Epeius, but it was Athené who put it into his heart. Tell us also how Ulysses contrived that it should be dragged up into the very citadel of Troy, after he had first hidden inside it the bravest of the Greek chiefs. Sing us now this song, and I shall know that the gods themselves have taught you."

Then the minstrel sang how the Wooden Horse was made, and how Ulysses, with certain of the bravest of the Greek chiefs, hid themselves within, and how the rest of the forces pretended to depart, burning their camp, and sailing away in their ships, but they did not sail farther than to a certain island that there was close by. Also he told how the people of Troy dragged the horse within the walls of the city into the public square where they used to meet and hold their Assembly; also how the people sat round it, and the chief men among them gave their advice what should be done with this strange thing. Some said: "Let us cleave it open, and see what there may be inside." Others said: "Let us take it to the brow of the hill and cast it down;" but some advised that it should be left where it was, as a thank-offering to the gods who had delivered the city from their enemies. And this counsel prevailed, for it was the doom of the city that it should be taken by means of the Wooden Horse.

So he sang, and the heart of Ulysses was melted within him as he listened, and the tears ran down his cheeks. But only the king perceived. And the king said to the singer: "Cease now from your singing, for ever since you began, this stranger has not ceased to shed tears: we are come together to make merry and to rejoice, and to give gifts to this stranger, and to send him to his home." Then he turned to Ulysses, and said: "Tell us now your name, O stranger: tell us also from what land you come, for if our ships are to take you to your home, they must know what course to take that they may carry you thither. For, indeed, our ships are not as the ships of other men. They have no need of rudders or steersmen, but they know of themselves which way they should go. Tell us therefore your name, and the name of the land from which you come. I did perceive that you wept when you heard the fate of Troy. Had you, perchance, kinsman, or brother, or friend among those who perished at Troy?" Then said Ulysses: "O king, what shall I tell you first, and what last, for I have endured many things. But first I will tell you my name. Know, then, that I am ULYSSES, King of Ithaca." And afterwards he told them the story of all that he had suffered from the day that he had sailed away from Troy down to his coming to the island of Calypso.

Ithaca

When Ulysses had finished his story, the king and all his people sat for a time saying nothing. After a while, the king said: "Ulysses, you shall have your wish; we will carry you to your home. This we will do to-morrow, for now it is time for bed." Then he turned to the princes and said: "This guest of ours is a brave man, and has suffered much; let us give him a special gift to show that we honour him. He has a chest full of clothes and gold already; and now let us give him kettles and bowls to use in his home. These you may bring to-morrow, and now you can go to your homes."

The next day the princes brought the kettles and bowls, and the king stowed them away with his own hands under the benches of the ship. When this was finished they all went to the palace, and sat down to a great feast. But Ulysses kept watching the sun, wishing that the day was finished, so much did he want to see his home again.

At last he stood up and said: "O king, you and your people have been very kind to me; and now send me home, I beg you. Let us have the parting cup, and then let me go." So the king told his squire to mix the cup. And the squire mixed it, and served it out. And all the people in the hall drank, and as they drank they prayed that the stranger might have a happy return to his home. And when the cup was given to Ulysses, he stood up and put it into the hand of the queen, and said: "O queen, farewell; I pray that you may be happy with your husband, and your children, and your people." And when he had said this, he turned and left the palace. The king sent his squire to show him the way to the ship; also some of the women who waited on the queen carried food and wine, and a rug on which he might sleep in the ship. The chest, with the clothes and the gold, was taken down also and put into the ship.

Then the rowers made all things ready. They put the rug in the hinder part of the vessel, and Ulysses climbed into the ship, and lay down upon it. Then the men unfastened the ropes which made the ship fast to the shore, and took their places on the benches, and began to row. As soon as ever they touched the water with their oars, Ulysses fell into a deep sleep. And the men rowed, and the ship sprang forward more quickly than a chariot with four horses travels over the plain. A hawk could not fly through the air more swiftly.

When the morning star rose in the sky, the ship came to Ithaca. Now there was a harbour in the island which the rowers knew very well. It was sheltered from the waves, and at the head of it was a great olive tree, and near the olive tree a cave. Here the men ran the ship ashore, and they took up Ulysses in his rug, for he was still fast asleep, and laid him down under the olive tree, and by his side they put all his provisions. After this, they got into their ship again, and started for home.

After a while Ulysses woke up from his sleep. Now Athené had spread a great mist over all the place, and Ulysses did not know where he was, so different did it look from what it really was. And he cried out: "Where am I? What shall I do? Where shall I put these goods of mine? Surely these Phaeacians have not done what they promised, but have taken me to a strange land. But first let me see whether they have left me the things which belonged to me." So he counted the clothes, and the gold, and the kettles, and found that nothing was missing. Still he was in great trouble, for he did not know where he was. While he walked to and fro, Athené met him. She had taken the shape of a handsome young shepherd. When Ulysses saw her, he was glad, though, indeed, he did not know that it was the goddess, not a shepherd, that he saw. He said: "Friend, you are the first man that I have seen in this country. Tell me where I am, and help me. Is this an island, or is it part of the mainland?"

Athené said: "You must have come from a very far country not to know this place, for, indeed, it is a country which most men know. This is the island of Ithaca, a good land, though it is not a good place for horses. Yet it is fertile, and gives good pasture for sheep and goats, and the vineyards bear good wine." Ulysses was very glad to hear this, still he thought it better not to let the stranger know who he really was. So he made up this story: "I come from the island of Crete. I got into trouble, for I killed the king's son, who would have robbed me of some of my goods. Then I made a bargain with certain Phoenicians that they should take me and my goods either to Pylos or to Elis. This they would have done but for the contrary winds which drove them to this place. So they put me out of the ship while I slept, and my possessions with me."

When Ulysses had finished his story, Athené changed her shape again, becoming like a woman fair and tall. And she laughed, and said: "O Ulysses, he would be a cunning man who could cheat you. Here you are in your own country again, and you are still making up these tales about yourself. Well, you are the wisest among mortals, and I am Athené, the goddess of Wisdom. I have always been used to stand by you and help you. And so I will do hereafter. First let us hide these goods of yours. Afterwards we will consider what should best be done. But you must be silent, telling no one who you are. So shall you come at last to your own again."

Ulysses answered: "O goddess, it is hard for any man to know you, for you take many shapes. You were always good to me when we were fighting against Troy, and you helped me the other day when I was among the Phaeacians. But now tell me truly: What is this place? You say that it is Ithaca, but it seems to me a strange country."

Then Athené scattered the mist so that Ulysses could see the place as it really was, and he knew it to be Ithaca, and he kneeled down, and kissed the ground, for he was very thankful in his heart.

And Athené said: "Now let us hide away your goods in the cave." So Ulysses took the clothes, and the gold, and all his other possessions, and stored them away in the cave, and Athené rolled a great stone to the mouth of the cave to keep them safe.

After this Athené asked him how he meant to get possession of his kingdom again. She told him how that there was a great crowd of princes from Ithaca and the islands round about, who had come hoping to marry Penelopé, and how they sat day after day in his palace and wasted his substance. "And how," said she, "will you, being one man, prevail over them who are so many?" "If you will stand by me, and help me," said he, "I will fight against a hundred, ay, and against three hundred."

Then said Athené: "I will so change you that no man shall know you. I will make the skin of your face and hands withered and cold, and take the colour out of your hair, and make your eyes dull. The Suitors will think nothing of you, and even your wife and your son will not know you. Now go to the house of Eumaeus, who looks after the swine, for he is faithful to you; I will go to Sparta and fetch home your son Telemaˇchus, for he is gone there seeking news of you."

Ulysses said: "Why did he go when you knew all and might have told him? Is he also to suffer what I have suffered?" "Nay," answered Athené, "it was only right that he should bestir himself, looking for his father. Be contented; all will be well."

So she touched him with her rod. And when she touched him, his skin withered, like the skin of an old man, and his hair lost its colour, and his eyes grew dim. And his clothes also looked torn and dirty. Also the goddess gave him a stag's skin, very shabby, with the hair worn from it. And she put a staff in his hand, and a battered wallet, such as beggars carry, which was fastened to his shoulders by a rope.

Eumaeus

W hen Ulysses went away from Ithaca to fight against the Trojans, he left in charge of the swine a certain man, whose name was Eumaeus. He was a slave, but nevertheless he was a king's son, and this was how he came to be a slave. His father was king of a certain island, and he had in his household a Phoenician woman, and this woman was nurse to his son. She had been stolen away from her home by some people from Taphos—the Taphians were great stealers of men—and sold to the king. When the child was some five or six years old, there came a Phoenician ship to the island, with rings and bracelets and other fine things which women love, and the Phoenician woman, because they were from the same country, made friends with them and told her story. They said to her that they knew her father and mother, and that they were rich people, and promised, if she would come with them, to take her to her old home. Then the woman said that she would come with them. And that she might pay them for her passage, and also have something for herself, she took the little boy, the king's son, with her. Also she carried away three gold cups that were in the house. So the Phoenicians sailed away with the woman and the child. On the sixth day she died, and they threw her body overboard, and carried the child to Ithaca, where they sold him to the father of Ulysses.

And now Ulysses went to the place where this Eumaeus lived and kept the swine. There were twelve sties round a very big courtyard, and in each sty fifty swine. Also, to keep away thieves, he had four watchdogs, very large and fierce. The swineherd was in his house, making a pair of sandals; he had three men who were looking after the swine in the fields, for though he was a slave, he had other men under him; a fourth was driving a fat hog to the city, which was to be killed and cooked for the Suitors. When Ulysses came into the courtyard the four dogs ran at him. So he dropped his staff, and sat down on the ground, for dogs, they say, will not bite a man that is sitting. Yet they might have hurt him, for they were very fierce, but Eumaeus heard their barking, and came out of his house, and drove away the dogs with stones. Then he said to Ulysses: "Old man, the dogs had nearly killed you. That would have been a great grief to me, and I have grief enough already. My lord has gone away, and no one knows where he is; perhaps he is wandering about without food to eat, and others all the time are eating the fat beasts that belong to him. But come into my house, old man, and tell me your story."

So Ulysses went into the house, and the swineherd made him sit down on his own bed. There was a heap of brushwood, with the skin of a wild goat spread over it. Ulysses was glad to find him so kind, and said: "Now may the gods reward you for your kindness to a stranger!"

The swineherd answered: "It would be a wicked thing not to be kind to a stranger. But I have little to give. If my master had stayed at home, I should be better off. He would have given me a house and land and a wife. Good masters, and indeed Ulysses was a good master, give such gifts to servants who serve them well. And I have served him well. Once there was not a man in all these islands who had better flocks of sheep and herds of cattle and droves of swine than he; but of late years there has been a great waste in his house, for the princes of the island assemble in his house and eat and drink, yes, and waste in a most shameful way."

Then he went out and took a small pig from one of the sties, and prepared a meal for the stranger, and mixed wine for him in a cup made of ivywood. And Ulysses sat, and ate and drank. Not a word did he say, for he was busy thinking how he might punish the Suitors who were wasting his goods in this way.

At last he said: "Friend, who was this master of yours, who you say has been absent from his home so long? Perhaps I may have seen him, for I have wandered over many lands, and have seen and known many men."

Then said Eumaeus: "This is what all the travellers say, but we hear no truth from them. There is not a vagabond-fellow comes here but our queen must see him, and ask him questions about her husband, weeping all the while. And you, I dare say, for a cloak or a tunic, would tell a wonderful story of your own."

Then said the false beggar: "Listen to me: I tell you that Ulysses will return; yes, he will come before the next new moon. And you shall give me a gift such as men give to those who bring them good news. You shall give me a coat and a cloak. But, till my words are found to come true, I will take nothing from you. I hate the man who tells lies because he is poor: I would sooner die than do such a thing myself."

The swineherd answered: "Old man, you will never get the coat and the cloak from me. But don't talk about these things any more. It breaks my heart to think of my dear master. And now I am in trouble about my young master, his son. For he has gone to some strange places, hoping to get news about his father. Surely he has lost his wits to do such a thing. For the Suitors, I hear, lie in wait for him to kill him as he comes back. And so all my master's house will perish. But let these things be. Tell me now, old man, who you are, and from what country you come."

Ulysses said: "It would take a long time to tell you all my story. We might sit here, and eat and drink for a whole year, while I told you of all my adventures. But something you shall hear.

"I am a man of Crete, and my father's name was Castor. He had other sons, whose mother was a free woman; but my mother was a slave. While he lived he treated me just as he did my brothers, but when he died they gave me a very small share of his goods, and took away my home from me. Nevertheless, I did well for myself, for I was brave, and my neighbors thought well of me, so that I married a rich wife. There was not a man in the country who was fonder of fighting than I was—yes, even of taking part in an ambush, a thing which tries a man's courage more than anything else. Nine times did I go with my ship—for I had a ship and a crew of my own—on various adventures. The tenth time I went with the king of Crete to fight against the city of Troy. And when we had taken the city, I came back to the country with the king. For a month I stopped at home. And then I went to Egypt; and this time I had nine ships, for there were many who were willing to go with me. We had a fair wind, and got to our journey's end in four days. But then my men did much mischief to the people of the land, laying waste their fields, and carrying away their wives and children. And when I wished to stop them, they would not listen to me. Then the Egyptians gathered an army and came upon us. They killed many, and they took the rest prisoners. But I ran up to the king of Egypt, where he sat in his chariot, and begged him to have mercy on me. And he listened to me. So kind was he that I stayed with him for seven years, and became a rich man. Would that I had been content! But in the eighth year a Phoenician merchant came to the place, and promised me riches without end if I would go with him. So I gathered all that I had together, and went with him. For a year I stayed with him. Then he put me in his ship, meaning to take me to Africa, and to sell me there for a slave. But the ship was wrecked on the way, and I was the only one on board that was not drowned. I caught hold of the mast, and floated on it for nine days; and on the tenth I came to the country of King Pheidon. And there I heard tell of Ulysses; for the king was keeping his goods for him while he was on a journey to inquire of an oracle. From this place I took my passage in a merchant ship, but the sailors planned to sell me for a slave. So they bound me, and put me in the hold of the ship. But one day, when they were having their supper on shore, I loosed myself from my bonds, and leapt into the sea, and, swimming to land, so escaped."

Ulysses, we see, had always a tale ready. The swineherd said: "Your story makes me feel for you, for, indeed, you must have suffered much. But I don't believe what you tell me about my master, King Ulysses. All the strangers that come to this place have something to say about him; for they know that it is what we want to hear. I live here alone, and take care of the swine. But every now and then the queen sends for me, saying that some one has come bringing news of the king. So I go, and I find the man, with a crowd of people round him asking him questions. Some of them really wish that the king would come home, but there are many who hope that he has perished, because they sit here idle and waste his goods. But I am not one of those who ask questions; I never have done it since a certain Aetolian cheated me with the story that he told. He had killed a man, he said, and had been obliged to leave his home, and I treated him kindly, and gave him the best that I had. And the fellow told me that he had seen my master with the king of Crete, and that he was then busy mending his ships, which had been damaged by a storm. He would come back, the fellow said, at the beginning of summer, or, at the latest, at harvest time, and would bring great riches with him. So, old man, do not try to please me with idle tales about Ulysses. I pity you, and try to help you because you are poor, but I wish to hear no lies about my master."

"Well," said Ulysses, "you are very slow to believe. But now listen to me; if your master comes back, as I say he will, then you shall give me a coat and a cloak. And if he does not come back, then your men may throw me down from a rock into the sea, as a warning to others that they should not tell false tales."

The swineherd said: "This is idle talk. What good would it do me to kill you? What would people say of me, if I took a stranger into my home, and then slew him? How should I ever pray to the gods again, if I had done such a thing? But enough of this. It is supper time, and I wish that my men had come back that we might sup together."

While he was speaking the men came back. And the swineherd said to them: "Fetch a fat pig from the sty, for I have a stranger here, and I should like to give him a good meal."

So they fetched a five-year-old hog, and they dressed the meat for their supper. And the swineherd gave to Ulysses the chine, for this was the best portion.

Now it was a very cold night, and it rained without ceasing, for the wind was blowing from the west, and this commonly brings rain in those parts. And after supper Ulysses thought he would try his host, to see what he would do; so he told this story:—

"A certain night when we were fighting against Troy, we laid our ambush near the city. Menelaüs and Ulysses and I were the leaders of it. We sat hidden in the reeds, and the night was cold, so that the snow lay upon our shields. Now all the others had their cloaks, but I had left mine in my tent. When the night was three parts spent, I said to Ulysses, who lay close by me: 'Here I am—I, without a cloak. I a leader, to perish of cold!' Now Ulysses was always ready, knowing what to do. 'Hush!' he said, 'lest some one should hear you.' Then he said to the others: 'I have had a dream, which makes me sure that we are in danger. We are a long way from the ships, and these are too far off us. Let some one run to King Agamemnon, and ask him to send us more men.' Then Thuas stood up, and said, 'I will run and tell him,' and he threw off his cloak, and ran. And I took the cloak, and slept warmly in it."

The swineherd said: "Old man, that is a good tale. And to-night, too, you shall have a cloak to keep you from the cold. But to-morrow you must put on your old rags again!" And he gave him his own cloak.

Ulysses and His Son

The next day, while the swineherd was making the breakfast ready, Ulysses heard a step outside, and because the dogs did not bark, he said: "Friend, here comes some one whom you know, for the dogs do not bark." And while he was still speaking, Telemaˇchus stood in the doorway. It should be told that he had landed from his ship at the nearest place that there was to the swineherd's cottage, for he knew that he was a good man and true.

When the swineherd saw Telemaˇchus, he dropped the bowl that he had in his hand, for he was mixing some wine with hot water for him and his guest to drink with their breakfast, and ran to him, and kissed his head, and his eyes, and his hands. As a father kisses an only son who comes back to him after being away for ten years, so did the swineherd kiss Telemaˇchus. The beggar, for such Ulysses seemed to be, rose from his place, and would have given it to the young man. But Telemaˇchus would not take it. So they three sat down, and ate and drank. And when they had finished, the young man said to the swineherd: "Who is this?" The swineherd answered: "He is a stranger, who has asked me for help. But now I pass him over to you, for you are my master, and I am your servant."

"Nay," said Telemaˇchus, "this cannot be. You call me master; but am I master in my own house? Do not the Suitors devour it? Does not even my mother doubt whether she will not forget the great Ulysses who is her husband, and follow one of these men? I will give this stranger food and clothes and a sword; but I will not take him into my house, for the Suitors are there, and they are haughty and insolent."

Ulysses heard the two talking, and he said: "But why do you bear with these men? Do the people hate you, that you cannot punish these insolent fellows as they deserve? Have you no kinsman to help you? I would sooner die than see such shameful things done in my house."

Telemaˇchus answered: "My people do not hate me, but they are very slow to help. As for kinsmen, I have none. For my grandfather, Laertes, was an only son, and so was my father Ulysses, and I myself have neither brother nor sister. So I have no one to stand by me, and these wicked men spoil my goods, with none to stop them, ay, and they even seek to kill me."

Then he said to the swineherd: "Go to my mother the queen, and tell her that I have come back safe. But see that no one hears you; and I will stay here till you return."

So the swineherd departed. And when he was gone, there came the goddess Athené, and she had the likeness of a tall and fair woman. Telemăchus did not see her, for it is not every one who can see the gods; but Ulysses saw her, and the dogs saw her, and whimpered for fear. She made a sign to Ulysses, and he went out of the house. Then she said: "Do not hide yourself from your son; tell him who you are, and plan with him how you may slay the Suitors. And remember that I am with you to help you."

Then she touched him with her golden wand. And all at once he had a new tunic and a new coat. Also he became taller and more handsome, and his cheeks grew rounder, and his hair and his beard grew darker. Having done this, she went away, and Ulysses went again into the cottage. Much did Telemăchus marvel to see him, and he cried:—

"Stranger, you are not the same that you were but a few moments ago. You have different clothes, and the colour of your skin is changed. Can it be that you are a god and not a man?"

"I am no god," said Ulysses; "I am your father, the father for whom you have been looking."

But Telemăchus could not believe what he said. "You cannot be my father," he answered. "No man could do what you have done, making yourself old and young as you please, and changing your clothes this way. Just now you were a shabby beggar, and now you are as one of the gods in heaven."

Ulysses answered: "Ay, but it is in very truth your father who has come back to his home after twenty years. As for what you so wonder at, it is Athené's work; it is she who makes me at one time like an old beggar in shabby clothes, and at another like a young prince, richly clad."

When he had said this he sat down, and Telemăchus threw his arms round his father's neck and shed many tears. After a while Telemăchus said to his father: "Tell me now, father, how you came back."

Ulysses said: "The Phaeacians brought me in a ship, and set me down on the shore of this island, and they brought many things with me, handsome presents that were made to me. These have I hidden in a cave. But now let us plan how we may slay these Suitors. Tell me how many there are of them. Should we make war upon them ourselves, or shall we get others to help us?"

Telemăchus said: "My father, you are, I know, a great warrior, but this thing we cannot do. These men are not ten, or twice ten, but more than a hundred. And they have a herald and a minstrel, and certain attendants."

Then said Ulysses: "To-morrow you must go to the palace, and take your place among the Suitors, and I will come like to a shabby beggar. If they behave themselves badly to me, endure it. Their time is nearly come; they shall soon be punished as they deserve. Be prudent, therefore. Also, when I give you a sign, then take away all the arms that hang in the hall, and stow them away in your chamber. And if any man ask you why you do this, say that they want cleaning, for the smoke has soiled them, and they are not such as Ulysses left them when he went away to Troy. And you might say also that it is not well to have weapons in a hall where men are used to feast, for the very sight of the steel makes men ready to quarrel. But keep two swords and two spears close at hand. These will be for you and me. And mind that you tell no one that I have come back—not my father, nor the swineherd, no, nor Penelopé herself."

While they were still talking, the swineherd came back from the city. But before he came into the house, Athené changed Ulysses back again into the shape of the old beggar man, for it was not well that he should know the truth until everything was ready.

Telemaˇchus said to him: "Have you brought back any news from the city? Have the Suitors who went out in a ship to kill me come back, or are they still watching for me?"

The swineherd said: "I cannot tell you this for a certainty. I thought it better to ask no questions in the city. But I saw a ship coming into the harbour, and I saw a number of men in it who had shields and spears. It may be that these were the Suitors, but I am not sure."

Then Telemaˇchus looked at Ulysses, but he was careful not to meet the eye of the swineherd.

Of the Dog Argus and Other Things

The next day Telema˘chus said to the swineherd: "I will go to the city, for my mother will not be easy till she sees my face. You will take the stranger with you that he may beg of any that may have a mind to give."

"Yes," said Ulysses, "that is what I desire. If a man must beg, 'tis better to beg in the city than in the country. And do you go first; I will follow a little later, when it will be warmer, for now I shall feel cold under these rags."

So Telema˘chus went on to the city, and very glad were his mother and the nurse to see him. He looked after certain business that he had to do, but all the time he had one thought always in his mind, how he and his father might kill the Suitors.

About noon the swineherd and Ulysses came to the city. Now just outside the wall there was a fountain, and there the two came across a certain Melanthius, who looked after the goats. When he saw the swineherd and his companion, he said: "Why do you bring beggars to the city? we have enough of them already." And he came up and kicked Ulysses on the thigh, thinking to push him over. But Ulysses stood firm. For a while he thought to himself: "Shall I knock out this fellow's brains with my club?" But he thought it better to endure. So the two went on to the palace. Now at the door of the courtyard there lay a dog, Argus by name, which had belonged to Ulysses in old time. He had reared him from a puppy, feeding him with his own hand; but before the dog had come to his full growth, his master had gone away to fight against Troy. While Argus was strong, men had used him in their hunting, when they went out to kill roe-deer and wild goats and hares. But now he was old no one looked after him, and he lay on a dunghill, and the lice swarmed on him. When he saw his old master, he knew him at once, and wagged his tail and drooped his ears, for he was too weak to get up from the place where he lay.

When Ulysses saw him, the tears came into his eyes, and he said to the swineherd: "Now this is strange, Eumaeus, that so good a dog, for I see that he is of a good breed, should lie here upon a dunghill."

The swineherd answered: "He belongs to a master who died far away from his home. Once upon a time there was no dog more swift or more strong; but his master is dead, and the careless women take no count of him. When the master is away, the slaves neglect their work. Surely it is true that a slave is but half a man." While the two were talking together, the dog Argus died. He had waited twenty years for his master to come back, and he saw him at last.

Then the swineherd and the beggar went into the hall where the Suitors sat at their meal. When Telemaˇchus saw them, he took bread and meat, as much as he could hold in his two hands, and bade a servant carry them to the beggar. Also, he bade the man tell him that he could go round among the Suitors and ask alms of them. So Ulysses went, stretching out his hand as beggars do. Some of the Suitors gave, for they saw that he was tall and strong, for all that he looked old and shabby. But when he came to Antinoüs, and had told him his story, how he had been rich in old days, and had had ships of his own, and how he had gone to Egypt and had been sold as a slave to Cyprus, the young man mocked him, saying: "Get away with your tales, or you will find that Ithaca is a worse place for you than Egypt or Cyprus."

Ulysses said to him: "You have a fair face but an evil heart. You sit here at another man's feast, and yet will give me nothing."

Then Antinoüs caught up the footstool that was under his feet, and struck Ulysses with it. It was a hard blow, but he stood as firm as a rock. He said nothing, but he was very angry in his heart. Then he went and sat down at the door of the hall. And he said to those who sat in the hall: "Hear, all ye Suitors of the queen! Antinoüs has struck me because I am poor. May the curse of the hungry fall upon him, and bring him to destruction before he come to his marriage day."

But Antinoüs cried: "Sit still, stranger, and eat what you have got in silence, or I will bid the young men drag you from the house, ay, and tear your flesh off your bones."

But even the Suitors blamed him: "You did ill to strike the stranger; there is a curse on those that do such things. Do you not know that sometimes the gods put on the shape of poor men, and visit the dwellings of men to see whether they are good or bad?" But Antinoüs did not care what others thought about him, so full of naughtiness was his heart. As for Telemaˇchus, he was full of anger to see his father so treated. But he kept it to himself; he did not shed a tear, no, nor speak a word; but he thought of the time when the Suitors should suffer for all their ill-doings. But Penelopé, when she heard of it, prayed that the gods might strike the wicked man. "They are all enemies," she said to the dame that kept the house, "but this Antinoüs is the worst of all." Then she said to the swineherd: "Bring this stranger to me; I should like to talk with him. Perhaps he has heard something of Ulysses, or even has seen him, for I hear that he has wandered far."

The swineherd answered: "Be sure, my queen, that this man will charm you with his talk. I kept him in my house for three days, and he never stopped talking of what he had seen and of his adventures. He charms those that listen to him, as a man that sings beautiful songs charms them. And, indeed, he does say that he has heard of Ulysses, that he has gathered much wealth, and that he is on his way home."

When Penelopé heard this, she was still more eager to talk with the stranger. "Call him," she said, "and bring him here to me at once. O that Ulysses would come back, and punish these wicked men for all the evil that they have done! Tell the stranger that if I find he tells me truth, I will give him a new coat and cloak."

Then the swineherd said to Ulysses: "The queen wants to speak to you, and ask you what you have heard about her husband. And if she finds that you have told her the truth, she will give you a new coat and cloak; yes, and give you leave to beg anywhere you please about the island."

Now Ulysses did not think that it was quite time to let his wife know who he was, and he was afraid that if he went to talk to her she would find it out. So he pretended to be afraid of the Suitors, and said to the swineherd: "I would gladly tell the queen all that I know about her husband; but I am afraid of the wicked young men, of whom there are so many. Even now, when that man struck me, and that for nothing, there was no one to stop him. Telema˘chus himself would not, or could not. Tell the queen, therefore, that I am afraid to come now, but that if she will wait till the evening, then I will come."

Then the swineherd went to the queen to give her this message. And when she saw that the beggar was not with him she said: "How is this that you have not brought him? Is he ashamed to come? The beggar who is ashamed does not know his trade."

The swineherd answered: "Not so, lady, but he is afraid of those haughty and violent young men; and, indeed, he is right. So he would have you wait till the evening before he comes, and then you can speak with him alone. It will be better so."

The queen said: "The stranger is wise, and it shall be as he says. Truly, these men are more insolent than any others in the world."

Then the swineherd went close up to Telema˘chus and whispered to him: "I am going back to the farm, to look after things there. Take care of yourself and the stranger. There are many here who are ready to do you harm. May the gods bring them to confusion!"

Telemaˇchus answered: "Go, father, as you say, and come again to-morrow, and bring with you beasts for sacrifice."

So the swineherd went away, and the Suitors made merry in the hall with dancing and singing.

Of the Beggar Irus and Other Things

This same afternoon there came a beggar from the town, whom the young men called Irus, because he carried messages for them, giving him this name because it is Iris who takes the messages of the gods. This fellow was very stout and tall, and a mighty man to eat and drink, but he was a coward. When he saw Ulysses sitting at the door of the palace, he said: "Old man, get away from that place, or I will drag you from it. The young men would like me to do so now, but I think it a shame to strike an old man."

Ulysses said: "There is room here for you and me; get what you can, I do not grudge it you; but you do not make me angry, lest I should hurt you."

But Irus thought to himself: "Here is a man whom I can easily get the better of;" and he said: "Get away from your place, or else fight with me."

Antinoüs heard what he said, and he called to the Suitors and said: "Here is good sport, the best that I have ever seen in this place. These two beggars are going to fight. Come, my friends, and let us make a match between them."

Then the young men got up from their seats to join in the sport. And Antinoüs said: "Here are two haunches of goats—we should have had them for supper. Now if these two beggars will fight, we will give the conqueror one of the haunches for his own supper, and he shall eat it with us, and he shall always have a place kept for him."

Ulysses said: "It is a hard thing for an old man to fight with a young one. Still I am ready. Only you must all swear that you will not give me a foul blow while I am fighting with this fellow."

Telemaˇchus said: "That shall be so, old man;" and all the Suitors agreed. Then Ulysses made himself ready to fight. And when the Suitors saw his thighs, how strong and thick they were, and how broad his shoulders, and what mighty arms he had, they said to each other: "This is a strong fellow; there will be little left of Irus when the fight is over." As for Irus, when he saw the old beggar stripped, he was terribly afraid, and would have slunk away, but the young men would not suffer it. Antinoüs said: "How is this, Irus? Are you afraid of that old beggar? If you play the coward, you shall be put into a ship, and taken to King Echetus, who will cut off your ears and your nose, and give them to his dogs."

So the two men stood up to fight. And Ulysses thought to himself: "Shall I kill this fellow with a blow, or shall I be content with knocking him down?" And this last seemed the better thing to do. First Irus struck Ulysses, but did not hurt him with his blow; then Ulysses struck Irus, and the blow was on the man's jaw-bone. And Irus fell to the ground, and the blood poured out of his mouth. Then Ulysses dragged him out of the hall, and propped him against the wall of the courtyard, and put a staff in his hand and said: "Sit there, and keep away dogs and swine from coming in at the door; but do not try to lord it over men, no, not even over strangers and beggars, lest some worse thing should happen to you."

Then Antinoüs gave Ulysses the goat's haunch, and another of the Suitors, whose name was Amphino˘mus, took two loaves from the table, and gave them to him. Also he gave him a cup of wine, and himself drank his health, saying: "Good luck to you, father, hereafter, for now you seem to have fallen on evil days."

And Ulysses had a liking for the young man, knowing that he was better than his fellows, and he tried to give him a warning. So he said: "You have some wisdom, and your father, I know, is a wise man. Now listen to me: there is nothing in the world so foolish as man. When he is prosperous, he thinks that no evil will come near him; but when the gods send evil, then he can do nothing to help himself. Look at me; once I was prosperous, and I trusted in myself and in my kinsfolk, and see what I am now! Trust not in robbery and wrong, for the gods will punish such things sooner or later. You and your fellows here are doing wrong to one who is absent. But he will come back some day and slay his enemies. Fly, therefore, while there is time, and be not here to meet him when he comes."

So Ulysses spoke, meaning to be kind to the man. And the man felt in his heart that these words were true; nevertheless he went on in the same way, for his doom was upon him that he should die. And now Athené put it into the heart of Penelopé that she should show herself to the Suitors, and this the goddess did for this reason. First, that the hearts of the young men should be still more lifted up in them with pride and folly, and next that they should be moved to give gifts to the queen, as will be seen; and, thirdly, that the queen might be more honored by her husband and her son. So Penelopé said to the old woman that waited on her: "I have a desire now for the first time to show myself to the Suitors, though they are quite as hateful to me as before. Also, I would say a word to my son, lest he should have too much to do with these wicked men, and that they should do him some harm."

The old woman said: "This is well thought, lady. Go and show yourself to the Suitors, and speak to your son, but first wash and anoint your face. Do not let the tears be seen on your cheeks: it is not well to be always grieving."

But the queen said: "Do not talk to me about washing and anointing my face. What do I care how I look, now that my husband is gone? But tell two of my maids to come with me, for I would not go among these men alone."

So the old woman went to tell the maids. But Athené would not let the queen have her own way in this matter. So she caused a deep sleep to fall upon her, and while she slept, she made her more beautiful and taller than she was before.

When the queen awoke, she said to herself: "O that I might die without pain, just as now I have fallen asleep. For what good is my life to me, now that my husband is gone?"

Then she got up from her bed, and washed her face, and went down to the hall, and stood in the door, with a maid standing on either side of her. Never was there a more beautiful woman, and every one of the Suitors prayed in his heart that he might have her for his wife.

First she spoke to her son: "Telemăchus, when you were a child, you had a ready wit; but now that you are grown up, though you are such to look at as a king's son should be, tall and fair, yet your thoughts seem to go astray. What is this that has now been done in this house—this ill-treating a stranger? It would be a shame to us for ever, if he should be hurt."

Telemăchus answered: "You do well to be angry, my mother. Nevertheless, I am not to blame; I cannot have all things as I would wish them to be, for others are stronger than I am, and will have their way. But as for this fight between the stranger and Irus, it did not end as the Suitors would have had it. The stranger had the better of him, and Irus now sits by the gate, wagging his head, and cannot raise himself on to his feet, for the stranger has taken all the strength out of him. I wish in my heart that all the Suitors were in as evil case as he."

Then said one of the Suitors to Penelopé: "O queen, if all the Greeks could behold you, there would be such a crowd in this hall to-morrow as never was seen, so fair are you above all the women in the land."

Penelopé said: "Do not talk to me of beauty; my beauty departed when my lord, Ulysses, went to Troy. If only he would return! Then it would be well with me. I remember how, when he departed, he took me by the hand, and said: 'O lady, not all the Greeks that go this day to Troy will come back, for the men of Troy, they say, are great spearmen, and skilled in shooting with the bow, and good drivers of chariots. And so I know not whether I shall come back to my home or perish there before the walls of the city. Do thou, therefore, care for my father and for my mother while I am away; care for them as you do now, and even more. And bring up our son, Telemăchus.

And when he is a bearded man, then, if I am dead, marry whom you will.' So my husband spoke. And now the time is come. For he is dead, for it is ten years since Troy was taken, and yet he has not come back; and Telemaˇchus is grown to be a man; and I am constrained to make another marriage, although I am unhappy. And I have yet another trouble. My Suitors are not as the Suitors of other women. For the custom is that when a man would woo a lady, he brings sheep and oxen and makes a feast for his kindred and friends, but these men devour my substance, and make no payment for it."

So spoke the queen; and Ulysses was glad to see how she beguiled the men, drawing gifts from them, while she hated them in her heart.

Then said Antinoüs: "Lady, we will give you gifts, nor will you do well to refuse them. But know this, that we will not depart from this place till you have chosen one of us for your husband."

To this all the Suitors agreed. And every man sent his squire to fetch his gift. Antinoüs gave an embroidered robe, very handsome, with twelve brooches and twelve clasps of gold on it. Another gave a chain of curious work, with beads of amber; a third a pair of ear-rings; and yet another a very precious jewel. Every one gave a gift. So the queen went back to her chamber.

Then said one of the Suitors to his fellows, scoffing at the stranger: "See now our good luck in that the gods have sent this man to us. How does the light of the torches flash on his bald head!" And he turned to Ulysses, and said: "Stranger, will you serve me as a hired servant at my farm among the hills? Your wages will be sure, and you shall work, gathering stones, and building walls, and planting trees. And you shall have clothes, and shoes for your feet, and bread to eat. But you do not care, I take it, to work in the fields; you like better to beg your bread and to do no work."

Ulysses answered: "Young man, I would gladly try my strength against yours. We two might each take a scythe in his hand and mow grass when the days grow long in the spring, fasting meanwhile. Or we might plough against each other, driving teams of oxen in a field of four acres. Then you should see whether I could plough a clean and straight furrow. Or if Zeus should order, would that you and I might stand together in the front rank! You think overmuch of yourself; but, verily, if Ulysses should come back, this door would not be wide enough for you and your fellows to escape."

The man was very angry to hear such words. "Old man," he cried, "you had better not say such things, lest I do you a mischief. Has the wine stolen away your wits, or is it your way to prate in this idle fashion, or are you puffed up by having got the better of Irus the beggar?"

And he caught up a footstool, and threw it at Ulysses, but Ulysses stooped down and escaped it. But the footstool struck a young man who was carrying round the wine, and hurt his hand so grievously that he fell back, and lay on the floor groaning.

Then said one of the Suitors to his neighbour: "I wish this fellow would go away. Ever since he came hither there has been strife and quarrelling in the place. Now we shall have no more pleasure in the feast." But Telemaˇchus said: "It is plain that you have had meat and drink enough. Now let us all go to rest." And they agreed and went away.

How Ulysses Was Made Known

Ulysses said to his son: "Now is the time to do the thing of which I spoke to you, that you should take away the swords and spears from the hall, and lay them up in the armoury."

So Telema˘chus said to the nurse: "Now shut up the maids in their rooms till I have taken away the arms from the hall and put them in the armoury. They are foul with the smoke, and it is time that they should be cleaned."

The nurse said: "I wish that all your father's goods were as well looked after. But who shall carry a light for you, if you will have none of the maids?"

Telema˘chus answered: "This stranger shall do it. He has eaten my bread, and he should do some work for it."

So the nurse shut up the maids in their rooms, and Ulysses and his son set themselves to carry the arms, the spears and swords and shields, from the hall to the armoury. Nor did they need any one to light them, for Athené went before them, holding a golden lamp in her hand. No one saw her or the lamp, but the light they saw. And Telema˘chus said: "This is a strange thing, father; the walls and the beams and the pillars are bright as with fire."

Now Ulysses knew that this was Athené's doing, and he said: "Say nothing, nor ask any question about it."

And when they had finished the carrying of the arms, Ulysses said to the young man: "Go now to your room and sleep; I wish to talk to your mother."

So Telema˘chus went to his room and lay down to sleep, and Ulysses sat in the hall alone, thinking how he should slay the Suitors. After a while, Penelopé came down and sat by the fire. Her chair was made of silver and ivory. The maids also came down and cleared away the dishes and the cups, and put fresh logs upon the fire. Then the queen said: "Bring another chair, and a cushion, that this stranger may sit down and tell me his story." So they brought a chair and a cushion, and Ulysses sat down. Then said the queen: "Stranger, tell me who you are. What was your father's name, and from what country do you come?" Ulysses answered: "Lady, ask me what you will, but not my name or my country. To think of these brings tears to my eyes; and I would not that any one should see me weeping. They will say, 'This is a foolish fellow, or he has let the wine steal away his senses.' "

The queen said: "I too have had many sorrows and have shed many tears since the day when my husband left me, going with the Greeks to fight against the men of Troy. And now I know not what to do for the troubles that are come upon me. For the princes of this island of Ithaca, and of the other islands round about, come hither, asking me to marry. And they sit here day after day, and devour my lord's substance. And I do not know how to escape them. For three years, indeed, I put them off, for I said that I could not marry till I had woven a shroud for the old man, my husband's father. And I worked at the weaving of this in the day, and at night I undid the weaving. But one of the maids told the thing to the Suitors, and I could not help finishing the work. And now I know not what to do, for my father and mother are urgent with me that I should marry, and my son sees all his substance eaten up before his eyes, which these Suitors eat and drink in his house. Then tell me, stranger, of what race you are, for you did not come from a rock or an oak tree, as the old fables have it."

Ulysses said: "Lady, if you will know these things, I will tell you, though it grieves me to the heart. I come from a certain island that is called Crete. It is a fair land, and rich, with many people in it, and ninety cities. I was the younger son of the king, and when my father died, then my elder brother became king in his place. And when the Greeks went against the city of Troy, my brother went with them. Some ten days after he had departed there came a stranger, who said that he was Ulysses, and that he, too, was sailing for Troy, and that the winds had carried him out of his course. And he asked for my brother, who, he said, was his friend. So I gave food and wine to him and to his people. Twelve days did they stay, for the wind blew from the north and hindered their sailing; but on the thirteenth day it blew from the south, and they departed."

When the queen heard this, she was much moved, and shed many tears. Ulysses pitied her when he saw her weep, but his own eyes were dry, as hard as if they had been of horn or iron. Then Penelopé said: "Stranger, let me ask you one question, that I may be sure that this man was in very truth my husband. Tell me now what were the clothes that he wore, and whether he had any companion with him."

Now this was a hard question, for twenty years had passed since these things happened, and a man might well have forgotten what clothes a stranger had worn. And even Ulysses himself might not bear them in mind, for women remember such things more readily than do men.

The beggar said: "I remember that he had a cloak, sea-purple in colour, made of wool, and double. And I remember also that it was clasped with a brooch of gold, and that the brooch was of this pattern—a dog holding a fawn. Wonderfully wrought it was, so eager to lay hold was the dog, and so did the fawn struggle to be free. And his coat was white and smooth. But whether he had brought these things from his home, I know not. Many men gave him gifts. I myself gave him a sword and a coat. and he had a comrade with him, a herald, older than he, with curly hair and dark skin."

When Penelopé heard this, she wept aloud, for she remembered every one of these things, and knew that the beggar had indeed seen her husband. "You tell a true story, old man," she said. "These clothes that you speak of Ulysses had; I folded them with my own hands, and put them away in his baggage. They were what he would wear at feasts and the like; others he had for travelling. And the brooch with the dog and the fawn I gave him. But, alas! I shall never see him any more."

"Say not so, dear lady," said the beggar. "Do not think of Ulysses as if he were dead; he will surely come again. And, indeed, he is not far away. He is with King Pheidon, and will soon be coming back, and will bring much treasure with him, enough to make this house rich for many generations. King Pheidon showed me these things. Ulysses himself I did not see, for he had gone to inquire of the god at Dodona, where there is the sacred oak, and the god answers by the voice of the doves that roost in its branches. He went to ask—so the king told me—whether he should come back openly or secretly. But be sure, lady, that he will come, and before this month is out."

Penelopé said: "May your words be found true, old man. If these things come to pass, you shall have gifts in plenty; you shall not want any more, as long as you live. But I have many doubts. But now the maids shall make a bed for you with a mattress and blankets, so that you may sleep warmly till the morning. And they shall wash your feet."

But Ulysses said: "I thank you, lady; but I will not have my bed made with blankets and mattress. I do not care for these things. Since I left the land of Crete, I have not used them. Nor do I care for the bath. Nevertheless, if there is some old woman among your servants, some one whom you trust, she shall wash my feet, if you will."

Penelopé said: "Such an old woman there is in the house. She nursed my husband, and cared for him, and carried him in her arms, ever since he was born. She is weak with old age; still she will wash your feet."

So the queen called the nurse, and said to her: "Come, nurse, wash this stranger's feet. He is one that knows your master Ulysses."

The nurse, when she heard this queen so speak, put her hands before her face, and wept. And she said to the stranger: "Willingly will I do this, both for the queen's sake and for yours, if you bring news of my dear master. Yes, and because you are like him. Many strangers have come hither, but never saw I one that was so like Ulysses."

Ulysses said: "Say you so? 'Tis what others have said before, that Ulysses and I were much alike."

So the nurse made ready the bath; and Ulysses turned away from the fire, and sat looking into the darkness, for he feared lest when the old woman should take his leg in her hands she should find a great scar that there was on it. Now the story of how the scar came about is this:—

When Ulysses was a lad of some eighteen years, he went to Parnassus to see his mother's father, Autolycus. It was this man who had given him his name, for when he was newly born the nurse had laid him on his grandfather's knee, saying: "Give this child a name." And Autolycus had said: "Let his name be Ulysses, and when he is grown up, let him come to me, and I will give him a gift that will be worth having." So Ulysses went to see his grandfather, and he and his grandmother and their sons were very glad to see him, and they made a great feast for him. The next day they all went hunting, and Ulysses went with them. They climbed up the side of the mountain Parnassus, and the time was about sunrise. The beaters came to a glade in the forest, and the dogs went before, following a scent on which they had come, and with them came Ulysses and his uncles, the sons of Autolycus. And the dogs brought them to the lair of a wild boar. A very thick place it was, so covered that neither sun nor rain could come through, and there was a great quantity of dead leaves in it. When the boar, which was a very great beast, was roused by the baying of the dogs and by the trampling of the hunters' feet, he sprang up from his lair, and his hair bristled on his back, and his eyes shone with a very fierce light. Now Ulysses was not used to hunting of this sort, for there were no wild boars in Ithaca, and, maybe, he did not know how great was the danger. But he was a very brave lad, and very eager for praise, and he rushed in before the rest of the company, holding his spear in his hand, for he greatly wished to be the one who should kill the beast. But the boar was too quick for him, for it charged him, thrusting aside the spear, and made a great wound in his leg, just above the knee, striking him with his tusk sideways. But the bone was not touched. Nor did Ulysses fail, though, indeed, he was greatly hurt; for he stabbed the boar in the shoulder, running the spear into the beast's breast, and it fell dead on the ground. Then his uncles bound up the wound, staying the blood with such things as were used for that purpose, and also singing a song of healing. So they went back to the house; and they kept the lad till the wound was healed, and they sent him away with many splendid gifts. But the scar of the wound was left.

When the nurse felt the scar, she knew that the stranger was Ulysses, and she said: "O Ulysses, O my child, to think that I knew you not." And she looked towards the queen, as meaning to tell her what she had found. But Ulysses laid his hand upon her mouth, and said in a whisper: "Mother, would you be my death? I am come back after these twenty years, but no one must know till I have got all things ready."

Then the old woman held her peace. After this Penelopé talked with him again. Many things she said to him, and among them was a dream that she had dreamt. "I thought," she said, "that I saw a flock of geese in the palace, and that an eagle came into the hall and killed them all, and that I heard a voice saying: 'These geese are the Suitors, and the eagle is your husband.' " "That," said the stranger, "is a good dream." After this she said: "To-morrow I must make my choice among the Suitors, and I have promised to bring out the great bow that was Ulysses', and he that shall draw the bow most easily, and best shoot an arrow at the mark, he shall be my husband."

"That, too, is well," answered Ulysses. "Let this trial of the bow be made at once. Truly, before one of these men shall bend the bow, Ulysses shall come back and shoot at a certain mark."

The Trial of the Bow

Ulysses lay down to sleep in the gallery of the hall. He lay with the undressed hide of a bull under him, and he took to cover him fleeces of sheep that had been killed for sacrifice and feast. Also the dame that kept the house laid a mantle over him. But he could not sleep, for he was thinking about many things, chiefly how he, being one, with but some two or three to help him, could slay all the company of Suitors.

While he turned from side to side thinking over those things, Athené came and stood over his head in the likeness of a woman, and said to him: "Why do you not sleep? Here you are in your own home, and you find that your wife is true to you, and that your son is just such as you could wish. What troubles you?"

Ulysses answered: "These things that you say, O goddess! are true. But I think how I, being one against many, shall be able to slay the Suitors. This troubles me; and this also, how, if I slay them, shall I escape the avengers of blood?"

The goddess answered: "Truly, your faith is weak. Should you not trust in the gods, for they are stronger than men? The gods are on your side; I am with you, and will keep you to the end. And now sleep, for to wake all night is vexation of spirit."

So she poured sleep on eyes, and left him.

When he awoke up in the morning, he took up the fleeces which had covered him, and laid them on a seat in the hall, and the bull's hide on which he had slept he carried outside. And as he stood, he looked up to the sky and said: "O Zeus, send me now a sign, if indeed, in bringing me back to my country, thou meanest to do me good?"

And even while he was speaking there came thunder from the sky, and Ulysses was glad to hear it. Also there came another sign to him, and this was a word which was spoken by a woman at the mill. Twelve women there were who ground corn for the palace, wheat and barley. Eleven of them were sleeping, for they had finished their task; but this one was weaker than the rest, and had not finished her part, but still was grinding. And when she heard the thunder, she cried: "O Zeus, may this be a sign of good to me! may it mean that I shall never grind wheat and barley any more for the Suitors!"

And now Telemaˇchus came down from the room where he slept, and said to the nurse: "Did you give to our guest food and drink and bedding as was fitting?"

Then nurse said: "The man ate and drank as much as he would, but a mattress and rugs he would not have. He slept on a bull's hide, and had the fleeces of sheep to cover him. But he had also a mantle over him."

After this the swineherd came, driving three fat hogs for the day's feast. He said to Ulysses: "Stranger, how have these young men behaved to you?"

Ulysses said: "May the gods deal with them as they have dealt with me!"

And after the swineherd came Melanthius the goatherd, bringing goats for the day's feast. When he saw Ulysses, he spoke roughly to him: "Old man, are you still plaguing us with your begging? We shall not part, I take it, till we have made trial of each other with our fists. Your begging is past bearing. Are there not other feasts to which you can go?"

Last came the neatherd, whose name was Philaetius, and he was driving a barren heifer; and this also, besides the pigs and the goats, was for the feast. He said to Ulysses: "Friend, I hope that you may have better luck in the time to come; for now I see that you have many troubles. Maybe Ulysses is wandering about, clothed in rags as you are and begging his bread. I weep to think of it. Ay, it may be that he is dead. That would be a great grief. Long ago he set me to take care of his cattle, and they have increased under my hand, yet it vexes me to see how these strangers are ever devouring them in his own home. Long ago I would have fled to some other place, for the thing is past bearing, but that I hope that Ulysses will yet come again to his own."

Ulysses said to him: "Philaetius, I see that you are a good man. Now listen to what I say: I swear that this day, while you are still here, Ulysses will come home. You shall see it with your eyes—yes, and the end of the Suitors also."

And now the Suitors came and sat down, as they were wont, to their morning meal. And the servants took to Ulysses a full share of meat and drink, for this was what Telemaˇchus had bidden them do. When Ctesippus saw this—he was one who cared neither for gods nor men—he said: "Is this fellow to fare as well as we fare? See now what gift I will give him!" And he took the foot of a bullock out of a basket, and threw it at Ulysses. But he moved his head to the left, and the foot flew by, and made a mark on the wall.

When Telemaˇchus saw this, he cried: " 'Tis well for you, Ctesippus, that you did not hit the stranger. Truly, if you had hit him, I had pierced you through with my spear, and your father would have had to make ready your burying, not your wedding."

"That is well said," cried another of the Suitors; " 'tis a shame to do wrong either to Telemaˇchus, or to his guest. Nevertheless, he must bid his mother choose out from among us the man whom she will marry, so that we may not waste our time any more."

Telemaˇchus answered: "My mother may marry whom she will; but never will I force her to leave this house."

When he said this the Suitors laughed, but their laughter was not as of men that were glad. And there came a darkness over the place, so that one of the men cried: "It is this stranger that brings bad luck with him. Let us send him away, for the hall seems to grow dark while he is here."

By this time Penelopé had taken down the great bow of Ulysses from the peg on which it hung, and she drew it out of the case in which it was kept, and laid it across her knees and wept over it. Then, after a while, she rose, and carried it to the hall, where the Suitors sat feasting. With the bow she brought also the quiver full of arrows, and, standing by the pillar that stood under the dome, she said:—

"You, who come here day after day, and devour my substance, pretending that you wish to marry me, see here; look at this bow and these arrows; they belong to the great Ulysses, and with these I will try you. Whoso among you that shall most easily bend this bow with his hands, and shall shoot best at the mark which my son shall set up, him will I take for my husband; him will I follow, leaving this house, which I shall never see again except in my dreams."

Then Telemaˇchus set the mark. And when he had set it, he made as if he would have drawn the bow himself; and this he would have done, for he was strong and worthy of his father; but Ulysses signed to him that he should not do it. So he said: "I am too young, and have not grown to my full strength; you that are older than I should try first."

Then a certain priest who was among the Suitors, Leiodes by name, made trial of the bow. He was the best among them, and did not like their ways; but for all that he stayed with them. He took the bow, and tried to bend it, wearying himself with it, making his hands sore, for they were soft and not used to work. At last he said: "I cannot bend the bow; and I fear that it will bring grief and pain to many this day."

But Antinoüs cried: "Why do you say such words?" And he bade the goatherd fetch a roll of fat from the kitchen, that they might make the string soft with it. And the Suitors rubbed the fat upon it, trying to soften it. But they could not bend it; they tried all of them, but it was in vain, till only two were left, Antinoüs and Eurymachus, who were indeed the strongest of them all.

While the Suitors were trying the bow, Ulysses went out into the court, and spoke to the swineherd, and the man who herded the cattle, taking them by themselves, and said to them: "What would you do if Ulysses were to come back to his home? Would you fight for him, or for the Suitors?"

They both answered with one voice: "We would fight for him."

Then said Ulysses: "Look now at me: I am Ulysses, and I have come back after twenty years. You are glad in your hearts to see me; but I know not whether there is any one else besides you who is glad. Come now, be brave men to-day and help me, and I will reward you; you shall have wives and lands and houses, and you shall lie near me, and Telemăchus shall take you for comrades and brothers. And if you want a sign that I am indeed Ulysses, look at this scar; this is the wound which the wild boar made on the day when I went hunting with my grandfather."

The men wept for joy to hear this; and they kissed Ulysses, and he kissed them. Then he said to the swineherd: "When the Suitors have tried the bow, bring it to me. Also bid the women keep within doors, and not move out if they hear the noise of battle." To the herdsman of the cattle he said: "Lock the doors of the hall, and fasten them with a rope."

Then he went back to the hall. Eurymachus had the bow in his hand, and was warming it at the fire. Then he tried to draw it, but could not. And he groaned aloud, saying: "Woe is me! I am grieved not for the loss of this marriage, for there are other women in Greece who may be wooed, but because we are all weaker than the great Ulysses. This is, indeed, a shameful thing." But Antinoüs said: "Do not lose heart. This day is holy to the god of Archers, and it does not please him that we are about this business. We will try again to-morrow, and first we will sacrifice to the god."

They were all pleased to hear these words, hoping that they might yet be able to draw the bow. But Ulysses said: "Let me try it; I should like to know whether I have still the strength which I had when I was young."

The Suitors were very angry that the stranger should dare to think of such a thing; but Penelopé said that the man should try the bow, and that she would give him great gifts if he could bend it. Then said Telemăchus: "Mother, this bow is mine, and I will give it or refuse it, as I shall see fit. And if it pleases me that this stranger shall try it, then it shall be so, and no man shall say nay. But now do you and your maids go to your rooms; these things are for men to settle."

This he said because he knew what would soon happen in the hall, and he would not have her there. She wondered to hear him speak with such authority, but she made no answer to him, and she went out of the hall, taking her maids with her.

Then Telemaˇchus gave the bow to the swineherd, and bade him take it to Ulysses. The Suitors were angry, and would have stopped him, but Telemaˇchus said: "Take it; it is mine to give or to refuse," and the swineherd took it to Ulysses. And when he had done this, he went to the nurse, and bade her keep the women within doors whatever they might hear.

Then Ulysses took the bow in his hand, and felt it to see whether it had suffered any hurt; and the Suitors laughed to see him do it. And when he found that it was without a flaw, then he bent it, and strung it, and he twanged the string, and the tone of it was shrill and sweet as the cry of a swallow. After this he took an arrow from the quiver, and laid the notch upon the string, and drew the bow to the full, still sitting in his place. And the arrow went straight to the mark. Then he said to Telemaˇchus: "Come, stand by me; there is yet another feast to be kept before the sun goes down." And the young man stood by his side, armed with a spear.

The Slaying of the Suitors

Ulysses cried aloud: "This work is done; and now I will try at another mark." As he spoke, he aimed his arrow at Antinoüs. The man was raising a cup to his lips. There was not a thought of danger in his mind: who could have dreamt that any man, though he were ever so strong and brave, should dare such a thing, being but one against many? The head of the arrow passed through the neck of Antinoüs; and the blood gushed out of his nostrils, and he fell, overturning the table that was near him. All the Suitors, when they saw him fall, leapt from their seats, but when they looked, all the arms had been taken down from the walls. For a moment they doubted whether the stranger had killed the man by chance or on purpose; but Ulysses cried out: "I am Ulysses! Dogs, you thought that I should never come back. Therefore you have devoured my goods, and made suit to my wife, though I was yet living, and have had no fear of god or of man before your eyes. And now a sudden destruction has come upon you all."

When they heard these words, the Suitors trembled for fear. There was only one man among them who could so much as speak. This was Eurymachus. He said: "If you are indeed Ulysses of Ithaca, you speak the truth. We have done great wrong to you. But the man who was most to blame lies dead here. It was Antinoüs who was the chief of your enemies. What he desired was not merely marriage with your wife, but to destroy your house, and to be king of Ithaca. But we will pay you back twenty times for all that we have taken of yours."

Ulysses said: "Talk not of paying back. You shall die this day, all of you."

Eurymachus said: "This man will not stay his hand, but will kill us all with his arrows. Let us make a rush for the door, and we will raise a cry in the city, and this archer will soon have shot his last."

As he spoke, he rushed on with two-edged knife in his hand; but Ulysses shot an arrow at him as he came, and he fell forward dead. And Telemaˇchus slew another with his spear; but he could not draw out the spear from the wound, lest the enemy should take him at a disadvantage as he stooped.

Now it was plain that when Ulysses should have shot away all his arrows, the Suitors would have the better of them. So Telemaˇchus ran to the armoury, and fetched down four helmets, and four shields, and eight spears. With these he armed himself and the two servants—that is, the swineherd and the herdman of the cattle. Now while Ulysses had yet arrows in his quiver, the Suitors held back, for the three bravest of them had been slain, and they had neither armour nor weapon. But the goatherd saw their need, and he crept secretly up to the armoury and brought down thence twelve helmets and shields and as many spears. When Ulysses saw this, he cried to Telemaˇchus: "There is treachery, my son. Have the women done this thing, or is it the goatherd?" Telemaˇchus answered: "It is my fault, father. I left the door of the armoury open." While some of the Suitors were arming themselves, the goatherd went again to the armoury, but the swineherd and his companion followed him, and caught him as he was taking arms, and bound him with a rope. As soon as they had done this, they hastened back to the hall and stood by the side of Ulysses. Then a certain Agelaüs said to the other Suitors: "Friends, we can overcome these four if we join together. Let six of us throw our spears all at once." This they did, but the spears went wide of the mark. But the spears of the four went not wide, for each slew his man, and this they did again and again. On the other hand, both Telemaˇchus and the swineherd were wounded, but not to their great hurt. The swineherd slew Ctesippus, and as he smote him, he cried: "Take that for the ox-foot which you gave to our guest." And all the courage that was in the Suitors left them, and they were as a flock of birds which is scattered and torn by eagles.

Leiodes, the priest, prayed Ulysses that he would spare him, saying that he had done no wrong, but had only served at the altar. But Ulysses answered: "It is enough that you have served at the altar of these wicked men, and that you have made suit to my wife." And he slew him without mercy. But the minstrel and the herald he spared. "Go," said he, "and sit by the altar." So they went and sat by the altar, fearing lest they also should be slain.

So the Suitors were slain, every one of them. And Ulysses bade the women come and wash the hall and the tables with water and smoke them with sulphur. And he said to the nurse: "Go now, and tell the queen that her husband has come back."

At Last

The nurse went to the queen's bed-room with the good news. She ran with all the speed that she could, even stumbling in her haste. She found the queen asleep, for she had been awake for a long time, and was weary. And now the nurse stood by her head, and said: "Awake, dear child, and see what you have longed to see for so many years. Ulysses has come back, and has slain the wicked men who troubled you."

But Penelopé answered: "Surely, dear nurse, the gods have taken away your senses. Why do you mock me, waking me out of the sweetest sleep that I have ever had since the day when Ulysses sailed away to Troy? Go to the other women, and leave me. If one of them had done this to me, I would have punished her, but you I cannot harm."

The nurse answered: "I do not mock you, dear child. It is indeed true that Ulysses is here. The stranger with whom you talked is he. Your son knew it, but hid the matter that the Suitors should be taken unawares."

Then Penelopé was glad, and fell upon the old woman's neck, saying: "Tell me now the truth. Has he indeed come back? And how did he, being but one, contrive to slay so many?"

"That," said the nurse, "I do not know. We women sat together amazed, hearing the groaning of men that were being slain. Then some one fetched us, and I found Ulysses standing among the dead, and these lay piled one on the other. Truly you would have rejoiced to see him, so like was he to a lion, stained as he was with blood and the labour of the fight. And now the women here are washing the hall, and cleansing it with sulphur. But come; now is the end of all your grief, for the husband whom you so longed to see has come back."

But Penelopé began again to doubt. "Dear nurse," she said, "be not too sure. Great, indeed, would be my joy if I could see him. But this cannot be he; it is some god who has taken the shape of a man that he may punish the Suitors for the wrong that they have done."

Then said the nurse: "What is this that you say? That your husband cannot have come back, when he is already in the house? Truly you are slow to believe. Now hear this proof, a thing that I saw with my own eyes. It is the scar of the wound that a wild boar gave him, when he was yet a lad. I saw it when I washed his feet, and I would have told it to you, but he put his hand on my mouth and would not suffer me to speak, for so he thought it best."

Penelopé said: "I am in great doubt. Nevertheless, I will go into the hall and see the dead Suitors, and the man, whoever he be, that has slain them."

So she dressed herself and went down, and sat in a dark part of the hall, while Ulysses stood by the pillar, waiting till his wife should speak to him. But she was in great doubt. Sometimes she seemed to know him, and sometimes not, for he was still in his rags, not having suffered the women to give him new clothes.

Telemaˇchus said: "Mother, you are indeed an evil mother, for you sit away from my father, and will not speak to him. Surely your heart must be harder than a stone."

Ulysses answered: "Let be, Telemaˇchus; your mother will know the truth in good time. But now let us hide this slaughter for a while, lest the friends of these dead men come against us. Let there be music and dancing in the hall. Men will say, 'This is for the wedding of the queen.' "

So the minstrel played and the women danced. Then Ulysses went to the bath, and washed himself, and put on new clothes, and came back to the hall; also Athené made him fairer and younger, such as he was when he left his home to go to Troy. And he stood by his wife, and said: "Surely, O lady, the gods have made you harder of heart than all other women. Would any other wife have kept away from her husband, when he came back after twenty years?"

But Penelopé still doubted. Then Ulysses said: "Hear now, Penelopé, and know that it is indeed your husband whom you see. I will tell you a thing that you will remember. There was an olive there in the inner court of this house, which had a trunk of about the bigness of a pillar. Round this I built a room, and I roofed it over, and put doors upon it. Then I lopped all the boughs of the olive, and made the tree into a bedpost. And I joined the bedstead on to this post, and adorned it with gold, and silver, and ivory. Also I fastened it together with a band of leather which had been dyed with purple: whether the bedstead is still in its place, or whether some one has moved it—but it was not an easy thing to move—I do not know, but this was as it used to be in old time."

Then Penelopé knew that he was indeed her husband; and she ran to him, and kissed him, saying: "Pardon me, my lord, that I was so slow to know you; I was afraid, for men have many ways of deceiving, lest some one should come, saying falsely that he was my husband. But now I know that in truth you are he and not another."

So they wept over each other, and kissed each other. Thus did Ulysses come home at last after twenty years.

Of Laertes

The next day Ulysses said to his wife: "You and I have suffered many things for many years. You wearied for my coming back, and feared that I might be dead, and I was kept from coming. And now we are together again, but there are some things still to be done. I see that the Suitors have wasted my flocks and herds, devouring them at their feasts. My loss I must make up. Some I will take from other lands, where my enemies live, and some shall be paid back to me by the fathers of the men who have robbed me. But now I will go and see my old father, who is very sad, I know, thinking that I shall never return. And there is another thing of which I must speak. The people of Ithaca will soon hear how the Suitors have been slain, and there will be great anger in their hearts, for some of them had sons and brothers among the men who are dead. Do you, therefore, and your maids keep close to your own rooms. Do not look out, nor ask for news. Only wait till I shall set everything right."

Then Ulysses put on his armour, and took his spear and his sword. His son, and the swineherd, and the keeper of the cattle did the same; and the four went to the place where the old man Laertes lived, Ulysses leading the way. It was a farm which the old king had cleared, breaking up the moorland, and cutting down the forest, and was now rich and fertile. Round the old man's cottage were huts in which his slaves lived, and in the cottage itself was an old woman of Sicily, who looked after him very faithfully and lovingly.

Ulysses said to his son and to the two herds: "Go into the house, and make ready a meal for mid-day, killing one of the pigs. I will find the old man, my father, where he is at work on the farm, and will see whether he knows me or not." So he put off his armour, and laid down his spear and sword, and went to the vineyard, for he thought he should find the old man there. Now all the men that worked on the farm had gone on an errand to fetch stones for building up the gaps in the vineyard wall. So the old man was left alone. Ulysses saw him as he stood hoeing round the stock of a vine. He had on a coat that was soiled with earth, and patched and shabby. He wore also leggings of leather that the briars and thorns should not hurt him, and hedger's gloves on his hands, and a goatskin cap on his head.

And when Ulysses saw the old man, his father, how feeble he was, and bowed with years, and sad, he stood still under a pear tree that there was in the place, and his eyes were blinded with tears. He doubted for a while whether he should go up to the old man and throw his arms round him, and kiss him, and tell him who he was, and how he had come back, or whether he should try him, and see whether or no he knew him. And this seemed to be the better of the two. So he came near him as he stood hoeing the ground by the vine-stock, and said; "Sir, you know well how to work an orchard or a vineyard; all is going well here. 'Tis plain to me that there is neither seedling, nor fig tree, nor vine, nor olive, nor pear, nor plot of herbs in the garden that you have not cared for. But there is no one, I see, to care for you, to look after your old age, or to see that you are decently clad. You are no idle servant that your master should neglect you; and, indeed, I take it that you are not a servant at all. You have not the look of such, but you are tall and shaped like a king. Such a one as you should have good food, and the bath when he will, and a soft bed. Tell me, now, whose servant are you? Whose is this orchard that you are working? But first tell me, is this truly the land of Ithaca? I asked this of a man that I met on the way, and the churl seemed tongue-tied, for he did not answer me a word. And another question I would willingly have asked him, but that he did not even stay to hear it. And this question was about a certain friend of mine in old days, for I desired to know whether he was alive or dead. And now, old sir, let me ask this same question of you. Years ago there came to my house a certain man, and was my guest. I loved him much—never has there been one of all the strangers that I have seen whom I loved so well. This man said that he was born in Ithaca, and he said also that his father's name was Laertes, and that he was king of Ithaca. Many days did I keep him in my house, and when he went away, I gave him splendid gifts—several talents of gold, and a great silver bowl, worked with flowers, and twelve cloaks, and as many coats."

When the old man heard this, he wept aloud: "It is so, stranger; you have come to the land of Ithaca. But, alas! it is in the hands of evil men. If you had found him of whom you speak, even my son, then truly we would have given you gifts such as you gave to him, and requited your kindness as was fitting. But tell me this: how many years have passed since you took my son into your house?—for, indeed, it was my son who was your guest. Alas! he has had evil fortune. He has died far from his friends and his country, for either the fish of the sea have devoured him or the ravens have pecked out his eyes, or the wild beasts have torn him; but his wife, the faithful Penelopé, did not close his eyes, nor weep over his body. Tell me this, and tell me also who you are, and from what country you have come, and who was your father, and whether you travelled hither in a ship of your own, or were brought in the ship of another?"

Then Ulysses answered, telling this tale, for a tale he always had ready for those that asked him: "I come from the land of Sicily, and I was carried hither by a storm. And as for the time of your son's coming to my house, know that it was four years ago. We thought that he would have good luck when he went, for all the signs were good, and I was glad that it should be so, and sent him on his way with good cheer and with great gifts."

When he heard these words, the old man Laertes was overborne with grief, and he stooped down and caught up the dust from the ground, and poured it on his white head, sitting and groaning the while. And when Ulysses saw this, his heart yearned towards the old man, and there was a stinging pain of tears in his nostrils, so that he could no more refrain. And he fell on the old man's neck, and held him close, and kissed him, saying: "My father, my father, look at me, for I am your long-lost son. I have come back at last after twenty years. And I have slain the Suitors in my hall, paying them back in full for all the wrong that they have done."

But Laertes stared at him, doubting whether the thing was indeed true, and said: "If you are indeed my son Ulysses, come back after all these years, show me some proof that may make me sure."

Then Ulysses answered: "Look now at this scar which the wild boar made when I went hunting with my mother's father long ago on the mountain of Parnassus. That is proof enough; but I will give you yet another, for I will tell you of the trees which you gave me many years ago in this orchard. I was a little lad, running after you, and you gave me ten apple trees and thirteen pears, and forty fig trees, and fifty rows of vine. And these I remember grew ripe at different times."

When the old man heard these words, his knees failed under him for very joy, and he threw his arms about his son, and his son clasped him close. But when his spirit revived in him, he said: "This is well that the Suitors have suffered for their evil deeds. Truly there are gods in heaven, but I fear greatly that the men of Ithaca and from the islands round about should gather an army, and come against us, for these men had kindred among them."

Ulysses answered: "Fear not, I will see to this. But now come to the house, for there a meal has been made ready for us."

So they went to the house. And the old man went to the bath and was anointed with oil, and was vested in a fine cloak. Athené also—for she was near at hand—made him broader and taller, so that his son wondered to see him, and cried: "Surely one of the gods that live for ever has done this thing for you."

After this they sat down to the meal; but before they began, came the old steward, Dolius by name, coming back from his work, and his tall sons with him. And when they saw Ulysses, they wondered who he might be; but Ulysses cried from his place: "Sit down, father, and eat; and you, my men, wonder no more. Here is the meal ready for you, and we would not begin till you had come."

Then Dolius came near, and caught his master's hand, and kissed it at the wrist and said: "Oh, my dearest lad, so you have come back at last to them who longed for you so sorely! Welcome to you! The gods themselves have sent you home; may they give you blessings without end. Does the queen know of your coming, or shall we send a messenger to tell her?"

Ulysses answered: "She knows it; but think not of other things. Let us eat and drink."

So they ate and drank, and were of good cheer.

How There Was Peace Between Ulysses and His People

Now all this time there went the news through the town how the Suitors had been killed. And the people came from all parts to the king's palace, crying and mourning; and they took up the dead bodies and carried them away and buried them. And the bodies of them that came from the islands round about, they gave to the fishermen that they might carry them each to his home. And when they had done this, they gathered together in the great square of the town till it was filled from one end to the other.

Then stood Eupeithes, who was father to Antinoüs, the man who was first killed by Ulysses, and said: "Friends, this man has done great evil to this land and this people. He took away with him many brave men in his ships when he went to Troy; twelve ships he took, and there were fifty men in each. All these he has lost; not one will you ever see again. But he himself has come back. Now, therefore, let us take vengeance on him, and on them that have joined themselves to him, before they flee to some other land. It will be a shame to us for ever and ever, if we sit still and suffer the men who have murdered our sons and our brothers to go free. For myself, I would rather die than suffer such disgrace. Let us go, therefore, before they take ship and escape."

Then Medon the herald stood up in the Assembly, and Phemius the singer with him, and said: "Listen now to me, men of Ithaca: all that Ulysses did to the Suitors, he did by the will of the gods. I myself saw one of them stand by his side—he seemed like to Mentor, but I know that he was a god—and he cheered him on and helped him as he fought, and he turned aside the spears of the Suitors."

Then a certain prophet stood up, a wise man, who knew all things that had been, and all that were yet to come to pass, and he said: "Listen to me, men of Ithaca, these dreadful things are the harvest, but you sowed the seed. For when the wise Mentor told you what you should do, that you should keep your sons back from doing this evil, you would not hear him. You suffered them to waste your king's wealth, and to make suit to his wife, laughing in their hearts, and thinking that he would never come back. See now the end. Listen, therefore, to me. Do not go against this man, lest you also should perish."

So the wise man spoke, and some listened to him, but more than half sprang to their feet, and shouted for the battle. So they armed themselves for the fight, and followed Eupeithes. Meanwhile Athené in heaven said to Zeus, her father: "What is thy will, my father? Must there be still more of war and of the shedding of blood? or wilt thou command that there be peace between Ulysses and his people?"

And Zeus answered: "My daughter, order it as thou wilt. It has been of thy doing that Ulysses has taken vengeance on the Suitors; now see that there be peace between him and his people. Let them forget that their sons and brothers have been slain; and that they be the more ready to forget, see that they have plenty and prosperity in their land."

Then Athené sped down from heaven to earth, that she might bring these things to pass.

Meanwhile they that sat in the house of Laertes had finished their meal, and Ulysses said: "Let some one go out and see what has been done, lest these people come upon us before we are ready." So one of the sons of Dolius went out, and lo! the crowd of armed men was hard at hand, and he cried out to Ulysses: "They are coming. Let us arm."

So they arose and armed themselves. Twelve they were in all—Ulysses and his son, and the swineherd and the herd serving at the table; and Dolius with his six sons, and old Laertes. And Athené came in the shape of Mentor.

Ulysses said to his son: "My son, now you take your place for the first time in the line of battle. Bear yourself therefore worthily, and shame not your father and your father's father."

And Telemaˇchus said, and when he spoke the light of battle was in his eye: "My father, you shall see what is in the heart of your son; never will I shame my father and my father's father."

Then the old man cried aloud in his joy: "Now I thank the gods that I have lived to see this day, for my son and my son's son contend who shall bear himself more bravely in the battle."

Then Athené said to the old man Laertes: "And pray to the father of the gods and men that he may strengthen your arm, and be you the first to cast your spear."

So the old man prayed; and then he cast his spear; at Eupeithes, the leader of the rebels, he cast it, and smote him on the helmet and broke through the brass, and pierced his brain. Heavily did he fall to the ground, and his armour rang about him. After this Ulysses and his son charged at the rebels, and Athené also lifted up her voice; and the others fled for fear of the heroes and of the voice. And as Ulysses would have followed them, Zeus cast down a thunderbolt from heaven, and it fell at the feet of Athené. And when Athené saw it she cried: "Hold your hand, lest you move the anger of Father Zeus."

So she came forward, having the shape and voice of Mentor, and she spoke to the people, and bade them remember how Ulysses and his father before had been good kings, and how the Suitors had behaved very badly, and had suffered as they deserved. "And now," she said, "he is willing to forget all that is past, and to rule over you as a just man should. Make your peace with him." And she herself inclined their hearts to do this thing. So Ulysses and his people were made friends again.

CPSIA information can be obtained at www.ICGtesting.com
Printed in the USA
BVOW01s0026260816

460018BV00002B/185/P